THE BEND IN REDWOOD ROAD

DANIELLE STEWART

Random Acts Publishing

Most days it's manageable. No more than a quiet wondering around the edges of her mind.

What has become of the baby she left behind?

Smiling through the pain and suffering in silence, Leslie Laudon marches forward. Embracing the life skillfully designed by her husband, Paul. Living right could be penance for an impossible choice she made. Dutiful and anchoring, Leslie pours herself into her other children. Nurturing them through infancy, protecting them as toddlers, guiding them as teens.

As her youngest child heads off to college with her suitcases and coordinating dorm room accessories, so goes Leslie's identity. The chaotic life of a busy working mother threatens to become dangerously quiet. *Quiet enough to hear the voices she's tried to silence for decades.*

Gwen Fox was adopted by two perfect people. Noel and Millie have always treated her the same as their two biological sons. Her parents' love is strong and unwavering, yet a soul-deep ache still lingers in her. Plagued by an unnamed, hard-to-explain longing Gwen could never shake.

Riddled with doubt and dragged down by the undertow of unanswered questions, Leslie and Gwen both find their lives suddenly upended. One seeks the truth about the day she was born. The other seeks herself, the woman she was before motherhood.

Before she made a choice to leave a piece of her heart lying asleep in the hospital nursery.

In this complex journey for answers, blame is abundant. Guilt is thick enough to choke on. Marriages are brought to the brink of disaster. As the ripples of the past vibrate through their lives, Gwen and Leslie realize there is no turning back. What they have put into motion cannot be stopped. The road toward the truth will be littered with casualties.

A special thank you to all those who contributed to this book. Lending your experiences and perspective was invaluable. It was a reminder that every journey and family is different. There is no right way to feel.

Mandy, Beth, Molly and Dawn: You helped propel this project forward. Brilliant notes and a ready red pen to slice and dice.

Thank you to Elizabeth Munyer for being my eyes and pencil as she explored the redwood trees. Your words are magic. I can't wait to read your book someday.

PROLOGUE

There was a tangible sinking feeling. A going under.

G wen's scalp tingled with a prickly heat. Goosebumps skittered up her arms, though the room wasn't cold. Her eardrums thudded to the beat of her pulse, turning the professor's lecture into a distant muffled sound. Breathing came quick but shallow. The body she'd been in control of her whole life was suddenly acting on its own. Ignoring the messages her brain was trying to send, like a petulant toddler flouting the rules.

These symptoms had all the hallmarks of a panic attack. She'd learned about it in psychology class.

While books and facts were always a comfort to Gwen, reading about it didn't do justice to the overwhelming sensations of the real thing. She clung to the information she had learned, hoping it would focus her mind. This reaction was only the culmination of prehistoric indicators of fear and danger.

Her thick brown hair fell in front of her face but she couldn't muster the control to sweep it away. The smell of her lavender shampoo was a reminder that it had been a normal morning, the fulfillment of her usual routine. If she tried hard enough she could explain these sensations away.

Slow your breathing Gwen. Pull yourself together. You're just scared.

Yes. What she was feeling was biological. Increased rate of breathing, accelerated heartbeat, boosted blood pressure. These physical signals were designed to be lifesaving. The gazelle's body responded this way when the lion approached. She grasped at the data but it wasn't enough.

This was not some primordial fight-or-flight situation. It was Thursday morning physics class. No reason at all for her body to be crushed by anxiety.

As her palms soaked with sweat and her pencil grew too slick to hold, she realized there might be no rebounding. No getting a grip. She may not be able to un-ring this bell. Her panic attack would be on display for everyone in class.

"I—" She breathed the word out as her chest caved to the vise closing around it. Tears spilled from her eyes in a flood. Her body shook and tensed. Dark spots formed as she tried to focus her vision on the room around her.

"I need—" Gwen reached for the arm next to her. It was attached to a man and currently propping up his bearded chin. Her grip was tight. Frighteningly so, judging by his twisted expression. She blinked hard to try to bring him into focus.

"What?" His voice was laced with confusion and annoyance. Someone woken from a dream by an unexpected bump in the night.

"I'm about . . . I'm falling . . ." Gwen edged the words out past the ever-growing lump in her throat.

"Falling?" His bushy brows knit together as he finally turned his body toward Gwen. Her eyes focused for a brief moment on his gray wool hat. It looked soft. Something she wanted to reach out and touch, but she had no more control over her body than she had over the sunrise. It was separate from her. Uninterested in what she wanted. What she needed.

Gwen was suddenly sorry she didn't know this man's name. Hadn't bothered to learn anything about him in the last two months they'd been sitting beside each other.

Now she couldn't. Words wouldn't form. You needed breath for that. You needed control for that. Instead the sobs erupted. Wild, hiccupping sobs that would be dramatic even for an actress in movies from years gone by.

Her hand flew to her chest, pushing against it as though it would take force to keep her heart from leaping out. Her bones, something she'd taken for granted, failed her. They turned to Jell-O as she slid sideways from her seat to her knees. The floor was hard and cold but something about that felt comforting. Solid when everything else was mush.

The tunnel vision taking over meant she couldn't see heads turning her way. Couldn't hear mumbles of concern from her classmates. But it must be happening. She was making a scene.

Classrooms now required everyone to be alert. You had to know where to run, when to hide, how to fight back. Active shooters had thrust everyone into a new level of cognizance. Well before children realized *why* they were hiding behind their desks, they knew how to. This generation had known lockdowns before locker rooms. Learned to hide under tables before they'd memorized their times tables. Trained in the art of huddling silently before the training wheels had come off their bikes.

Gwen's disturbance would rightly be met with everyone's attention. They would think fast. Measure the threat and remember all the drills they'd been forced to do since they were children. Soon enough they would realize she was not a disgruntled student. She was just a woman on the floor of their class falling to pieces. She was sure that would flood them with relief.

Lucky them.

"What's going on?" Professor Yarro's voice swam into her ears and right back out. "Miss, are you hurt?" She could feel him crouched down beside her. His cologne was reminiscent of Thanksgiving spices, and she tried to cling to the warmth of it. But that too faded.

She was sure he didn't know her name. Not at the moment. Gwen wasn't a problem student or a standout academic. There would be no reason for her professor to discern her from the other sixty people in the class. *Now she'd be someone he would remember for all the wrong reasons.* A war story he'd tell his colleagues over a beer on Friday night.

The fellow student she'd clung to finally wrangled his arm free. But he didn't run off. He instead knelt in front of her, inspecting her face. "She can't breathe."

"Allergic reaction?" Professor Yarro asked as though Gwen's classroom neighbor might somehow know. He shrugged and looked helplessly back at the professor.

Gwen's tears fell in uninterrupted rivers cutting their way down her cheeks. Carrying her mascara along like debris swept away in a torrent of rain. Her body curled small around itself. Legs pulled into her chest, her forehead planted on her knees. She rocked. Shook uncontrollably. Gasping for breath. She hadn't completely passed out but a kind of blackness overtook her senses.

Any other details about that day had to be recounted to her by others. Eyewitnesses to her collapse. Front row onlookers to her darkest moment told her an ambulance was called. The classroom evacuated with an abundance of caution. Professor Yarro had accessed her file through the student portal and provided her emergency contact person.

Her mother.

Gwen was transported to Mayfield Regional Hospital without

answering a single question. Without uttering a word. Everyone she encountered pleaded with her. Was she allergic to any medications? In any acute pain? Had she taken any drugs? She provided nothing. Not even a nod.

Her jaw was locked shut. Clenched so tightly her muscles ached. At the edges of her mind she heard them label her as unresponsive. Noncompliant. Gwen had never been a rebel. She didn't go through that teenage phase where getting in trouble was a sport. Normally, she did what was right, what was being asked of her. Lying on the gurney, she was unable to give them what they wanted.

Hospital staff tried to unlock her like a safe whose combination had long been lost. Tough love from brash nurses didn't work. Sweet attempts from kind-eyed doctors had no impact. Their urgency grew as it took a little while for her mother to be reached. An advocate for cell phone etiquette, her mother was sitting in the hospice wing of the local nursing home and wouldn't dare bring that device in with her. Finally, when her mother made it back to her car, the connection was made.

Suddenly, the doctors were aware Gwen was a healthy twenty-five-year-old woman with no history of drug use, no allergies, and only a few mild childhood illnesses. No signs of depression or mental illness. Her mother reported on Gwen like a student presenting on a well-researched person in history. She gave the facts, as she knew them. Superficial vignettes that only scratched the surface of who Gwen really was. George Washington and his wooden teeth. Gandhi and his hunger strike. Information that brought them no closer to knowing why Gwen seemed unable to speak. Unable to stop crying.

What her mother couldn't provide was a family medical history. Those forms Gwen avoided at every doctor's appointment she'd been to as an adult. The checklist about maternal and paternal predispositions to various illnesses and diseases. There was no road map of genetics she could trace back on her family tree. History of cancer, diabetes, mental health issues? She didn't know. No one in her life knew.

The irony, even in her state of utter disarray, was not lost on Gwen. The hysteria she was thrust into was not likely caused by some genetic health problem passed down from her biological family. The ache in her heart was the result of not knowing what flaws these strangers had passed to her. The black hole she was falling into was the shape of the family who didn't want her. The people she didn't know at all.

When the frenzy wouldn't pass. When the hives and the shaking didn't improve, the doctors sedated Gwen. A slow wave of medicated calm filled her like water poured quickly into a glass. A rush of relief. A letting go.

A tangible sinking feeling. A going under.

CHAPTER 1

Gwen

"I do enjoy quiet time." Dr. Bethany Charmrose was tapping the back of her pen to the notepad propped on her lap. Her hairstyle was painfully outdated. Teased and hair sprayed in all the wrong places. Volume clearly her goal rather than keeping on trend.

The navy blue dress she wore was long and adorned with substantial shoulder pads. A lace collar that buttoned tight to her neck. The uniform of a workingwoman in the eighties.

Gwen pushed aside her superficial judgments and instead took in the doctor's warm eyes and beaming doughy face. Welcoming. Open. Kind. And apparently she was highly acclaimed in her field. Dr. Charmrose was not the university counselor who had been recommended to her by the doctor at the hospital. Instead, she was a sought-after expert who Gwen's mother had somehow tracked down and secured an appointment with. Because that's what she did for her children. They'd sound the alarm and she'd jump into action.

Swimming in the awkwardness of the silence she was creating, Gwen glanced around the small office again. It would not pass the HGTV test. Where was the personality? The essence of the owner? Dr. Charmrose looked like she might have a collection of some sort. Porcelain clowns or little cherub dolls. Her office reflected none of that spunk that was clearly present in her eyes. She was inviting. A walking, talking warm hug. Yet her office was drab and nondescript.

Did therapists all shop at the same store?

Some big warehouse with uninteresting art and lackluster trinkets. Firm, sterile-looking furniture. Large yellow notepads. Substantial pens with her name engraved. Beige walls. Windows with dusty white blinds always pulled shut. Yuck.

Dr. Charmrose leaned in a little and her obtrusive old-lady perfume shot to Gwen's nostrils. The brown leather chair shifted under her weight and the springs groaned. "I can sit here and make my grocery list. I can doodle little pictures on my pad. Quiet time is nice, but spending our hour together in silence won't be a productive long-term strategy."

This was Gwen's second visit. The first was spent tight-lipped and straight-backed. She was inexplicably angry at the idea of being mentally dissected by a stranger. The appointment was just a box she could check off. As far as a long-term strategy for success, Gwen was far less optimistic. This second appointment however, the anger had subsided. She saw this wasn't an affront but a well-meaning attempt at help.

"I don't want to waste your time," Gwen admitted, fidgeting in her chair like a child dreading a haircut. Not at all impressed by the tiny lollipop promised to her at the end. She knew already the hour would be wasted. The juice was not going to be worth the squeeze.

"You're paying for my time. Or someone is. I get the money either way. It's not a waste for me." She pulled her blue thick-rimmed glasses off and placed them on the notepad. "Tell me, what's brought you here today, Gwen?"

She knew the question was a setup. A trap. But Dr. Charmrose didn't seem ready to give up anytime soon. A formidable opponent.

"My mother was worried. I knew she'd feel better if I were seeing someone. She found you, so I came." Gwen thought of her mother. Mariam Fox. Millie to her friends. And everyone was her friend. A sturdy woman. Not in stature but in spirit. Reliable. Steadfast. Dedicated to mothering the way a soldier is devoted to his mission. Tunnel vision.

Millie had curly hair. The kind that sprang up wildly from whatever means she tried to use to tame it. Hats. Headbands. Ponytails. They were laughably useless for her blonde ringlets. Other than a wrestling match with her hair, her morning routine was simple. She didn't bother with makeup. Her bright blue eyes never looked tired so it wasn't necessary. Her skin was smooth and porcelain pale. A button nose. Perfectly straight, gleaming white teeth. Flawless without much effort. Inside and out. Gwen often wished she did have Millie's genetics. They were impressive. If she were born to this woman, how lucky she'd be.

Gwen wondered what it would be like if her parents had never told her she was adopted. She didn't closely resemble Millie or Noel, but some families didn't always have strong features handed down. Unlike Millie, Gwen had thick, straight brown hair and deep brown eyes. She was taller than Millie by five inches, but her brothers were tall. Where Millie's hips were narrow, Gwen had curves. She was the only one in the family who would tan in the summer rather than sunburn. But surely the Fox clan could have conjured up a story about a great aunt who had the same figure, same slightly darker complexion. She'd likely have believed them.

Though there were endless ways to parent, Millie was a modern and enlightened mother. The bake sale queen. The loudest in the stands at the championship basketball game. Explained the homework. Showed up. Beamed with pride. Everything a child could want or need in a parent. When she failed, she admitted it. When she had a misstep, even with her children, she apologized. Her lessons came in many forms, but the best ones were always those she taught by example rather than words. The Fox children were lucky children.

Dave, Nick, and Gwen were the reasons Millie woke in the morning. The reasons she stayed up worrying at night. Would David ever lose his lisp? Years of carting him to speech therapy ended in success. How would Nick ever learn to overcome his fear of sleepovers? She solved that too. Magic monster spray. Pictures of the family packed in his overnight bag. Could Gwen manage to take more risks and make a few mistakes? It was ages of conversations and hard lessons, but even that Millie Fox had helped to improve. There was nothing she couldn't do. More than that, there was nothing she *wouldn't* do. It's what made sitting in a therapist's office feel even worse to Gwen.

Dr. Charmrose smiled softly. "Do you think your mother would want you sitting in silence in here or would she like you talking and trying to understand what's going on?"

"Nothing is going on right now." That was true. Since her release from the hospital Gwen had felt fine. She'd managed to get herself together. But this wasn't a space for facts. Gwen was here to dive deep into feelings. To face the illogical storm of emotions that she was swept up in.

No thanks.

"I'm glad that you feel well right now." Somehow Dr. Charmrose had already found something to write in her notebook. "But you had a significant psychological event less than two weeks ago. It's important that we try to get to the root of that so we can ensure you are prepared if it happens again. Do you want it to happen again?"

"No."

"So do you agree we should try to understand why it happened the first time? That would be the best course of action for preventing it."

Gwen cursed her love of logic. It was her weakness. Hard to debate an obvious truth. But she decided to try. "It was a panic attack brought on by nothing. That happens doesn't it? Spontaneous attacks with no triggers. People do experience those? It's different than an anxiety attack."

"You've done some reading?"

"A bit."

"Well that tells me you have the desire to understand this better. That's good." Another note jotted down. "Tell me about your workload at school. You're a grad student? It was close to exam time correct? Writing your thesis? A lot of students can feel pressure about the coursework or even the ending of something that's been a part of their life for years. The unknown of what's to come after college."

"My workload is manageable. It was close to exam time, and I missed a few of them but went back last week and was able to make them up. Being the crazy crying girl earned me some extra time."

"Do you think you are the crazy crying girl?"

"No."

Dr. Charmrose nodded and waited for Gwen to offer up some more information. "I'm satisfied with my grades. I have enjoyed college, but I'm ready for it to be completed. After I graduate I'll go on to earn an additional certification. I already have a job lined up at a lab where I've previously done some hands-on study. I'm sure there are plenty of students you see who experience those feelings you're describing, but I'm not one of them. I'm not nineteen and homesick. I'm twenty-five. I have a fine apartment. Some friends. A great family."

"That's good. You seem to have a very healthy outlook on your future and your experiences at college. How about relationships? Can you tell me more about the people in your life?"

"I'm not dating anyone right now. I was with someone for a long time, but we broke up last year. It was amicable. No drama."

"How long were you together?"

"Three years."

"That's a long relationship. Do you keep in touch?"

"No. Ryan was a year older. He graduated last year and moved to California to work on his tech start-up with some buddies."

"Long distance relationships can be difficult."

"We broke up before he knew he was moving. The relationship had run its course, and I could see he was starting to compromise himself to stay in my life. If we were together when the job opportunity came up, he never would have taken it and moved to California. He'd have waited for me. I don't think that's healthy."

Dr. Charmrose nodded. "So it ended amicably. Do you feel you have moved on from that relationship?"

"Yes. I'm telling you, these are not triggers for me. School is good. I'm not broken-hearted."

"So why do you think you were crying on the floor of your classroom to the point where an ambulance needed to be called?" She cocked up a brow and leaned back in her chair. Clearly she'd decided it wouldn't do to dance around anything. She torpedoed her direct question right into Gwen's hull.

Gwen had studied psychology. Obviously not to the extent Dr.

Charmrose had, but she knew the widely accepted rules in the field. Dr. Charmrose was breaking them. The "why" questions were taboo. Being too direct and leading toward an answer wasn't supposed to be part of the journey. But maybe that was what made her a standout in her field. Occasionally ignoring what the books said. Or maybe she was actually terrible at this and no one had figured it out yet. Either way, there were thirty minutes left in this session, and Gwen had no intention of storming out and ending it early. So she decided she had better give her something.

"I don't know what caused it. Like I said, it was biological. No triggers—it just happened. And it hasn't happened since. I feel fine."

"Let's try an exercise. Tell me what you did that morning. Tell me what you did the day before."

"Why? It won't make a difference."

"Humor me. Sometimes we are so close to a situation we can't see our own triggers."

"It was a normal day. I woke up. Left my dorm. Got my same coffee at the same coffee shop. Dropped something off at the post office. Walked to class. Sat down."

"And then started crying?"

"Apparently." Gwen tossed her hands up like a middle school kid who was asked not to put her feet up on the coffee table. She wasn't trying to be obstinate, but she wasn't trying that hard not to be either.

"What did you mail?" The doctor's pen hovered over the pad.

Gwen's mouth sprang shut like a bear trap. The suddenness of her movement was too obvious to be ignored.

"Do you usually stop at the post office?" Dr. Charmrose knew she was onto something.

Gwen cleared her throat and tried to right herself. "When I have something to mail, I go to the post office."

"That was outside your normal daily routine? What did you mail that day?"

"Is that important?"

"Is it important to you?"

Gwen picked at her already raw cuticle and averted her eyes. She'd been caught. She could lie. She owed nothing to Dr. Charmrose. The truth however had been needling her. Pinpricks against her brain. She didn't want to fall apart again. She didn't want to be the crazy crying girl. If there were a chance this would help, maybe it was worth the truth. "It was my DNA test for an ancestry site."

"I did one of those last year." Dr. Charmrose tried to lighten her expression as she put her pen down. The illusion of two friends chatting. "I found out some really interesting stuff about my heritage. My mother had been a good bookkeeper when it came to our ancestry but my father's side of the family was harder to track down. A lot of their records had been destroyed in a fire. But the DNA results helped us narrow down the town our ancestors were from and then we found a parish that had some amazing documents. I'm seventeen percent Eastern European. That was news to me. What do you hope to find?"

Gwen dragged her sweaty palms over her jeans. "I'm adopted."

"Oh." Dr. Charmrose didn't pick up her pen. Gwen was sure it was a calculated move. "So you don't know much about your genealogy?"

"I know nothing."

"But you want to?"

"Doesn't everyone?" There was a snap in her voice. She felt the urge to qualify the situation. "My parents are amazing. I have a really remarkable family. If you asked me to sit here and come up with a list of things they've done wrong, I couldn't. My life has been very good."

"That's wonderful. Most people I work with come in with the list in hand."

"I'm very lucky."

"But you still want to know more about your origins?"

"I love my parents very much," Gwen stressed.

"What you're feeling, the conflict of emotions, can be common with adopted children. I'd like to explore this more."

"I know other people who are adopted. They have no interest in seeking out their birth families. They feel like they are exactly where they are meant to be with the people they are meant to be with." Gwen reported this as though it was the only obvious emotion someone should have.

"Some people do feel that way as well."

"The good people." Gwen didn't look up from her hands.

"These emotions don't make people good or bad. They make them different from each other. Was there a certain event or situation that made you want to find your birth family?"

"No." Gwen felt her chest tighten and her throat closed around the lie like a snake smothering its prey. She wasn't ready to speak it out loud. She wasn't ready to point to the part of her life that shifted everything.

"So you just have a general desire to explore more about yourself?"

"There is nothing to explore. I sent off my DNA test. It'll be six weeks. Then I'll know more about myself than I ever have."

"You'll know more about your structural DNA. Not more about who you are as a person. Do you see those things as separate?"

Gwen tried to fight a smug expression. Her competitive streak reared its head often, and it took restraint to keep it at bay. "I'm a grad student. I'm studying for my Master of Science in genetic counseling. My thesis is on current genetic counseling practices and barriers in relation to sourcing medical history for adoptees. I have lived and breathed this field for nearly six years. I understand the nature versus nurture debate, if that's what you're asking."

Dr. Charmrose pursed her lips and gave a tiny nod that expressed she was impressed. "You're twenty-five?"

"Yes."

Again the doctor jotted something down. Gwen was desperate to know what her age meant. What she might have written down. "You've worked very hard in this field. You are clearly knowledgeable. What I'm asking is what you think knowing this information will mean. Let's say you're thirty percent Italian. Or you're predisposed to some food allergy. What does that information mean to you?"

"I don't know. I don't have the information yet."

Dr. Charmrose looked unimpressed with her deflection. "You're a smart girl. We've established that. How about you go out on a limb and try to imagine how you will feel when you get the results."

That technique could not have been in the psychology books.

Gwen gulped. She hadn't imagined the aftermath of getting her DNA results. She wouldn't now. "I'm not sure."

"All right. Tell me about the DNA kit. You purchased it?"

"Yes."

"Recently?"

"No."

"How long did you have it before mailing it in?"

"A year." Gwen's cheeks flushed. The older she'd gotten the better she'd become at hiding the truth, but every now and then her complexion betrayed her. "It's not even that detailed. I paid a hundred dollars and spit in a tube. The results will be fairly unreliable and superficial." She folded her hands in her lap as the doctor's pen and paper connected again, a little more frantically this time.

Or maybe that was just her imagination.

"What I hear you saying is you've been considering it for a while and on that day you finally sent it off. Then the wheels were in motion. How did that make you feel?"

"I tried to get it back." Gwen let the words out like a panther stalking quietly through the tall grass.

"What do you mean?" Dr. Charmrose tipped her chin to the side and brought her thin, penciled-in brows together a bit.

"I went back to the post office half an hour later and tried to get them to give it back to me. They said they couldn't. It had already been labeled for shipping."

"How did that make you feel?"

Gwen bit her bottom lip as she conjured up the image of the frightened postal worker who tried to patiently explain to her why she couldn't have the package back. Her tears couldn't sway him.

When Gwen didn't answer Dr. Charmrose continued. "What made that day *the day?* You'd been hanging on to it so long. Looking at it. Thinking about it. But that day was the day you knew you wanted to send it. Was there some significance to the date?"

"No. I thought I was ready."

"But then once you were settled in class did you second guess yourself? Second guess your choice?"

"Yes."

"What about the DNA test worries you? Are you afraid of what you might find?"

"Yes."

"Why?"

"It's a database. People find biological family members on there. Suddenly you turn into the deep dark family secret that's been uncovered. Once it's in motion you can't stop it. You can't control it."

"You like having control?"

At this, Gwen rolled her eyes dramatically.

"You take exception to that question?" Dr. Charmrose waved as though she was giving Gwen the permission to speak freely.

"Everyone appreciates some level of control in their lives. The way you said it sounds cliché and textbook. The psychologist equivalent of a coach telling someone to keep your eye on the ball."

She jotted something else down as she moved on, not addressing Gwen's criticism. "Have you talked to your parents about this?"

"No."

"Do you think they would be supportive?"

"Of course. That's all they ever are. I've known I was adopted for as long as I can remember. We had a very open dialogue about it. When I was very young, my family went to support groups, even my brothers. My mother made it her mission to make sure I had a healthy relationship with the idea of adoption and the journey. But when I hit my teen years I was done with that. I didn't want to talk about it anymore. I didn't want it to be a part of my identity. Kids at school were asking weird questions. I wanted to feel normal. So my parents backed off. It never felt like the right time to bring it up again."

"Even though your parents are very supportive?"

Gwen remembered her mother's expression the first time she'd said she didn't want to talk about being adopted anymore. "My mother seemed relieved to know I didn't want to ask any more questions. As if I'd finally made the decision to completely accept them as all the family I would ever need. I'd always accepted them as my family. Asking questions didn't mean I didn't love them. My mother knew that. And she never said anything, but I could see it in her eyes. She was happy." Gwen laughed humorlessly. "So I'm a control freak and people pleaser, I guess. You can check off those two boxes for me."

"That's not at all what I'm here to do."

Gwen shrugged as though it didn't matter. Because, frankly, it didn't.

"Let's go back to when you were having an open dialogue about your adoption; did you ever ask them specifically for details about your biological family?"

"I didn't have to ask. My mother volunteered all she knew when I was about eight. They don't know much. I was left at a clinic in Rhode Island by a Jane Doe the day I was born." In the last year, Gwen wondered endlessly about those few hours she was with her birth mother. What had happened? Had her mother held her? Nursed her? Kissed her? Was her father there somewhere? Did he know about her at all? Or had they been immediately separated from their baby?

In the last couple of months, a little voice, one completely devoid of logic or reality, would whisper much darker questions. *What had I done in such a short time to make her leave me there? Was I a bad baby?* When she was a child, the support groups had been quick to squash that narrative. To remind her that she was a perfect little baby in an imperfect situation. There was nothing she could have done or been to change it. Easy to say, hard to believe.

"Millie and Noel, my parents, had no plans to adopt." Gwen could practically hear the house phone ringing in the middle of the night. She could picture how her parents would have reacted to the call about the baby in need. They would look at each other and know they would love her instantly and ferociously.

"They had two boys of their own already. Dave was four. Nick was almost two. As they tell it, they had no plans for any more kids. The nurse at the hospital, who was responsible for my care that night after I was abandoned, was a high school friend of my father and, even though they hadn't seen each other in years, they had kept in touch. The baby would need to be nursed and my mother was just starting to wean Nick. Without much of a plan, the nurse reached out to my parents. My mother recounts the story with a smile every time. She says it's the best phone call she never expected. They were immediately in the car, dropping the boys off to my grandmother and driving straight to the hospital. I was in her arms within hours, and she knew she'd never let me go again." Gwen took great pride in recounting this story. In telling people that she may not have been wanted by one mother but the other, not even expecting her, jumping into action.

"You sound close with your parents."

"Very."

Dr. Charmrose moved one hand to her chin, contemplatively. "Yet you feel like it's important to keep this part of the journey from them. Is it fair to assume their support would help you process these emotions and keep them from bubbling over in unhealthy ways?"

"When I was growing up it was always implied that I wouldn't be able to find my biological family. My birth mother was a Jane Doe. My father was a mystery. My father's friend, the nurse, died of cancer a few years later. If someone came back looking for me there, no one would be around to tell the story. It was a very small clinic. Long since closed. She was the only night nurse. My mom and dad took me home that night. The adoption process was expedited by a lawyer my father is friends with. Nothing about our situation was traditional. I wasn't given a name at birth. Initially no birth certificate was filled out. On paper I was born Gwen Dorothy, to Millie and Noel Fox. I was abandoned. Abandoned children have the lowest percent chance of reunification."

"I didn't know that statistic."

"I've done a bit of reading on that too." Gwen sighed, remembering the quiet nights in the library where she pretended to be studying for school. Instead she was looking for any road that might lead toward her past.

"When I was a child there was no access to things like these DNA tests and the public databases that are now available. Anyone can use those now for a small fee. And if either of my biological parents have committed a serious crime, their DNA may be available in the national CODIS database. A familial DNA match could connect us. But that isn't something just any person could have access to."

"Would a genetic counselor have access?" Dr. Charmrose didn't yell *checkmate*! But she might as well have, considering her gloating expression.

Gwen folded her arms across her chest. "Depending on the field I pursue or the lab I work with, that could be part of my role."

"Was that on your mind when you picked your career path?"

Gwen squirmed even though it really hadn't been on her mind in an obvious way when she picked the field. It wasn't about finding her birth family. But maybe it had been about finding herself. "I've always been fascinated by the building blocks that make people. How the science has evolved into tools to solve crimes. Save lives. Reunite people."

"Your parents, Noel and Millie . . . would you consider talking to them now that we're unearthing some deeper emotions? They know what field you are going into. It could be more of a clinical conversation about your work to start with."

"It feels like a slap in the face to my parents, the people who upended their lives for a baby they never planned to have. They answered the phone one night and there I was, the youngest of their children. They already had a toddler in their only crib. They were changing enough diapers. They paid for the degree I'm about to get. Now I'm supposed to tell them: thanks for every-thing, but I'd like to use this science and knowledge to find the people who didn't even want me. Sorry, Millie and Noel, I know you went into this with the understanding that there would be no one looking for me, and no one I could ever find. You guys were great, gave me all of yourselves, but it's just not enough."

"It sounds as if they have been enough."

"Of course they have," she snapped defensively.

"Then perhaps there is a way to make sure they know that, even while you pursue this next phase of your life." Dr. Charmrose softened her expression and uncrossed her legs so she could lean in closer. "Gwen, I hear you. I hear the pain in your voice and the concern you have for how this might make your parents feel. But it's important for you to know that everything you are feeling right now can be common with adoptees. It doesn't make you ungrateful. You want to understand how you came to be and who, biologically, you came from. I don't know how your parents will feel. But to be fair, neither do you. You haven't given them the chance to show you."

Gwen let the advice bounce off her like a dodge ball. It connected with a sting, but then rolled away. "The DNA results may not tell me a thing. I might find out what my genetic material says about my ethnicity. And it could stop there. The odds that I will find anything of substance that could lead me to my biological family are quite low. Why should I put my parents through that, just to find out there was nothing there to begin with? I won't hurt them for an unlikely possibility. They don't deserve that."

Dr. Charmrose nodded but not in agreement. In understanding. "What do you see as the next step then?"

"I'm going home for Christmas break. I had originally planned to stay on campus to finish my thesis and only go home on Christmas Eve. Now I think my parents will feel better if I stay for the whole break."

"And where is home?"

"Connecticut."

"Are you looking forward to being home?"

Like all the ones before it, this was a complicated question. Old Wesley was equal parts comfortingly familiar and claustrophobic. When people thought Connecticut they usually imagined posh Greenwich or bustling Hartford. People she met rarely knew of her tiny coastal town dotted with historic lighthouses. It had inns and estates that drew tourists in the summer and fall, but enough snow to keep everyone else away the rest of the year. It became popular due to the downtown area, which was waterfront and nostalgic. The town gave people the illusion of old-world charm without any of the inconvenience. Cute rustic signs at the breakfast place were great for esthetics but people wanted fresh brewed exotic coffee options. Everyone loved the old-time soda fountain pharmacy but also expected the latest options in medicine available there. The tiny eclectic bookstore was full of character, but on demand, they ordered the latest blockbuster book people were anticipating.

It was a show, put on by the town and fully appreciated by the tourists and residents alike. The idea that she'd be getting in her car and heading that way soon sent her further into conflict. She was hungry for the warmth of her mother's arms but worried about bringing with her the emotional tornado that was chasing close behind.

"I'm not here to tell you what to do, Gwen, but I'd be remiss if I didn't encourage you to find some support while you are home. If not from your family, then from your friends or a support group. I can recommend one in your area. This will not just go away if you bury your head in the sand."

"Thank you," Gwen said, watching the clock over Dr. Charmrose's head ticking away the last minute of their time. "I'd appreciate the information on the support group. That's a good option."

Maybe they both knew the business card she'd handed Gwen

with the phone number scratched on the back would be tossed in the trash. There would be no community center with metal folding chairs in her future. No Styrofoam cups filled with stale coffee. There was a good chance the doctor's advice was correct. But being right didn't always matter. Sometimes it was just about survival.

CHAPTER 2

Leslie

"Are you feeling those empty-nest blues creeping in yet?" Claudette Marchland swept into the tiny coffee shop and slid into the booth with the grace of a ballerina. She was tall and slim. The envy of most women whose bodies had begun betraying them in their fifties. With no work at all, she'd maintained her figure. Claudette's sharp features made her look far more serious than she was. People wouldn't guess she was always good for a giggle. To Leslie, it was a characteristic that made her the perfect friend and confidant over the years.

Claudette and Leslie had met at a toddler music class and bonded over the ridiculousness of paying thirty dollars for their young daughters to bang on drums. Over a cup of coffee Claudette had remarked that they could hit a pot with a wooden spoon at her house and she'd only charge Leslie ten dollars. And as the best ones usually are, a friendship was born out of the mutual dislike of something they found silly.

Now, like almost every Thursday morning for the last decade, they were in the corner booth of the coffee shop about to dish on everything good, bad, and ugly happening in their lives. Leslie made a habit of going into the office later those days and somehow she always felt supercharged. That's what Claudette did. She juiced people up like a current of electricity.

Leslie slid the cup of coffee toward her friend and sighed. "It's not even Christmas yet. We're months away from graduation. Then we have the whole summer together."

She faked a formal southern drawl. "But, Mrs. Leslie Laudon, you are always ahead of the game when it comes to worry." Claudette shot a knowing look.

She was right.

"Empty-nest blues are legit but so are the my kid is driving me nuts and is it time to drop her at college yet blues."

"Cheers to that," Claudette said with a breathy laugh as they clinked their coffee mugs together. "I love my Janie, but I swear I might send her to military school instead of her senior year of high school next fall. She only looks up from her phone long enough to roll her eyes at me."

Leslie didn't know why commiserating felt so damn good. Having someone look at you and feel your pain, as trivial as it was, was a magical thing. "I hear you. Kerry is a good kid but she has some serious attitude lately. The girl drama is real. I asked her if she wanted to do some Christmas baking with me this weekend and you'd think I'd asked her to burn all her textbooks and quit school. She thinks the only thing she has time to do is study. Heaven forbid I gently remind her she's already going to be the top of her class. Suggesting that she relax gets my head bitten off."

Leslie had fallen into the rhythm of her life. The familiar routine. More than that, she was good at it. Not supermom, but somehow everyone managed to have what they needed when they needed it. She didn't knock the socks off the other PTA moms. For the bake sale she'd make some basic chocolate chip cookies or even buy something from the bakery if she was short on time. Nothing fancy. Not an overachiever but certainly consistent. Dependable.

First her role was to sort out the kids and their schedules. Then she'd dutifully turn up at her job. Always meeting the expectations of her bosses but never quite having time to exceed them. Every eighteen months or so, her superior would pull her into a conference room and explain how perfect she'd be for an open position at the firm. How excited they'd be to promote her. But could she travel? Could she attend a conference in Portland? Put in some more hours while they launched the new branch of their business? She'd beam with pride and then gracefully decline. Her husband already traveled so much for work. He was the COO of a large banking firm. There just wouldn't be a way for her to take on more work while her children were small. Then again when they were tweens, they just needed so much. And teens needed more attention than babies.

There was never a right time.

The last slice of her life would be left for her husband, Paul. She'd listen to his gripes about his work travel and the way they'd ignored his last proposal in the boardroom. Ensure his suits were pressed. His car was serviced. Prescriptions filled.

Paul was a great father, but she was the primary parent and keeper of the to-do list. It was expected that when one of the children was sick, she'd stay home. It's what she and Paul had decided was *the perfect plan.* And their lives had turned out exactly as they'd designed. How lucky they were to be able to say that.

This next phase, the letting go of her youngest child, had snuck up on her. The suddenness of saying goodbye to her sweetheart daughter was crushing.

"You're an old pro at sending the kids off to school by now. You've done it twice already," Claudette said, eyeing the table next to them the way only she could. She had this keen robot-like detection system. People-watching wasn't some casual pastime for her. It was a life skill she honed daily. Leslie didn't know what was setting off her friend's judgment radar but she knew it wouldn't be long before she found out. Half the fun of checking people out, dissecting their nuanced movements and hushed conversations, was chatting about it with friends.

Leslie sipped her coffee and thought about how Kerry would be sitting in a coffee shop like this one, hundreds of miles away soon. She'd be hunched over a stack of textbooks trying to navigate her freshmen year courses. It made Leslie's stomach ache with anxiety. Kerry was shy, sometimes painfully so. What if her roommate in her dorm was rude? What if she didn't make any friends?

"It was different with the boys," she admitted. "They were always closer to Paul even though he worked more than I did. They had sports and usually went to him for advice. Each of them had at least two buddies going off to the same schools. And they were never that far away. Less than two hours. She's going to California. Why does she have to go so far? What's wrong with right here in New Hampshire? I'd even settle for one of the colleges in Massachusetts like her brothers chose. Kerry is my homebody. My buddy. I can't imagine not sitting down and having a cup of tea with her in the morning before school."

"Don't start crying," Claudette demanded with a firm point of her finger in Leslie's face. "If you start, I'll start and we'll get kicked out of here again for making a scene."

No one had ever *actually* kicked them out of the coffee shop before. Not technically. But there had been a couple of occasions where they were carrying on so animatedly they'd been asked, quite nicely, if they would be moving on soon.

"I've done my share of crying already. My tear ducts need a break. I'll be fine. I'm glad she's going off to college. Maybe it's what she needs." Leslie understood this was one of the lies one tells themselves, hoping if it's repeated enough it might ring true.

"Kerry is going to blossom in college," Claudette said. She put her hand over Leslie's and squeezed. "She's ready."

"At least one of us is."

"Think of how much time you and Paul will have to reconnect. That's what I keep focusing on for when Janie leaves. Lucas and I will be strolling around the house naked. Turning her room into a gym. Traveling without wondering if the kids are going to drink our beer. You have to look for the silver lining."

Leslie worked up a little smile. She and Paul had been good parents. She knew that. Dedicated to their children and their needs. Building their character intentionally. Reading the parenting books, following the expert advice. What they hadn't done since the kids had transitioned to busy, smelly teens, was dedicate time for each other. There had been a few times they'd snuck off for an adults-only trip. Date nights, when both of their work and home schedules allowed it, were rare. Having three kids was a commitment. Now that the commitment was changing, it was time to look at their marriage and do a thorough needs assessment.

She silently scolded herself for the work lingo. That was one of Paul's main criticism of her: using her work lingo at home. He hated that.

"That does sound great," Leslie agreed, swallowing the lie with a sip of her coffee like a pill she struggled to get down. "Paul and I will be good empty-nesters I think. He's slowing down at work. He's changed his travel schedule in the last six months. He's still years away from retiring, but at his level he's finding time to work remotely and actually delegate. He's been home a lot more."

"And how about your schedule? Will you be slowing down?" Claudette propped her pointy chin into her delicate long fingers and awaited her answer.

"I've slowed down on my career for the last twenty-five years. I'm ready to ramp it up. I don't want to be one of those old ladies who looks back and realizes she never chased her dreams."

Claudette made a harrumphing sound. "You're the director of communications at a prominent medical supplies company. Don't act like you're some slouch. I'm here in yoga pants every day, and I don't do yoga. You wear power suits and pin your hair up." Claudette waved her hand at Leslie's styled hair. "You should be very proud of your career. Your company loves you. How many times have you been offered a promotion?"

"And how many times have I turned them down?" Leslie planted her mug on the table with a thud.

"But they offer. And that says a lot about you."

Leslie was tired of the consolation prizes. A better parking spot. A beautiful floral arrangement on the anniversary of her hire date. It wasn't enough.

"I'd be a Senior VP there if I'd have been able to travel and work all the hours my colleagues did over the years. Look at the trajectory of Paul's career. He's been able to give a lot more of himself to his work than I have and it shows."

"Since when does that bother you?" Claudette took note of the young couple that walked in and then refocused on her friend. "You've always seemed very fulfilled with your career. You managed the kids-and-work balancing act better than anyone I've ever met."

"I wouldn't change a thing about the last couple of decades," Leslie said, adding to the lies like inches of snow in a blizzard. This particular lie, that she didn't regret her missed opportunities at work, had been something she'd been lying about for as long as she could remember. "Maybe it's my time now. I'm still young enough to pursue my career goals, right?"

"Damn right you are. I feel terrible I didn't realize this was on your mind. What exactly would that look like for you, chasing these dreams?" Claudette leaned in attentively.

"I have no idea," Leslie admitted with a lighthearted laugh. "I could travel more. I'm overdue on attending trainings and conferences. If I started now and found the right company, I could land a CEO position in the next five years."

"Well, hot dog. I love that. You deserve to run the show and any company would be lucky to have you. What does Paul think of all this?"

Leslie didn't have to answer. Her sheepish expression gave her away.

"Why haven't you told him? Paul absolutely lights up when he talks about you. It's like having your own personal cheerleader. He's very proud of you."

That was partly true. In public he did tend to talk highly of her. But it wasn't the whole picture.

"When he talks about me as a mom and wife but not when he talks about my career. It's actually an old point of contention for us. We had some trouble and it caused a big rift for us. Way back before you and I met."

"Was there really a time before we met?" Claudette tipped her head back in a dreamy way.

"Surprisingly, yes. And I could have used a friend like you back then. It was ugly. We were young. Paul and I realized we both couldn't be ambitiously pursuing careers and have a big family. It works for some people but it wouldn't work for us. We hit a crossroads and it was a really hard period for our marriage. I feel like when I bring this up it'll stir up so much of that old pain. He's gotten quite used to being the primary breadwinner and the one who holds the bigger title at work. He's not a petty man or anything, but like I said, there is history there for us."

"You're being silly. Paul would love to see you move up that corporate ladder. You deserve it and he knows it. If he doesn't I'll have a little talk with him." Claudette cracked her knuckles and tried to make a threatening face. "You know he's scared of me."

"He really is," she agreed with a smirk. "So are all the other people on the PTA, half the teachers in the school, and that one woman at the grocery store who goes on break every time she sees you get in her checkout line."

"I can't help it if I'm intimidating. People misinterpret what I say. I'm misunderstood."

"You told that poor girl if she crushed your bread with the milk again you'd crush her spirit."

"Bread isn't cheap," Claudette remarked, forcing a serious expression.

"You are a nut. Forget me. I'm surprised you aren't the CEO of something yet."

"I am perfectly happy working at the floral shop and making enough money to buy extra shoes for myself. I have no idea why you'd want to take on any more in some stuffy corporate office. But I don't need to understand it to support you. If my girl wants to run the world, I'll lace up my sneakers and run right beside her."

"I don't know what I would do without you." The barista came by and topped off their coffees. As she moved to the next table, Claudette leaned in. That was the signal. Juicy gossip was coming her way.

"Burnie is sleeping with the owner. They got caught in the storeroom last week. Everyone figured he'd fire her but apparently not. He might make her a manager."

"Isn't he married?"

"Aren't they all? I swear Lucas would be swimming with the

fishes if he messed around on me." Claudette tightened her hand into a fist.

Leslie had never worried about Paul. Not because he was infallible, but because she knew secrets didn't make you a bad person. Or she hoped that to be true.

"Poor Burnie. That must be so awkward. I'm sure the other girls are all giving her a hard time now."

"You know it. I can't even judge her. I did my share of very stupid things when I was twenty. Didn't you?"

The question wasn't posed as an accusation but still Leslie felt guarded. Instead of answering she just raised a knowing brow and sipped her coffee. She let Claudette continue.

"I still blame the men though. These girls are young, just getting out into the world. The men should know better. Dirt bags."

"Absolutely."

"Would you do it over again if you could?"

"What?" Another question Leslie felt compelled to dodge. Her list of regrets was long.

"Go back to being twenty. I would. Gosh I regret half of my choices then. I thought I had life all figured out. I honestly believed I'd work at the ice cream shop forever and marry Skip Zilling. Then for no good reason I cheated on him with some guy who drove a dirt bike. I can't even remember his name now. It was so dramatic and messy. I still have my diary from back then. I only hope Janie makes better choices than I did."

"Janie has a good head on her shoulders, and you know better than anyone she has a strong will. She's not going to do anything she doesn't want to do."

"Yes, but she's going to do everything she wants to. That worries me too."

"Look at us. We screwed up plenty and we turned out fine." Leslie offered a playful grin.

"You were a goody-two-shoes. Don't lie."

"I made my share of missteps. Trust me." Her cheeks flushed hot.

"Look at those snotty girls whispering about her." Claudette groaned, pointing at the other baristas who were throwing side eyes toward Burnie. "We talk about the war on women but damn, sometimes girls like that are the biggest enemy."

"I'm glad we have each other." Leslie's chest warmed as she thought of the years they'd spent supporting each other. Laughing. Even fighting each other's battles. Over a couple of bottles of wine, Leslie had considered telling Claudette just how bad she'd screwed up in her twenties. For some reason it seemed more natural to tell her than to tell anyone else. But still, she hadn't.

"You're stuck with me forever. There are enough of those witches out there. We don't need that in our lives."

Leslie had buried her secrets deep down. Bottom of the ocean kind of deep. The doctor who'd prescribed her the antidepressants hadn't even asked why she needed them. Most days she could sit across from the people she loved and be the person they believed she was. She could separate herself completely from the past. It was a lifetime ago. That flawed and damaged person had more than paid her penance over the years. Or so she told herself.

It hadn't been perfect. Unexpected moments had rocked her stability. The birth of Kerry had sent her to a dark place. But Paul was by her side. Her mother insisted postpartum was nothing to be ashamed of. And the circle of people who loved her closed in and carried her back toward the light. When she'd hit the change of life, she was surged with emotions she'd long buried. But Claudette had been going through the same things. It was normal. They were experiencing what so many other women went through before them. Now these terrible bouts of sadness she was feeling would just be chalked up to empty-nest syndrome.

And every time someone excused her bleak outlook and debilitating sadness as a normal response, she wanted to scream. To tell them they didn't understand why her pain was different. Why her secret was too heavy to carry alone.

But just like her career, there hadn't been a right time to tell them. There hadn't been a moment that seemed perfect to claim for herself. So she powered through and tried to make peace with the fact that part of her would always be hidden. Hidden from Claudette. From Paul. From her children. All her children. Even the one she didn't know.

It wasn't only that she'd put a child up for adoption. It was how. It was why. It was when. There were versions of these scenarios people could swallow and excuse away. Socially acceptable reasons to make the decision. People wouldn't understand. And sometimes, when she looked back on her choice, they shouldn't.

CHAPTER 3

Gwen

The Fox house was small by modern standards. Built in 1921, the ceilings were low and the doorways narrow. The galley kitchen was not wide enough for two people to pass. Yet every Thanksgiving, Noel and Millie Fox found a way to prepare a feast to feed a crowd.

Minor changes and clever storage techniques helped with the cramped feeling, but the one bathroom, three-bedroom cottage was always going to look more suited to hobbits than people.

What it lacked in square footage it more than made up for in charm. Millie had always loved the farmhouse theme, adorning the tiny kitchen with metal jugs and wire racks filled with fresh fruit. The wood cabinets had been painstakingly painted to a weathered finish one hot summer when Millie was struck with the urge to get creative. A picture in a magazine had been all the inspiration she needed. It always seemed as though there was nothing she couldn't do when she put her mind to it.

It was home to Gwen. Unshakably stable. Unchanged in the most important ways. The musty earthy smell of the basement. The hand-carved original banister spools. The vent cut out of the upstairs floor that could, and often was, used to pass notes or eavesdrop.

The house was in her bones. Like a womb. She'd been formed there. Shaped by the necessary closeness that came from cohabitating in such a cramped space.

They had one unwavering and often quoted rule. *You can always come home.* There was no mistake too big. No problem too complex. Within the walls of 64 Redwood Road you were safe. You were loved. And you had a team behind you.

As Gwen turned her key in the door, she was struck by the silence. The house was never quiet. Because it was old, every creak of the floorboards or popping of the radiators created a soundtrack. If someone flushed the only toilet, it rattled the pipes in three other rooms. And when they were younger the sound of rowdy children reverberated off the walls. But right now, with the house empty, there was nothing.

Her mother and father had gone into Boston for a follow-up appointment with his back surgeon and planned to stay the night, not expecting Gwen home until the next morning. When she realized she could sneak in for a day of peace and quiet, she packed up and headed home early.

Moving into the tidy living room was bittersweet. As a teenager having this place to herself was a dream come true. Control over the remote. Ability to blast her music. But now she felt like she was seeing an X-ray. The lifeless bones of the place without all the things that brought energy to it. Laughter. Smells of food cooking. She even missed the messy piles of sports gear her brothers would leave around.

"Hello?" a voice called from the kitchen, and she closed her hand tightly around her sharp car keys. "Millie? Noel?"

Her breath caught in her throat as she backed against the closest wall. The likelihood that this was some robber who called his targets by name was low. But she wasn't ready to see any acquaintances either. Her plan was to hide out the first couple days and settle in.

"The door was open," the voice called, getting closer. "It's me. I'm just dropping off the truck. I took that load of stuff to the dump for my mom."

She peeked her head around before he could find her hiding. "Griffy?" Long sleeping parts of her brain sparked to life as she drank in his face. It stirred her soul like sweet cream mixed into coffee.

She stood staring at one of her closest childhood friends and remembered their long days of fun. Digging up worms. Climbing too high in the trees. Playing pretend. Rolling at lightning speed down a grassy hill.

A sense of freedom and ease washed over her. The smile he flashed was laced so tightly with the happy memories that she felt compelled to pull him in for a tight hug. But she didn't. Too many years had passed between them to make that natural. Still though, Griffy was a pillar that held up the most carefree parts of her life.

"Gwen?" he asked, twisting his face in confusion. "I didn't know you were home from school so early."

"Wow. Look at you." She leaned back and put a hand over her heart. "You cut your hair. Where are your curls, Griffy?"

"I put them the same place I put that nickname." He chuckled that familiar laugh, and she felt it hug around her. "I mostly go by Griffin now or Griff."

"Oh." She rolled her eyes. "Of course. No respectable financial consultant to the stars would be called Griffy. And they probably wouldn't take you very seriously with that mop of black curls you always had. My mother keeps me up to date on all your latest conquests at work."

"I'll be honest, I miss the curls." He ran his hand over his nearly shaved head and sighed.

"And being called Griffy?"

"Not so much."

Griff had on a pair of dark denim jeans and a faded gray shirt. His shoulders had filled out more since the last time they'd seen each other. A tattoo peeked out from his shirtsleeve, but she couldn't make out what it was.

The scar over his eyebrow seemed more prominent now that he was older. She remembered how he cried when he got hit by the hockey stick during a contentious street game. It wasn't the pain that worried him but the fact that he'd gotten blood on his school shirt. His father would be furious.

Relieved for the company, she waved him to the table and pulled out a chair for each of them. "Can you stay for a bit? I'll make coffee."

He eyed her bag still on her shoulder. "Are you just getting in? I don't want to keep you."

Tossing the bag to the floor, she waved off his objection as she filled the coffee pot. The galley kitchen connected to the small dining area, and it was easy to hold a conversation from one space to the other. "My parents are in Boston, following up with my dad's doctor. They won't be back until morning. I was just going to unpack and hang around. Do you need to head out?"

"I can stay for a bit. My mom was getting rid of a bunch of stuff so your dad lent me the pickup so I could take a load to the dump."

"She's getting rid of things finally?" Gwen gave a hopeful look, but he shot it down. There hadn't been the word *hoarding* in their vocabulary when they were younger. But now, looking back, she understood that was what his mother was doing. It made the house more chaotic, which was impressive considering how dysfunctional it was to begin with.

"Not as much as she needs to get rid of. She has stacks of newspapers no one will read. Dish sets they won't eat off of. It's just something for the two of them to fight about. The stuff I dumped today was to make the living room livable again for a while."

"Where'd you park? There's no flashy sports car out front." She looked out the small window over the sink.

"I was going to walk home after dropping the truck off. The walk will do me good; I'm in no rush to get back to that madhouse." He stood under the arched door frame of the galley kitchen, and she couldn't get over how much of the space he filled. If he weren't leaning, he'd have had to duck.

"How long are you here from Florida?" She glanced over her shoulder just long enough to see his pained expression rise then settle into a smile. There had always been something pained in his eyes. Long before she knew hearts could break, she sensed Griff had more weight to carry than the other kids she knew.

"I'm up here indefinitely," he reported flatly.

"Why?" She grabbed the cream and sugar and handed them to him so he could put them on the old farmhouse table where all her memories soaked into the rough wood. Her father had made it, and though it was imperfect, she couldn't imagine them ever having some shiny new one in its place. "You're not working for Pipeline Investments anymore?"

"No. No one is working for them anymore. They went under." He bit at his cheek and then shrugged again.

"I hadn't heard." She poured hot coffee into two chipped mugs with some silly sayings on them, and they both sat down. "I'm sorry to hear that. So you came back to Old Wesley? Why?"

"I keep asking myself the same question. I've been here a few weeks." He plastered on a smile she knew was fake.

"Then what?" She examined his familiar hazel eyes and

marked all the things about him that had changed in the years since she'd seen him. Griffin was her oldest brother's friend. A fixture in the Fox house her entire young life. He'd gone off to college when she started high school. It broke her heart to lose both her brother Dave and Griffy to adulthood before she was ready to join them. She was left at the station as the train pulled away.

"I don't have a plan just yet. It was complicated. I was getting promoted quickly at the firm. Taking on big time clients. Lots of responsibility."

"I know. The last time we saw each other was my parents' anniversary party years ago. You were really excited about the job. Then I heard from my parents how well you were doing."

"I should have known no one gets moved up the ladder that quickly. I didn't realize things were already going bad for the company. I was promoted so I could be the fall guy. It got really ugly." He stirred sugar into his coffee and was lost for a moment in a memory that seemed too painful to share. "The FEC was involved. Clients were scammed out of their retirements. I thought I might actually get jail time. It was bad."

"Griff, I had no idea. I'm so sorry." It struck her as strange that they'd once known so much about each other, and now, when life was actually challenging, they'd lost that connection. Wasn't it far more important now than when their biggest problem was how to sell enough lemonade for a new hockey stick?

"I kept it quiet. I didn't want my father to hear. I knew he'd be so disappointed."

"That's ridiculous. You didn't actually do anything wrong. That's not you. You are one of the best guys I've ever known. You wouldn't steal from anyone or do anything that might hurt some-one's future. Your dad is an idiot if he believes otherwise."

The expression on Griff's face matched the wonderment of

seeing a majestic sunrise. As if he was right in front of those cotton-candy pink clouds and blood orange streaks of light that steal your breath. A gratitude expressed so authentically it made her blush. He opened his mouth to speak but closed it instead around the rim of his coffee mug, offering a little nod of appreciation.

"You'll land on your feet," she promised him. "Any company would be lucky to have you."

"Not quite. I'm blacklisted. My name is now associated with a scandal. No one will want me. I need to find a new career. Something outside of the world of finance."

"Is Laura here too? Is she doing all right with this?"

He winced, taking a few extra beats to pick his words carefully.

"She didn't weather the storm well. It's understandable, she didn't sign up for the hell I went through. I don't blame her. She was working at a small advisory firm and couldn't be associated with me if she wanted any future there."

"Griff." Gwen tipped her head to the side. "You must be a wreck. On top of all that you're staying with your parents?"

He chuckled. "I can't stay much longer. You know how things are with me and my father. It's why I was at your house so much growing up. I couldn't be home then and I can't be home now. I don't know why I even came back. I have plenty of savings. I could have gone anywhere. I was stupid enough to think coming back here was going to be comforting or nostalgic or whatever."

"Me too." She groaned, tipping her head back and looking at the ceiling. "But it's not the place we were trying to come back to. It's a time. And that time is gone. This"—she waved around the house—"isn't going to magically fix things in our lives."

"Now you tell me. I could be hiding out on a beach in Fiji right now."

"We had a lot of good times here." She nudged him with her

elbow, accidently spilling some of his coffee. "Sorry. I'm still the little annoying kid messing up all your stuff."

He grabbed a napkin from the center of the table and mopped up the spill. "You were never that. You were a great kid."

"Oh please. I know you guys didn't want to take me around with you. My brothers hated it, but you always told them to let me come. Why? It would have been easier to just tell me to buzz off."

"I just never wanted you to feel—" He cut his words short and shook his head. "I don't know."

"Say it." Her brows knit together and she put her hand on his arm. "I've always wondered why you stuck up for me. You may not have known it, but it meant a lot to me. It was like having another big brother but without all the sibling drama."

"I was afraid you'd think we left you out because you were adopted. Like that was why they weren't including you. It was stupid. You hit the family lottery. Of course you knew you were loved. Even if they didn't want you to come fishing with us, you knew they had your back no matter what."

Now she was the one rendered speechless, using her coffee as an excuse to be quiet.

He covered her hand with his. "You weren't that annoying. I liked having you around. I hated being an only child. I would have loved having a kid sister. I swear there are some days the Fox family literally saved my life. I wouldn't have made it if it weren't for this house and your family."

"Did he hit you?" It was a question she'd always wanted to ask. The whispers about Griff and his father were always too quiet for Gwen's little ears to decipher.

"I don't think my parents ever planned to have kids. I was probably an accident. They were both well into their thirties by the time they had me." Griff squirmed in his chair and she released his arm, letting him grip his mug with two hands and hide behind it for a second. "He's an angry guy who had a hard time in Vietnam. His brother came to visit us once and told me my dad was a nice normal guy before that. He came back screwed up."

Gwen didn't point out how Griff hadn't answered the question. He didn't owe her the answer and she wouldn't push. If he hit Griff back then, she was certain that wasn't an issue now. His dad, Bill, was not a big man. Griff had long since passed him in height and weight. "We were always glad to have you here. You were part of the family from the beginning. One of the boys."

"Speaking of which, when are Nicky and David coming in?"

She smirked. "I guess growing out of a name is more common than I thought. Nicky is Nick now. David is Dave."

He laughed. "Yeah, of course I knew that. I've kept in touch with them. We trade emails. If our paths cross on business trips we always try to meet for a drink. But seeing you, it just made me remember them as Nicky and David."

"They'll be glad to spend some real time with you. They won't be here for another week. I wasn't supposed to arrive this early either. I don't know what the hell I'm going to do until they get here."

"Probably spend every waking moment reassuring your mom you're all right." He cocked a brow up in a knowing way. The expression was reminiscent of a game of truth or dare years ago. He always knew when she wasn't telling the whole story.

"What did she say?" A hot wave rolled up her back. Her mother didn't gossip and rarely spread her kids' business around. She was sure her brothers had been informed of her episode in class, but was surprised to know Griffin had been told. Had they stayed closely in touch too?

"Your mom and I have been talking a lot since I got back here. She's been one of the only things keeping me sane. I was here the day she got the call. She was a wreck. I drove her and your father to the hospital. They were both emotional, and I was worried about them driving. Your dad's back isn't great yet."

"You drove them to the hospital? I didn't know you were there." She felt suddenly nervous that he'd seen her that day. Hair wild. Tear-stained cheeks. Clenched fists.

"I just dropped them at the door. I offered to come back and pick them up, but they had friends nearby. They stayed at their place and then caught a ride back with them. I was worried about you, but I didn't want to intrude."

"There was nothing to worry about. My mother is being dramatic. I took on too much for school and got dehydrated or something like that."

He nodded, completely unconvinced. "And where was Ryan for all this? Couldn't he bring you a bottle of water to keep you hydrated while you studied?"

"I guess my mother doesn't spread all my business around. You missed that we broke up. He's in California. He moved last year after he graduated." She picked at her cuticle and welcomed the sting of pain.

"What? You two broke up? I don't believe it." He gave a small smirk she couldn't pin down. He looked a little pleased at the news.

"Why not? People break up all the time. You and Laura broke up."

"She left me because things imploded. That's different. You and Ryan were different."

"What makes you think that?" Her lips curled up. She was intrigued by his assessment of her relationship with Ryan.

"Because you brought him to your parents' anniversary party, and he was madly in love with you. Every other word out of his mouth was your name. When I saw Dave two years ago, he said you and Ryan were going to get married after college. Your brother was sure of it."

"Well we're not getting married. Ryan graduated before me and moved to California for a tech start-up. It's going very well and his new girlfriend seems lovely according to social media. He's very happy."

"Social media? You mean the thing you use to stalk him because you still love him?" He slapped his hands together victoriously.

"I don't stalk him, and I'm not in love with him." That was mostly true. Nothing she did met the standard for actual stalking, and what she felt for him now couldn't really be considered love. Gwen's face went to stone, and she used every ounce of her energy to let Griff know she was serious. This was not a topic they were going to cover.

"Prove it. Who have you dated in the last year then?" Griff leaned back and flashed a smug expression. She could smell his cologne and hated how grown-up it was. She much preferred when they both still smelled of summer sun and sticky melted popsicles.

"I've been on a couple dates." It sounded pathetic when she said it out loud.

"But no relationships? None for a year? That's because you're pining over Ryan in California. So maybe you need to take a trip out there and get him back. Make him wait for you to graduate and then move out there with him and kick out the new girl." He waggled his brows playfully. But this was no joke. She'd built a convincing narrative for her family around her breakup with Ryan. The less she talked about it the better.

"I don't have any feelings for him anymore. None." Gwen cut her hand through the air decisively.

"Then what happened? He would have waited for you I'm sure. You are worth waiting for. I think you should—"

"Griff, please. I can't talk about it." Her words were chopped up like peppers under a chef's sharp knife. "Ryan and I are done. Something happened. I just can't talk about it."

Griff's face fell deathly serious as he planted his coffee mug down on the table. "Oh, Gwen, I'm sorry. I was just teasing you. Did he do something to you? Or cheat or something?"

"Let's talk about something happier, please. Our failures are bumming me out. I just need to laugh the way we used to. Do you remember how we would get Dave to shoot milk out his nose by telling that same old joke about the seagulls?"

"You want to laugh?" Griff lit with a mischievous smile. "I have an idea. But you'll have to trust me. We'll need rations. How mad do you think your dad would be if we stole some of his beer?"

"Not as mad as he would have been when we were underage. Why? What's this great idea?" Gwen leaned back skeptically. "Your big adventurous ideas didn't always work out."

"My career is a good example of that. But this will be fun. I promise."

"Remember when I was eleven and you promised me I would enjoy that horror movie about the ghost clown? I didn't sleep for a month."

He grabbed her coffee mug and put it in the sink. "Good thing you aren't eleven anymore. I say we go to the tree house. We've got to check it out. Think it could still hold us?"

"I doubt it, and it's cold out there."

"It's fifty-three degrees. That's basically a spring day here. Don't be a wimp."

"That stuff doesn't work on me anymore. People have called me far worse, and I don't do the peer pressure thing."

He reached his hand out and waited for her to take it. Still sitting, she considered her options. She could dig in and risk him leaving. Sitting alone in this house all night had sounded appealing before, but now that she was here it wasn't as promising. When she really considered it, she knew she didn't want him to go. Reaching for Griff's hand, she let out a dramatic sigh.

She knew it was her job to try to talk some sense into him. "I don't know if the tree house is even structurally sound anymore." His warm hand closed over hers as he pulled her up to her feet.

"Nerd," Griffin teased.

"Reckless dummy," she shot back.

Just like the good old days.

"I think it would be fun to find out if we can still get up there. We practically lived in it during the summers. It was our castle. I could really go for feeling like the king of something right now."

She pulled open the fridge and handed him two beers, grabbing two for herself. "You're going up first. And if the thing collapses I'm going to do exactly what I did when you fell off the rope swing and broke your arm."

"Run away and hide under a pile of tires instead of getting help for me?"

"Yes."

They slid open the back door and stepped out onto the deck her father had built with Dave during his freshman year of high school. As usual, Griff had been around, and so he had helped. Gwen's job had been handing out nails and lemonade while trying not to mix the two things up.

"Remember building this deck?" she asked, tapping her foot on the solid wood. She pulled her sweater closed tight as a cool breeze blew by. It was mild for December, but she still felt the chill run up her back.

"Your father taught me everything I know about working with my hands. Remember this?" He crouched down and pointed at a board in the far corner that had twelve nails in it. "I overdid it a bit on this one. I thought the more nails the better. Your dad laughed and told me sometimes moderation is the best option. He went on to give me all sorts of examples of how less is more. Your dad is such a patient guy."

"He's perfect. So is my mom." Melancholy crept in at the corner of her mind until she shook it off. Having wonderful parents wasn't something to feel bad about. She was blessed. The fact that she had to keep reminding herself of that was the problem.

They cut across the yard and Griff spun around with a curious expression on his face. "How is this so small now? When we were kids we played out here for hours. Soccer. Football. It couldn't have been this small. It's a postage stamp. Did it shrink?"

"We got bigger."

"We got bigger and significantly more depressing." He shook his head as though the passage of time disappointed him. She could understand the sentiment.

"I want to be a kid again." Gwen stood in the familiar space, marking in her mind all that had changed. The corner where the swing set had been. The ring in the grass that always got left behind after they drained and put away their blow-up pool. Her mother's garden that they'd steal cherry tomatoes out of. It was all gone. This was only a space behind the house now. No longer a backyard adventure land for kids.

"We start with the tree house." He pointed up at the wooden structure perched in the large oak tree at the edge of the property. The branches had woven across the windows and one of the railings had snapped in half. Otherwise it looked pretty sturdy.

The ladder was made of wood planks nailed into the trunk of the tree, leading up to a hole in the floor of the house.

"That hole we're supposed to climb through got a lot smaller." Griff eyed it skeptically. "I don't know if I'm going to fit."

"I am not going up there first. If you don't fit, that's too bad. I'm not calling the fire department to pry you out."

"That look on your face takes me right back." He put his hand

49

on his chest and chuckled. "If you put braids in your hair and wore those weird pink shoes you loved, I'd be transported back fifteen years. You always got that look on your face when you were afraid."

"And you'd all cluck like chickens at me. Are you about to do that again? I had hoped you'd matured some."

"I had no idea you were still afraid of your shadow."

She dropped her gaze to the ground and shifted her foot over a moss-covered rock. "I'm not afraid of my shadow. But the list of things that scare me is still long," she admitted quietly. Gwen had never been a risk-taker. They'd all jump off the highest wall at the reservoir and she'd stay behind. Never sledded down the most dangerous hill at the park. Never tried the big tricks on her bike.

"Don't look sad about it," he groaned, nudging her gently with his elbow. "I was only kidding. You weren't a chicken. You were four years younger than us. You shouldn't have been doing all the crazy stuff we were. You were right to say no."

"But four years later when I grew up, I didn't do that stuff either." She handed him her beer and he spun the top off, handing it back with a smile. "Griff, I missed out on a lot. I always wanted to be good. I felt like my parents deserved that. They took me in. Why should they have to deal with me disappointing them or breaking the rules? You, Dave, and Nick, you had a lot of fun. I just watched."

"Noel and Millie wouldn't have been disappointed in you even if you did screw up. Trust me, your brothers did plenty, and somehow they always found a way to work it out. It would have been the same for you."

She wanted to tell him that she was different from her brothers. Whether anyone wanted to admit it or not, it was true. Gwen knew she was loved. But she also knew she was different.

He put his two beers in his pockets and tentatively tested the first couple boards up to the tree house. They were shockingly secure.

"We're really going up there?" She leaned in to try to get a better look but got distracted by the muscles of Griff's flat stomach as he stretched his arms up. When she was a little girl she spent five years obsessing over Griff and his every move. It was puppy love. Somewhere around the age of eleven, she realized he made her stomach flutter. It kept on fluttering right up to the day he left for college.

Over those years, when her crush first started, she cried buckets of tears for the love that would never be. She doodled his name near hers. Wrote, and then tore up, dozens of letters to him. The blessing was her brothers never knew. If they had, they'd have told Griff, and her world would have crumbled in around her.

Gwen knew now, with years of experience passing between them, it was just a childhood crush. How many little girls thought of their big brother's friends in that dreamy kind of way? It was normal. And though Griff was still handsome, they were strangers to each other now. Those feelings were gone.

He climbed the rest of the way tentatively and then turned his body sideways to slide up through the tree house floor. "Wow. How did we all fit up here?"

"We were little," she called up to him with a laugh.

"Chug that beer so you can climb up here. It's great. Better than I imagined."

"Seriously? You might be overselling it."

"My standards are a little low right now. It's been a rough couple of months. But I'm telling you, it's great. Come up."

"I'm going to fall through the floor. Or sit on a nail. You do remember how much of a klutz I am, right?"

He leaned his head out the hole and called her name. "Gwen." The cool and familiar tone brought her back through all the years to when things made sense. In her mind his stubbled chin morphed back to a soft dimpled one. His large smooth hands transformed to smaller calloused ones, best used for climbing trees and handling a fishing pole. His designer jeans were suddenly department store clearance rack, the knee ripped from a fall off his bike. By saying her name that way he was the boy she loved again. Just for a moment.

Griff stared down at her with a silly expression. "When have I ever let anything bad happen to you? I am the one who stomped on that snake that almost bit you when you were nine. I told Jordan McNeil not to pull your pigtails anymore or I'd pop him one."

She pointed up at him accusingly. "And right after that you pulled my pigtails."

"You know the rule; *no one picks on Gwen but us*. We were tough on you, but I never let anything bad happen to you, and I won't now." He waved for her to come up.

Gwen wished her only problems now were garden snakes and pigtail pullers. She kicked back her beer and let the cold fizzy drink run down her throat. She wasn't much of a drinker and knew this would give her a little buzz. Maybe enough liquid courage to actually climb this tree. She finished quickly and had to catch her breath on the last sip. Tucking the unopened beer under her arm she started climbing toward his wide grin. He looked as shocked as she felt that she'd actually do it.

"I was so mad when I couldn't camp out with you guys anymore. That whole boy/girl sleepover thing really ruined it for me." She popped her head through the hole in the floor and looked on with joy at the relics of her childhood. A wooden crate filled with checkers and chess pieces. A lone action figure turned sideways in the corner. Christmas lights hung across the ceiling even though there was no place to plug them in. They'd always had big plans up here that usually flopped during the execution phase. Enormous ideas. Less follow through.

"The blankets are still here." Griff couldn't stand up fully without hitting his head. Crouched over, he moved to the tiny table and chairs. "Your mom used to come up here and fold these things all the time. She'd put them neatly back in these giant plastic zipper bags." He tugged at the zipper and pulled the cartoon-covered blankets out, unfolding and spreading them across the floor to sit on.

"Do you think she knew the last time she came up here, it would be her last time?" Gwen imagined her mother shimmying up the ladder to clean up their mess. Rarely a complaint. She was always just so glad they were being children. Millie often remarked that she wanted them to stay young as long as possible. She'd bake them cookies and replace the flashlight batteries for as long as they wanted her to. Whatever would drag out the summers with them hanging around, rather than running off somewhere else.

Griff had a contemplative look on his face. "I don't think it works that way. You rarely know when it's the end of an era until much later. I came by to talk to your mom when I first got back here and she said that was the best part of her life so far. When we were little and running around, keeping her busy. She loved that the most."

Gwen crouched down and took a seat on the fluffy blanket with her favorite cartoon character all over it. Griff opened his beer and then hers as he took a seat.

"Cheers." He clanked his bottle to hers. "To the good old days."

"To when things used to make sense." She took a long sip of her beer and felt his eyes on her.

"What is it, Gwen? What's going on?"

"I'm not giving you the latest gossip to report back to my

mom." She leaned her back against the wooden plank wall and closed her eyes. It smelled the same as she remembered it. The sap of the tree, the cedar planks her father had used to make the floor. The blankets that had been tucked away in plastic had retained the fresh smell of the laundry detergent her mother used to use.

"I wouldn't say a word to her or anyone else. I'm just worried about you." He kicked his foot gently to hers. "Come on. I told you my messed-up story. It can't be worse than that. No threat of jail time for you, I'm sure. What happened at school?"

Taking a long swig of her beer, she looked him over from head to toe. He looked like a giant crammed into a tiny little house. Laughably out of place yet somehow seeming very comfortable.

"Swear it with the code." She watched his eyes twinkle with delight as the memory dislodged from the wrinkly back part of his brain and came into focus.

"The code."

"Do you still remember it?"

"It's been a long time. I think I do. Do you?"

She nodded proudly. "I still remember the first day you guys let me in on it. You wanted me to swear not to tell my mom about the cigarettes you found at the park and brought up here."

"We never actually got the courage to smoke one. But we did burn a couple of them in the fire pit while your parents were at the store."

"That's the first day you let me do the code. You let me in the club. I was eight, and I'd been following you all around for two years desperate to be a part of the club."

"You don't know, do you?" He chuckled and looked on with pity. "There was no code before that day. Dave made it up to make you think it was some big deal. It was a way to keep you from tattling."

"No." She shot up, sitting straighter. "No he told me you guys had a club and you'd all sworn a blood oath to the code. He cut my finger with that stupid pocketknife."

"He made the whole thing up on the spot. But after that day we kept it going. We really did do the blood oath afterward. So you were actually the first one in the club."

"I was such a fool. I believed anything you guys told me."

"You were sweet and you looked up to your brothers. I've waited my whole life for someone to look at me the way you looked at them. They were your heroes."

"I was looking at you too," she corrected. "Griff, you meant just as much to me as they did."

"Maybe that was true. But then life changed, and I had to face the fact that I wasn't actually a Fox brother. It was fun for me to come here after school. For the summer sleepovers. But it's not like I was going to come back for Thanksgiving. Or when your grandpa died. I wasn't really family."

She had the urge to apologize, but she knew that wasn't what he was looking for. "I wish I had kept in touch with you. I could have used a friend outside the immediate Fox family over the last couple years. An objective voice for advice."

"I'd have been busy tanking my career and ruining my reputation, but I'm sure I could have made a little time for you. I'm surprised to hear anyone would need anything besides this family."

"They're amazing, but sometimes you need something separate."

"I would have picked up the phone if you called."

"We'd have loved it if you came to Grandad's funeral. He liked you a lot. I think my parents just didn't want to put pressure on you since you were in Florida. I promise, the next person who croaks, you're invited to come eat finger sandwiches and collect casseroles with us."

"I won't have far to travel." The pain on his face was impossible to miss. Being fired and having all his hard work dismantled had taken a raw and unmistakable toll on him.

"The code?" she asked, jutting her chin out at him. "If you say it I'll tell you what happened."

He straightened up and put his hand over his heart. "I solemnly swear to keep the secrets that are told to me by those who follow the code. To hide the treasures found by the code followers."

"That's not the whole thing," she said accusingly, pointing at him. "You don't remember it all."

"I drank a lot in college. Not all my childhood brain cells made it this far. What is it?"

"I'm not telling you. But," she said, contemplatively touching her chin, "it's close enough for now."

"You're going to tell me what happened at school?" He looked surprised but hopeful.

She'd tell him the parts she could comfortably speak out loud. The easier truths to face.

"I sent off my DNA to one of those genealogy sites. I've been trying to do it for a year."

"Trying?"

"Trying to work up the courage. Or talk myself out of it. I don't know which."

"What are you worried about?" He pulled the box of old toys closer to him and gave her the grace of not having his full attention while she talked. He pulled out a legless action figure whose head wouldn't spin back the right way. Griff busied himself trying to fix it.

"I'm worried about finding my birth family. Or maybe, not finding my birth family. I'm not exactly sure how I feel. I just know I'm screwed up about it right now. Enough to cry like a fool in the middle of class."

"I've never heard you talk about your birth family before. Growing up, you never mentioned them."

"Most of my childhood I didn't have much desire to find them. It's different now."

"Why?"

"It just is." She knew that wasn't a proper answer. Yet somehow it summed things up perfectly. The real reason she wanted answers wasn't something she was ready to talk about.

He shrugged. "You'll know soon enough. Your DNA might match you with someone and then you go from there. You can find a first or second cousin and then back into the answers you're looking for."

"You make it sound so simple. Things haven't been simple since this was my favorite hangout." She patted the floor of the tree house. "I don't want to sit around and wait for these results to pop up on my computer. This week, being home, I think I made a mistake."

"I'm certainly not one to convince you being back here is right. I've had my bags packed and ready to leave for a week. Yet, I'm still here."

"We should go." She dropped her face into her hands and laughed. "I haven't unpacked yet. Let's just get out of here. We can get in the car and leave."

"Right. I'm sure your mom would love that." He snorted out a laugh.

"Are you kidding, she loves you. If I took off on my own she'd freak out, but with you, she'd think I was in good hands."

"Are you being serious? Where would we go? A random road trip?"

"No, we'd go to Rhode Island."

"Because?"

"That's where I was born. A clinic on the coast. We should go."

"You're crazy." He scoffed and kicked his head back, leaning it against the wooden planks as he appraised the ceiling. "What would we do there?"

"I'm not exactly sure."

"But you want to go?"

"I know I don't want to sit here for a week with my mom scrutinizing my every move, worrying herself to death over my freak-out. I feel like when I mailed that DNA sample I lost control of the situation. I want to get it back. I want to know more about myself than some test could tell me."

"And you want me to come because you don't want your mom to worry?"

"Partly."

"And the other part?" He dropped his gaze from the ceiling to her, looking straight in her eyes.

"You ground me. You are a part of a time of my life I loved. Maybe if you're around I can keep things together." Her words felt heavy and serious, mismatched to their surroundings. She offered levity. "Plus you're a hot mess right now. You've got nowhere else to be. If you stay much longer you might never leave. Are you ready to be in your parent's basement the rest of your life?"

"Hell no."

"Then let's go. We can take my car." Her grin was so big it felt like a muscle she hadn't flexed in ages. "We'll hide out for a week until my brothers get here. At least then there will be commotion and holiday stuff going on. It'll be the perfect time for us to roll back in. You have to admit it's a good plan."

"I don't have to admit that." He shook his head. "But I might concede it's better than the alternative. I was going to move into the tree house and hope no one noticed. When are your parents back?"

"Tomorrow morning."

Griff grabbed another one of the blankets and rolled it up tightly. He tucked it under his head as he lay down. His legs didn't stretch to their full length before hitting the other wall. "I'm camping out right here tonight. If you haven't changed your mind by morning, I'll go with you."

"You'll freeze up here. You need better blankets. It'll be so uncomfortable on this floor."

"I guess we'll find out."

"We? I'm not sleeping up here." She huffed and twisted her face up, asserting her point.

"Sure you are. It'll be fun. We might need more beer though. The rope is still here; we can lower this basket down like we used to." He took a long sip off his bottle and winked at her. "I'm not going for your crazy plan if you don't go for mine."

"We would need sleeping bags and real pillows."

He snapped his fingers together. "And snacks. Beer. Snacks. Sleeping bags. Do you think your brother still has his comic books somewhere? Oh we need the boom box and the CDs."

"It's all still in Dave's closet." She rolled her eyes and waited for him to explain he was only kidding. When his face stayed serious, she smiled. "You really want to sleep up here? You could easily take the boys' room for the night if you don't want to go home."

"It's not about avoiding going home. I don't want the last time I slept up here to be the last time. I don't even remember it. Did we tell scary stories? Read comics? Talk about girls we wanted to kiss? I didn't know it would be the last time. I didn't pay attention. I didn't appreciate it. I want a do-over."

Gwen pulled her hands through her hair and pretended to be more annoyed by the idea than she was. He was right. There was something empowering about going into an old experience with new eyes. "Fine, but I'm not talking about the girls I want to kiss."

"You can keep your secrets. I have plenty too." He meant his words to land as a joke but something serious flashed across his eyes, and she knew her expression must have been the same. They'd play lighthearted pretend. Tuck themselves into the tree house, listen to the soundtrack of their youth, and flip through comic books. Then they'd take off before dawn for a haphazardly planned road trip. It would be nothing more than a time-out. A break from what would be waiting for them back here. Pressing pause on her pain. She knew it, but still, she welcomed it.

CHAPTER 4

Leslie

She was a January baby.

L eslie looked at the family ring Paul had given her for their fifteenth wedding anniversary. She wore it every day, a way to show him how thoughtful and special it was. The ring had a birthstone for each of them planted in the gold. Two emeralds for her and Kerry, their May birthdays only two days apart. An opal for Stephen. Ruby for Cole. Topaz for Paul. She wondered what it would look like with a garnet added. Would Paul even notice? Would any of them?

Twisting the ring around she stared mindlessly out the bay window. Paul had insisted on the larger house. To her, five bedrooms seemed excessive, the mortgage higher than she would have liked. But they could afford it. Even though the house was new when they bought it, Paul always sought out projects and upgrades. Every time Leslie thought they'd get a break from it, he'd come up with another one. Perpetually unsatisfied with what they had.

One particular project she never understood was the koi pond. Paul's theory was that it would be peaceful and add a nice focal point for the yard. To this day, eight years since they'd put it in, none of them had ever sat on the little bench and found any level of intended serenity. It was a chore to keep up and a tax on their electric and water bills. But Paul had wanted it. Envisioned it bringing them happiness. So there it was. That's what it was like to be the family decision-maker. The one who made the most money. The one who'd been touted as logical and strategic. His plans always found a way to fruition no matter how she tried to talk him out of it. So eventually she stopped trying.

"What's so interesting out there?" Kerry laughed when her mother jumped. "Sorry. I didn't mean to scare you. What are you looking at?"

"The koi pond," Leslie replied with a forced smile as her now-cold coffee turned to sludge in the bottom of her mug. She wasn't sure how long she'd been sitting there staring out the window. "It's so beautiful."

"Dad loves that thing." Kerry filled a glass with juice and popped two slices of bread into the toaster.

Leslie considered explaining how exactly Paul loved the koi pond. The way he loved the idea of it more than the actual thing. How his plans were usually fueled by excitement and then fizzled like a rocket losing power and falling to the earth. There was no value in talking Paul down to their daughter, so she let it go.

Leslie straightened up and made sure her voice was singsong and happy. "What are you planning today? More studying?"

"Don't say it like that," Kerry complained. "I have to study. Most parents wish their kids worked as hard as I do in school."

Leslie hadn't infused her words with even the slightest judgmental tone, but teenagers heard what they wanted to. "I'm glad you're studying. I'm sorry I was giving you a hard time about it this week. Maybe I can help."

"Come on, Mom. Be serious. You stopped being able to help me in ninth grade. All we did was fight about how they teach math now."

"We both got the same answers," Leslie protested. "Why does it matter how we got them?"

"It matters now." Kerry shrugged as she buttered her toast and threw a few grapes on her plate. Leslie could tell by the way she was balancing her dish in her hands, Kerry intended to take the food back to her room.

Didn't she know she'd be gone soon enough? Didn't she understand this time at home was precious and fleeting? Of course she didn't, because everything was ephemeral to teenagers. They were all tunnel-visioned and self-centered. Even the good ones like Kerry couldn't see the big picture.

She strained to drink her daughter in before she disappeared upstairs again. Kerry's hair was baby soft and, even though it was long, it spiked up in places it shouldn't. Not overly concerned with fashion, her daughter opted for comfy clothes rather than the latest trends. Kerry was awful at sports so Leslie never bothered to sign her up for any of the things the boys had been into. It had always been books for Kerry. It had always been about being the top student. The winner of the spelling bee. The science fair state champion. Leslie had been average at best in school. It made connecting with Kerry hard sometimes. How could you relate to your child who you couldn't help? When they surpassed you in so many ways, what was left?

Leslie stabbed at the thought that rose to the top of her mind. Was her other daughter this way? Would they have had more in common? Would they be baking those Christmas cookies right now?

What kind of monster thought of such things?

Paul's dress shoes clicked across the shiny wood floor, and Leslie drew in a deep breath as he approached. This funk she was in wasn't Kerry's fault. The blame didn't lie with Paul either.

"Morning, Dad," Kerry said as she put one slice of her toast in her mouth and left it hanging there. Paul leaned in, avoided the toast, and kissed her cheek.

"Morning, sweetie. Good luck with the studies today. Don't forget to take breaks."

Kerry nodded and rolled her eyes as she disappeared out of the kitchen. Paul grabbed the morning paper and made his way to the table next to Leslie. "See that's the key, you have to tell her stuff while her mouth is full. She can't get sassy that way."

"Very wise," Leslie replied, leaning into his kiss. He smelled like Paul. Clean. A dash of cologne. Mouthwash. "What do you have planned this morning?" she asked coolly.

"I need a haircut and I want to stop by the office to pick up some documents. I should have grabbed them yesterday and forgot."

"Forgetting things? You're getting old," Leslie teased. She'd resigned herself to cheering up. Nothing could be done to change the way things were. It was a waste of the day to stay in the low dark place she had started in.

"Actually I've had something else on my mind. Want to hear about it?" Paul settled back into his chair and pushed the newspaper aside. A wash of panic took over. Some kind of alarm buzzed in her mind though she didn't know why. Perhaps it was the excited look on his face. The flicker of exhilaration in his eyes. She stood and started making two fresh mugs of coffee just the way they liked it. Leslie felt compelled to keep her hands busy. When Paul was this kind of happy, something big was about to happen. That wasn't always good.

"You want to hear it or what?"

"Sure. Though it sounds a little ominous."

He waited for her to bring the coffee over and sit back down. "No, it's a good thing. A great thing actually. You know I've been adjusting my work schedule these last six months. Well, I've gotten an opportunity to transition out of my role and move onto the board. The package they are offering is incredibly lucrative and my role on the board would mean I could work remotely most of the time. More money. More stock options. Less hours."

"That's fantastic," Leslie chirped, feeling like her response could be a good model for him when she broke her news. She'd booked a trip to a conference in Toledo after Kerry left for college. It would be like a relaunch of her career, and she hoped he'd be as supportive as she was in that moment.

"And I did something a little impulsive. I know that's not like me."

It was indeed very much like him. Paul was dynamic and confident and in that he made quick decisions and asserted what he wanted. She had a feeling this would be no different.

He took her hand in his and looked deep into her eyes.

This was trouble.

"You've been such an amazing mother and wife over the years. I don't know what I would have done without you. I certainly never would have been able to get where I am in my career. Getting the kids off to college, ready for the world, that's mostly been you. You are the rock in this family. I wanted to do something special for you."

"Special?"

"I negotiated a month off into my transition. I'll be taking the next six months to help my successor get up to speed and then after Kerry is settled in at school, I'll be free for a whole month."

He could come with her to Toledo.

It wasn't the sexiest city on earth, but they could find ways to make it fun. "A whole month," she beamed. "That's exciting. I wanted to talk to you a bit about after Kerry goes to school. I have some ideas."

"Hold that thought," Paul said, straightening up his back and taking out his phone. "I want to get all the details right. You'll have a lot of questions. Brace yourself. I've booked us on a three-week tour of Europe. All the spots we've always wanted to hit. Venice. Rome. Paris. London. I worked with a travel agent for a month to get everything perfect. The tours. The reservations at the finest restaurants. When I go over it with you I think you'll be so pleased."

"Europe for three weeks? Which three weeks?"

"September. It'll be beautiful weather still, don't worry."

"But, work—my work."

"That's the best part." Paul was beaming with pride. "I called Roland and told him the situation. He said if anyone deserves a break it's you. They'll have it all worked out so you can take the time off. He said not to worry at all."

"You called my boss?"

"I know, crazy right? I feel like you've done all the planning and organizing of everything for decades. I wanted this to be completely handled for you. You have nothing to worry about." He smiled expectantly, but she didn't smile back. It was a few long beats before he realized she wasn't going to.

"I appreciate the thought," Leslie gulped out. "It must have been a lot of work. But—"

"But?" Paul asked, his eyes wide with surprise, his voice tinged with anger. "What could possibly be wrong with this?"

"I had made plans for the time after Kerry leaves for school."

"Oh my gosh, don't tell me we both did the same thing? Did you book a trip for us? How funny." Paul's face softened, and she felt terrible for the blow she was about to deliver.

"I have a conference in Toledo in September. I thought you could come. We could make a week of it."

"Toledo, Ohio? A conference?" The creases in Paul's forehead deepened. "I don't understand. We're talking about Europe. A dream vacation. Maybe you're just in shock. You need time to process it all. When I get back from the office I'll show you the entire itinerary, and I know you'll love it." His grip had loosened, and he slid his hand away.

"Paul, I wish you would have talked to me about this first. I've been giving a lot of thought to my career. The conference in Toledo is the largest in my industry, and I plan to network. I want to switch companies and really invest in my future in the business. I want to be all-in on it. If I don't go, I won't have this kind of opportunity until the following year. You said it yourself, I've kept everything around here going. I'm ready to take some time to see how far I can go in my career."

Paul winced as she explained. "All right, I hear what you're saying. That's a larger conversation and one we should definitely have. I didn't realize you were considering ramping up your career. I had hoped we'd slow down together. But I'm open to that discussion. This trip to Europe is separate. Maybe we can even talk about it when we're riding a gondola or standing under the Eiffel Tower."

"Paul, you shouldn't have gone to my boss and asked for time off without talking to me. The last thing I want to do right now is have them question my commitment to the company. This trip sounds amazing, but it's not the right time for it. I'm sorry. I really am."

"Leslie." Paul chuckled dismissively. "It's not a refundable trip. Just take some time to think about it and we'll talk later." He stood and tucked the paper under his arm. No kiss goodbye. As a consolation he gently squeezed her shoulder before grabbing his keys and leaving.

Her eyes drifted back to the koi pond, the water spilling over the fake rocks. The flowers the landscaper had just planted around the edge. The like-new bench no one ever bothered to sit on. Paul had made their decision all those years ago. He'd laid down the framework for their life as parents of young children. If she wasn't careful, he'd do the same for this stage of their life. She wasn't ready to give that control away. Not again.

Her guilt morphed to anger as she thought of Paul talking to her boss, smugly planning her vacation time. Assuming she wouldn't be missed for nearly a month. With laser focus she stood and stepped out the sliding glass door to the backyard.

That damn pond.

It had cost thousands to build. Even more to maintain over the years. The fish had been devoured multiple times by birds. Replaced as though they were cherished family pets rather than a nuisance no one wanted to deal with. Kneeling by the bubbling fountain Leslie took two handfuls of the flowers and yanked them from the fresh ground they'd been planted in. Ripping them away felt cathartic. The rage building inside her had a place for a moment. A function.

Clawing at the rest of the flowers, she upended each with growing force and vigor. When they all lay in a pile by her legs, she realized it had not been enough.

Knocking rocks to the side, she stood, rolling them out of their place. Toppling them over and exposing the rough unfinished cement surface below. Letting out a primal growl, her stare fixed on the bench. The stupid unused bench that Paul had spent weeks researching and picking out. Then a whole Saturday afternoon wasted assembling it. Just so it looked nice. Just so people could coo and comment on the space.

With two hands she stood behind the bench and shoved it forward. Her anger fueled her strength and the bench moved with ease, scraping across the stamped concrete and plummeting into the pond with a silly *sploosh* noise. Music to her ears.

Tears rolled down her cheeks as she took in the aftermath. Her hands ached where thorns and sharp-edged stones had cut and scraped her.

Paul would want an explanation. And maybe it was finally time to give him one.

As Leslie brushed at the dirt on the knees of her white slacks she heard the sliding door open behind her. She'd misjudged one part of this outburst. Forgotten the impact it might have on someone else.

"Mom?" Kerry's voice shook. "What are you doing?"

Leslie dropped her head and looked down at the mess, before slowly turning to see Kerry.

How much had she seen?

"I hate this thing," Leslie admitted in a hushed and quivering voice. "I just hate it."

"The koi pond? You hate it?" Kerry sounded confused but gentle and worried too.

Leslie nodded.

"Your hands are bleeding." Kerry moved in closer, wide nervous eyes examining her mother. "Come in and I'll get the bandages."

"No, you need to study. I'm fine. I should clean this all up before your father gets home. I can replant some of the flowers. I'll tell him I found some other ones I liked better. The rocks will go back up. I'll fish the bench out of the water. It'll all be fine."

Kerry hummed out a funny noise. "Mom, come clean up those cuts. Forget this mess. If you hate the koi pond, get rid of it. I never understood why we had the thing to begin with. No one sits out here. It's just more work for you, as if you didn't already have enough to do."

Leslie used the back of her hands to wipe her cheeks dry. "I shouldn't have done that."

"Maybe it's exactly what you should have done. Maybe you should have done it a long time ago." Kerry put her arm around her mother and led her into the house. She was always her sweet girl, a heart so true, flooded with empathy and understanding. Leslie had never wanted to need her children this way. Kids weren't supposed to have to pick up the pieces of their parents and put them back together.

"I don't know what came over me." They stepped back into the kitchen and Kerry guided her mother to a chair. Watching her daughter retrieve the first aid kit from under the sink was a surreal moment. Up until today it had been her job to bandage the boo-boos and calm the tears. She hadn't imagined the roles would ever reverse.

"Did he tell you about the trip to Europe today?" Kerry's lips pursed angrily. She looked like a woman suddenly. Her expression was mature and stoic.

"You knew?"

Kerry looked suddenly guilty. "He told me yesterday. I should have given him my opinion then, but he looked so happy. I had a feeling you wouldn't want to go."

"You did? Why?" How had she taken her nose out of a book long enough to know how Leslie would feel about the trip?

"I used your laptop the other day to print off some study material I needed. You had your résumé up and some job boards with listings for senior leadership positions. You want to work. Right? You've been supporting Dad all these years and going to his dinner meetings with the CEO and his wife. Hosting clients. You've been taking days off to get me and the boys where we needed to go. You're not looking to retire, are you?"

"No." There was apology in her voice. No one had ever told her before she had children just how much guilt came with the job. Thousands of diaper changes, bedtime stories, and packed lunches. Accompanied by failures and a mountain of remorse. Admitting she wanted to work more somehow made her sound ungrateful for all the years of mothering she was lucky enough to do.

"I wouldn't want to go on that trip either." Kerry crouched down in front of her mom and began wiping the tiny scratches clean. "This might sting."

"You wouldn't want to go? Why not?"

"The same reason I'm not spending all my time trying on a hundred formal dresses and aiming to be prom queen. I want to study. I have an idea of what I want out of my life, and I have to work for it. I think Dad's heart was in the right place, but he doesn't get it. He doesn't get you. And to be honest, after all these years of marriage, maybe you're going to have to toss a couple benches into the koi pond to get him to realize that."

Leslie turned her hands up to let Kerry wrap the bandages gently around her fingers. "Does this hurt?" Kerry winced apologetically as she wiped the cuts on her palm with alcohol swabs.

Leslie didn't flinch. She couldn't feel anything more than she could feel her anger and pain. "Your father and I made promises to each other many years ago. We made tough choices. He's not ready for those agreements to change."

"Dad's been around long enough. He should know everything changes eventually." The edge to Kerry's voice was unsettling. She was angry on Leslie's behalf and there was something nice about that.

"He's not used to things not going his way."

"Trust me I know that. He'll get used to it. He'll have to. You deserve whatever you want. Don't forget that." She patted her mother's leg gently. The role reversal was actually comforting. It was nice to see her child able to give comfort.

"Did you get so smart from all your books?" Leslie leaned her head in and touched her forehead to Kerry's.

"Some things you can't learn in books. You have to learn them from watching your mom."

CHAPTER 5

Gwen

"**M**aybe we should have waited for them." Gwen anxiously fiddled with the radio knobs. The note they'd left for her parents seemed wholly inadequate now that they were on the road. She could only imagine what they would think when they found it.

"We're grown people. We don't have to tell our parents where we're going or why. Relax." He rolled his neck, clearly trying to get rid of an ache.

"I guess that tree house floor wasn't as comfortable as you imagined it. Regretting it now?" She beamed with a gloating smile.

"I've been trying to live without regrets lately." He ran one hand over the steering wheel as they pulled up to a red light. "I have a little pain in my neck. It was worth it to hang out with my old friend, the pain in the ass."

"We could have hung out in a bigger space with better structural integrity. Some memory foam mattresses and indoor plumbing." He used the steering wheel buttons to turn the radio off and she huffed, getting the hint. Her nervous energy was bugging him.

"And we could have gone anywhere today, but you picked Rhode Island. A part of it which might be exactly as sleepy and dull as our town. We have no real plan. We're just winging it."

"That's not true." Gwen reached into her bag and pulled out her phone. She was waiting for it to ring and her mother's name to pop up. The fact that it hadn't only meant her parents weren't home yet. "I did a little research, and while the clinic I was left at closed down, it was associated with the Women and Infants Hospital in the city. There is a social media page dedicated to the main hospital. There were two posts about the clinic, and one woman commented that she worked there during the years I would have been left. I got her information. I want to talk to her."

"Great job Nancy Drew." He cast a sideways glance her way. "Now what?"

"She still works at the main hospital. I found her on a business networking site, and she is currently listed as working first shift in the pediatric wing. We'll go talk to her." She was intentionally trying to sound light and breezy about the plan. As if it was no big deal. She was sure he could see right through that.

"There's a very good chance I misjudged whether or not you are of sound mind. I wanted to sleep in a tree house. You want to stalk strangers and ask them questions from twenty-five years ago?"

"Scared?" She twisted her mouth into a playful smile even though her own emotions were as tumultuous and dark as a stormy sea. It wasn't the time to put that on display. She wanted to seem confident in her plan.

His face fell serious and she noticed his hands tighten on the steering wheel. "What if you don't like the answers you get?

There are a million variables. You could find out something you don't like."

"You think I don't know that? My biological parents could be dead. They could want me. They could reject me. The story of why they gave me up could be admirable or despicable. I could be the product of rape. The horrible reminder of a crime. Maybe they're such heinous people I'll regret ever having looked for them. I could spend the rest of my life plagued by thoughts of my own genetic poisons they created by having me. Every single romanticized idea I've had about finding them could be demolished."

"Right." Griff nodded as though relieved she was finally getting it. "Are you really prepared for that? Because the simple idea of sending off your DNA to be analyzed sent you to the hospital."

"It's not too late to go back," Gwen said, reaching out and touching his arm until his grip on the wheel loosened. "I can do this on my own. You don't have to get involved. Especially when things have been so rocky for you already."

"I don't want you to do this alone. I'm just not sure how I can actually help you. If things go bad, then what?"

"Maybe you can't help." Gwen shrugged and put her feet up on the dash, hoping a relaxed posture might beget relaxed feelings. "I might crash and burn. This could break me. And there's a chance all you'll be is a spectator. But I think that might still be better than being alone."

"I'm better than nothing."

"Exactly."

"I made a playlist," he grumbled. "I no longer think it matches the tone of this road trip." Griff's lips curled up slightly. "It's very upbeat. I should have picked songs with a little more doom and gloom."

"Actually, I'm feeling quite upbeat at the moment." Her phone vibrated in her hand, and she quickly sent it to voice mail. She'd wait for her mother to get desperate enough to text her.

They passed a familiar spot, and she couldn't help but reminisce. "Remember when we used to pile in the car for the drive-in movies?"

"Your father enjoyed a bargain, and he took it very seriously when they told him it was eight dollars a carload. He loaded that car. A dozen of us crammed into their station wagon. Popped our own popcorn. Your mom bought discount candy and put it in little plastic bags with our names written on it."

"And we'd go there early. Do you remember why?" She leaned toward him, waiting anxiously for his answer. There was nothing quite like sitting with someone who'd experienced life through the same lens. They had a language. Inside jokes. Hiding spots. Shared secrets. Epic fights. Negotiated forgiveness. It was thrilling to be with him again.

"Your dad made us walk around and pick up any soda or beer cans so he could cash them in for a nickel. We'd look for spare change that might have fallen out of people's cars. I swear some nights he ended up net neutral on the eight dollars he spent to take us there."

A moment after their laughter subsided, Griff's phone rang. "It's your mother," he reported nervously. "She already called you?"

"I think you should pick it up." She challenged him with sly grin and slowly batted her lashes at him.

"I might pick up," he threatened.

"You should."

He grunted and put his phone on speaker. "Hey, Millie."

"Are you with Gwen?" Millie asked, sounding out of breath. She felt bad her mother was worried. But relieved to not be in the house right now. Under the scrutiny of her mother's endless concern.

"Yeah, we left you a note. Did you get it?" She watched his grip tighten around the steering wheel again.

"I got the note. It just seemed strange. We weren't expecting Gwen until this morning, and we came home to find she'd gone off with you. What's this about?"

"I was dropping the truck back off at your house and ran into her. We started catching up and realized we didn't have much to do before the holiday. It sounded like a good time to hang out." He gulped and gave Gwen a dirty look for putting him in this position.

Gwen covered her mouth to stifle a giggle.

"She didn't answer her phone." Millie's words were curt and full of frustration. "Does she have her phone?"

Griff saw his chance to get her back. "Oh yeah, she has her phone. I don't know why she didn't answer. She's right here. You're on speakerphone. Gwen, say hi to your mom. Tell her why you didn't answer your phone."

Her laugh melted into an angry glare. "Hey, Mom. We're fine. Like Griff said, it just seemed like a good idea. Impulsive, but you know how he is."

"Where are you going?" Millie sounded abundantly worried. She could practically see her mother wearing a path in the linoleum floor.

"Griff says he knows this great spot in Rhode Island. It's all decorated for the holidays. They even do a gingerbread house contest. It sounded fun so we just decided to head out. I know it's spontaneous, but I really wanted a break from school."

"Oh," Millie sang, sounding more upbeat. "I do want you taking a break. That sounds nice. I like the idea of you and Griffy catching up. Just be safe and don't stress out about anything. And pick up your damn phone when I call."

"I'll make sure, Millie," Griff replied confidently.

"And you," Millie said brightly, "make sure you spend time

with us over Christmas, Griffy. We miss you. I'm glad you're back in town."

"Talk to you soon, Mom," Gwen said, reaching for the phone and hanging it up after a quick goodbye.

Griff focused on the stretch of road ahead and made a disapproving noise. "Gingerbread house contest?"

"What's wrong with that?" Her cheeks were hot with nervousness.

"I think you should have come up with something a little manlier for me to have suggested. Maybe I found a cool ski lodge. Or a concert we were going to check out."

"People break their necks skiing. There are big crowds at concerts. I was trying to think of something that would cause my mother absolutely no reason to worry. What's the worst thing that could happen at a gingerbread house contest?"

"We won't lose a limb, but I could get my dignity amputated. And now I'm caught up in a lie with your mom. I can't lie to her."

"It wasn't really a lie. I booked us a room at the Chalon Resort. It is decorated for the holidays and people come from all over to see their displays of gingerbread houses."

"And it's in close proximity to the hospital, I'd imagine."

"Three miles away."

He nodded, trying not to look impressed. "What's the best-case scenario for you in this?"

"In looking for my birth family?"

"Yes, what would you want to happen?"

"I don't have any expectations."

"You must."

"I can't. I can't allow myself to wish and hope for one particular outcome. The odds are stacked way too high against me. I'd be setting myself up to fail."

"Do you want some kind of ongoing relationship with them?

If it all falls into place and they aren't bad people, do you want them in your life?"

"I'd like the opportunity to consider it. I don't know how that would look. Or logistically how I'd manage that with my parents and my brothers. But people do it. And the Fox family knows how to do hard things. If it works out, I wouldn't mind having people who look like me or share my DNA around in my life sometimes."

"Isn't that funny?"

"What?"

"I've got loads of people. My parents. Two grandparents. Aunts. Uncles. Cousins. Second cousins. They all live within fifty miles of Old Wesley. We've got this thick brow thing going on. And I swear we all have the same curly mop of hair until we get smart and decide to chop it off. I've spent most of my adult life trying to avoid them. I just think it's funny how we all want what we don't have."

She leaned in and turned the radio back on. The *grass is always greener* speech was just around the corner. She could feel it. Instead she found a station that played music from when they were young and laughed as they stumbled over the lyrics. Griff had always been a superstar air guitarist, and she got a stitch in her side watching him drive while he violently strummed the pretend instrument.

"This is all I wanted," she gasped out. "I haven't laughed like this in the longest time." Gwen reached for his arm, trying to get him to put the air guitar to rest before she wet her pants. "You have to stop."

Griff bit at his bottom lip as the song hit the best guitar solo. "I can't be stopped. You can't stop this magic."

Forcefully taking his hand in hers she laced their fingers together. It wasn't meant to be intimate, only playful. It started that way, at least. Her laughs trailed off and his other hand dropped back to the steering wheel.

"We're holding hands," he said, as if he was reporting on the weather. "Actually you're holding my hand."

"To stop you from playing air guitar. You looked like you were going to hurt yourself." She squeezed his hand. "This is purely for your own safety."

"Oh I see. So we should let go then now that I'm safe?"

"If you promise to put the air guitar back in the air case." He opened his mouth to reply but she shot back. "All air instruments must be put away. I've seen your attempt at the saxophone. The drums. Trumpet. None of that. If you promise, I'll let your hand go."

Griff groaned as the radio switched to an old slow song. One she remembered being featured at her eighth-grade winter formal. A dance she wished he could have taken her to but a senior wouldn't be caught dead there. "This one has a sweet flute solo in it. I can't promise you I won't attempt it."

"Then I'm not letting you go." She clutched him tighter. "Sorry."

He feigned annoyance and dramatically huffed. "Fine. You can hold my hand."

"I'm not holding it as much as I am holding it hostage. When you are ready to hand over all your air instruments as ransom, we'll talk."

"I'm not ready to negotiate. Not yet. Maybe on the next song." A few beats passed, and then he squeezed her hand back.

This should have required more discussion. Dissection of intent and meaning. Was this the start of something? Just the filling of a need? Pure comfort in a time that so deeply required it?

She didn't know.

Gwen guessed he didn't know either. But as the flute solo

started he groaned in disappointment. "I'd have killed it on the flute."

"Or I'd have killed you for trying it."

Music became the focus of the rest of the ride. No heavy questions. No deep speculation into the future. Just memories rooted in familiar beats.

Like a bird flying through the sky, his presence was the lift that cut beneath her wings. For the last year she'd been fighting against every obstacle to merely get up off the ground. Now, without even trying, she was soaring.

CHAPTER 6

Leslie

It all fit in a tiny box.

T he box used to be under the extra winter blankets in the
linen closet but at some point, as the kids got older, it
wasn't safe to keep it there anymore. Paul wouldn't ever stumble
upon it. She wasn't sure he knew the house had a linen closet.
He'd be much more likely to subscribe to the idea the linen fairy
came every week to change out their towels and sheets.

The real risk of discovery came from the children. They could
snoop for Christmas presents and stumble upon it. Or they'd get a
spark of ingenuity and decide they wanted to build a blanket fort
in the living room, heading straight for the linen closet for
supplies. It would be too difficult to explain the contents of the
small box to anyone.

That's why, fifteen years ago, Leslie opened a safety deposit box at the local branch of her bank. She didn't lie to Paul about it. Instead, remarking on how an old acquaintance of hers had just lost their house to a fire. They should be smart and move their irreplaceable documents to a safety deposit box. To Paul it sounded like something responsible sophisticated people would do. Always wanting to seem prepared, of course he was on board.

Leaving the mess in the backyard, she kissed Kerry's forehead and thanked her for the insightful and kind words. With bandaged fingers, she grabbed her car keys and decided it was time to visit the bank again. Years had passed since the last time she'd spun the key into the lock and slid the metal box from the bank wall.

It was always anticlimactic when she did go. It wasn't as though there was much time to spend with its contents. You couldn't park yourself in the bank lobby and reminisce with relics of your past. For those reasons there had been plenty of times she'd talked herself out of going. She'd start driving there and then detour for coffee instead.

I'll just stir up the old pain. It doesn't do me any good.

It was different this time. The old pain was already stirred up, on display like the exposed roots of a toppled tree. There was no threat of a simple visit doing more damage. With the same focus that fueled her to destroy the koi pond, she drove unwaveringly toward the bank. Pulling into a parking spot she flung the car door open before even putting it in park. When her feet hit the pavement she realized something that most days would have been laughable.

She'd slid her feet into two different shoes. They were both backless clogs. One was black the other brown. If she was lucky it would not be noticeable to the average person passing by.

Her reflection in the car window made her cringe. Leslie tried to smooth her unkempt hair. She wasn't one to leave the house without running a comb through her hair and at a minimum sweeping on some mascara and under-eye concealer. The years had been better to her than most. The wrinkles around her eyes were few. But still she wasn't feeling very presentable right now.

An hour ago this had just been an average, quiet morning in the Laudon household. Her to-do list mostly consisted of trying to find a way to keep a grip on holiday traditions no one else in the family cared about.

She'd dug her nails into the rituals and clung to them with all her might. She'd fought against time and distance, which tried to pull them away. Like every year before, there would be holiday cookies shaped like elves even if she had to bake them alone. There would be popcorn strung for the tree, even if it meant working her fingers raw. No one would keep her from making the magic she'd been in charge of for decades. The holidays were meant to be busy. Bustling. Almost unmanageably chaotic. Yet this year threatened to be serene if she let it. For the first time ever, her sons weren't coming home. Schedules and excuses were keeping them away. The fact that she wouldn't wake up Christmas morning with her whole family hadn't really sunk in yet.

There wasn't really a need to put on the big holiday she always had. What really worried her was that she'd managed to go twenty-something years without being bored, and now was not the time to let the devil have hold of her idle hands.

Now those traditions would have to wait. Wait for her to stabilize her mind. The way she'd had to do so many times before. Push it down. Manage it.

The bank door was heavy and she struggled to pull it open, feeling weakened by the emotions coursing through her. Obediently falling into line, Leslie waited patiently for the next teller to be available. Technology had made trips to the bank in general a rare event for her. At most she'd deposit the occasional check into the ATM. Looking around the lobby Leslie missed how orderly and quiet it was there. How predictable and unchanged the bank was. Reliably so.

A teller with springy gray hair and cat-eye glasses waved her up. There was a grumpiness to her demeanor that Leslie felt grateful for. There would be no idle chitchat about the weather with this woman. Leslie had learned how to fake being okay, but it didn't mean she wanted to. Not right now.

"I'd like to open my safety deposit box." Even though it was hers. Even though Paul knew about it, Leslie still felt a pang of guilt as she announced her intent.

"Number?" the teller asked curtly, not looking up from her computer.

"Two twenty-one."

"Follow me." She circled around the counter and moved toward the room in the back. Leslie followed quickly, her tight grip on the key making her hand sweat.

"You can open the box and take it into that room there." She pointed to a small windowless room with only a hard bench in it. "When you are ready to close it up, just ring that buzzer."

"Got it," Leslie said, spinning her key in the lock and pulling the long steel box out of the wall. She nearly explained why she was there. Created some story about needing her daughter's birth certificate for college applications. But the woman was gone before the lie fully formed in her mind.

God bless her for not giving a damn.

Leslie rubbed her hand over the top of the closed metal box as though she were petting a friendly dog. Settling onto the rigid bench, she placed it on her lap and slowly flipped the lid open. Something in her was disappointed by how few things were there. The events took up huge real estate in her heart and her mind, but this tiny box was mostly empty. It's not as if somehow the contents would have duplicated or grown by now. A seedling that sprouted into a beautiful flower, watered by her tears.

Nothing had changed. Nothing had grown. It was all where she'd left it.

First, she fingered the little pink-and-blue striped cap, remembering how she'd tucked it in her pocket before leaving the hospital all those years ago. Bringing it to her nose, she drew in a breath, desperately searching for the hint of a scent that had long since faded.

Rubbing her thumb across the tiny hat she felt the tears forming. Blinking them back, she reached for the hospital bracelet. The one with the words Jane Doe typed across the front. She'd pretended to be no one, because that day, she felt like nothing. Like she didn't deserve an identity at all.

A little inked footprint and handprint on a piece of paper lay at the bottom, and she scooped it up. The swirls and lines in the tiny toes and fingers made her body ache. At the time the ink print was made Leslie didn't know just how special they were. Now she understood how those were formed. Why everyone's fingerprints and footprints were unique. Those ridges, the whorls and valleys were developed in a mother's womb. Solidified and unchanged for life. A gift, one of the only ones she could say she gave her baby. There had been so many days Leslie wished she could just peek in on her daughter's life. A bird's-eye view, then swoop away. Just to know she was all right. Cared for. Something to show Leslie she'd made the right decision.

But because of how she'd handled things, there had been no way to do that. No bread crumb trail to lead her back. Maybe that's why she'd been able to convince herself it was what she wanted. Hoping to see her daughter was impossible. And hoping for something impossible was always easy, because you never had to worry about the consequences, since it would never happen.

She consoled herself with the knowledge that there had been a need to move quickly. This was what was best for the baby. It was at least better than the alternative. Leslie's mind wandered to the face of the woman who'd saved her daughter's future.

Ivy Sue Chantal was as southern as her name implied. A long singsong drawl made her words, even the difficult ones to hear, sound buoyant and upbeat. As a nurse at a small clinic, Ivy made Leslie promises well outside the bounds of her job. Promises she was in no position to make. At great risk to herself, she gave Leslie more than she was in a position to give. And nearly every day, Leslie said a little prayer of gratitude for that.

Twenty-five years ago, the haze of labor pains and a broken heart had beaten Leslie to a pulp. When she prayed for it all to end, it was Ivy's hand in hers. Words of encouragement whispered in her ear. Ivy had been what got her through.

"You can do this, girl. You can do this." Her sterile smelling hands were dry and cracked from long hard days of work and too much hospital soap. Rough but easy to grip. Her hair, the lush black coils, were pinned back from her face. Her dark skin was rich and smooth. *"Miss, this baby is coming. You're going to be just fine and so is this baby."*

More promises. Ones Leslie was desperate to believe.

At that point Leslie didn't know if she was having a boy or a girl. She'd told the doctor at the adoption agency who provided her prenatal care that she preferred not to know. The temptation to look up baby names or stroll through the baby clothes department at the store lessened that way.

Though she couldn't indulge in the fun parts of her pregnancy, she did take the rules seriously. She knew to take the vitamins. To steer clear of certain foods. No smoking. No drinking. The doctor at MCA didn't do much besides the basics. No bells and whistles that she would have gotten at her own doctor. She was lucky enough to have good health insurance, but it was important to her that this didn't go in her medical records.

The unfriendly doctor at MCA didn't know her medical

history. To him she was a belly glazed with ultrasound jelly and legs in stirrups. That suited her fine considering the circumstances.

When labor began and she found herself at the tiny clinic it helped to remind herself that women had been giving birth for generations without modern medicine. It helped to not focus too much on the outdated equipment and tiny rooms. It had to be this way in order to keep her secret. It plagued her with worry. But in that moment, as she pushed and breathed and cried, she believed somehow Ivy was right. She'd survive this. Her baby would too. It was almost over.

When her daughter was born, there was a rush, a whooshing. Maybe it was only physical. But it felt deeper than that. A release of something. A strangling grip that had finally let up. There was guilt, but there was also a sense of freedom.

"Will you hold her?" Ivy asked, the swaddled baby in her own arms. What Ivy knew that no other employees in the room did, was this baby wouldn't be going home with her mother. Maybe others could guess as much, but Ivy had been the only person Leslie had spoken to since going into labor six hours earlier.

For Leslie, the draw to the infant was hypnotic and unstoppable. Crumbling away from her plan to keep this clinical and as simple as possible, her arms opened without a second of hesitation. As she drank in the smell and soft skin of her daughter, the maybes started flooding her mind. Maybe she could make this work. Maybe she could fix what she'd broken. Maybe she'd overreacted to the situation and how afraid she was.

The doctors cleared the room eventually, leaving just Ivy there, leaning over Leslie's shoulder. "She's perfect. Very healthy. You did well. You tore a bit; the doctor put in a couple stitches but nothing major. You'll recover quickly."

"Thank you," Leslie breathed out, ignoring the tears on her

cheeks. They rolled down freely and met at her chin, dripping down on to the baby's blanket.

Ivy's voice was soft in her ear. "You have options here. I know you feel as though you don't, but I can help you. We can call the police. Tell them what's going on with the agency you contracted with. There have been rumors about them for years. With the police and a lawyer, you could protect yourself."

"No." Leslie felt reality move like a wrecking ball through all the maybes she'd stacked up. "I can't get the police involved. I can't be this baby's mother. I can't be. Not now."

"I understand," Ivy said, patting her hand gently. Leslie questioned how this woman could possibly understand something so impossibly convoluted. But looking at Ivy's gentle face, Leslie knew somehow she did. "They won't allow you to stay here as a Jane Doe. Because we're a small clinic they're able to be more understanding than the main hospital, but soon they'll insist you tell them who you are or they will involve children's services. The baby will go into the foster system. You could be in some trouble."

"I don't want that, but the agency I thought I'd be working with can't know she's here. They can't have her. Not now that I know who they really are."

"I agree." Ivy lowered her voice as two other nurses passed by the door. "I know about them. Preying on women and children in need. It's despicable."

"Then what do I do?" Her words caught in her throat like a scared child, and she clutched her daughter tightly. "There must be something."

"You can leave." Ivy drew in a deep breath, and her own eyes filled with tears. "It's not a very easy-to-swallow option. But I'm worried for you and about these people at that agency. I don't know what might become of your daughter with them."

"What happens if I just leave?" Leslie gulped as she conjured

up an image of her shimmying out of the window in the dark of the night.

"I know of a couple, very good friends of mine. They might be able to help. They're good people. The best really. I think they would take her. Especially if I called and explained the situation"

"They want to adopt?"

"All I can say is, if I were in this situation, they would be who I would call. They're that special."

Leslie tried not to be wounded by the fact that she was on this end of the situation. If not for some missteps she could be the special person worthy of this kind of praise just like Ivy's friends were. "I signed papers with the Mission Crest Agency. What if they come for her? What if they can legally take her?"

Ivy brushed Leslie's hair off her sweat-soaked forehead. "They won't know who she is. They won't know where she is. Because you are a Jane Doe and so is she. When you leave here she won't be connected by name to you in any way. She'll be safe. It'll be a fresh start for her."

"A fresh start." Leslie whimpered as she squeezed her baby tightly and kissed her tiny nose. "And these people—you said they are good people?"

"The best. They have two boys of their own already."

"She'd have two big brothers?" Leslie asked hopefully. "I want her to have brothers."

"Yes."

"Where do they live?"

"I don't think I should tell you that." Ivy averted her eyes nervously as someone in the hallway stirred. It was clear if anyone else came in things would be out of Ivy's control. "I think if you do this, it should be a fresh start for you both. A part of your life you move on from. With MCA involved, the less you know the better."

Goose bumps moved up her arms as she considered how she

ended up here in the first place. *"How can I trust you? I trusted the last person who came into my life and said they'd have the perfect family for my baby. I was a fool to believe them."*

"People's words shouldn't be enough to make you believe something. When money is involved, people will say anything to get their way. I guess it's the telling of things that is easy. Anyone can do it, say whatever they like to convince people of their lies. The only thing I can say is, I have been a labor-and-delivery nurse for twenty-three years. I have watched first breaths, last breaths, no breaths at all. There have been joyful births and sorrowful deaths. I have celebrated and consoled. Counseled and prayed. I know, deep in my soul, life is precious, and I treat it as such. I'm asking nothing of you and taking a risk to do so. That's the only proof I can give you. It's up to you to decide if it's enough."

"Don't you want to know why I don't want my baby?" It seemed a natural question for someone in her situation. It felt strange that Ivy hadn't insisted on knowing before offering her help.

"You do want your baby," Ivy said, in a nearly scolding tone. *"I see it in your eyes right now. I hear your voice. You want your baby. That's different than not being able to keep her."*

That had been the moment Leslie knew how genuine Ivy's heart was. How truly able she was to understand.

"Could you call them? Ask them if they will take her?" Her words were broken up by tiny sobs. She'd known she'd let her child go. She'd known there was no other way. But it was starting to feel terrifyingly final now.

"I would be honored to make that phone call." Ivy used the back of her hands to wipe her tears away and drew in a deep breath.

"It doesn't usually work like this does it?" Butterflies raged in

Leslie's exhausted body as information came quickly and a new plan formed out of the ashes of her old one.

"No this isn't the way it normally works. But if you leave her, the child will need to be nursed. She'll need to be cared for. There would be a place for her in foster care but once she left here, I'd know nothing about what becomes of her. I have a very close relationship with the hospital's liaison in child protective services. She and I have been working together for over a decade. If I tell her this is the best option, she'll look into it, see the same thing, and help move the process along. The parents have fostered before their boys were born. They're in the system. It'll move quickly. Your baby will be all right. I'll make sure of it."

"I could tell you who I am," Leslie blurted out urgently. "Then if it doesn't work out with them you can call me and let me know what's happening."

Ivy held a hand like a stop sign. "I can't know more about you than I do right now. I'm an honest woman. A God-fearing woman, and I won't lie if someone asks me about you. Don't tell me who you are. Please."

Leslie nodded as her daughter squeaked and shifted in her arms. She made an instinctive sweet shushing noise and gently rocked her arms.

"You're a natural," Ivy commented with a bright smile as she busied herself with the beeping machine next to her.

If she only knew why this all came so naturally to Leslie. The truth might send Ivy running in the other direction. Maybe her understanding and empathy would dry up like sun-scorched earth. No one would be able to understand how Leslie ended up here with all she had waiting for her at home.

"Get some rest," Ivy said, opening her arms for the baby. "I'll make a phone call. It'll all be better soon."

"Can I keep her here while you do?" Leslie examined every inch of her daughter. Trying to imagine what these plump doughy *features would look like as the years flashed by. Some distinguishing feature she could remember forever. There was no birthmark shaped like Texas. No constellation pattern of freckles she could commit to memory.*

"How sure are you about this?" Ivy's weathered face examined the mother and daughter closely. "Maybe it doesn't have to be this way."

"I am all out of maybes," Leslie replied sadly. "I'm out of time. This is the only thing that will work. It has to be this way for everyone involved."

"Then I'll be back soon." When Ivy had shuffled her tired feet out of the delivery room, Leslie knew things were about to be put into motion. A landslide that couldn't be stopped. She'd have to leave without her baby in her arms. But Ivy had promised she'd be with good people. The best people. Her daughter would have the life she deserved. A life she could fit into, not like the one Leslie had now where there was no room at all.

A loud laugh in the lobby of the bank broke her out of the memory. A hardy, big-bellied man with red suspenders and dirty work boots passed by the door, the joke she hadn't heard still stirring up his laughter. Clearing away the tears on her cheeks she turned her face away. This wasn't the clinic. It was the bank, and she'd need to get it together before people started to worry.

It was hard to stuff it all down. It had always been hard. The ache radiating from her body was reminiscent of a bad sunburn. She was both hot and cold. Sensitive to the slightest touch. A tiny shift of her own body felt excruciating. Hyperaware of every nerve she possessed. Because a broken heart hurts all over.

"Why now?" she whispered to the empty room. She'd known her triggers before. Obviously giving birth to Kerry, another baby girl, would prompt her to break down. All the pink dresses she never got to buy her first daughter. Then it was the hormonal surges and ending of her childbearing years made sense. Menopause felt so final. But what was it now that had her reeling with guilt and sadness? Kerry leaving? The empty nest?

No.

A knot tightened in her stomach as she let the answer rise to the top like cream.

Being alone with Paul.

Leslie had been so busy. Busy raising their children. Balancing their schedules. Supporting his career. When the dust settled, when the responsibilities she'd been charged with were complete, how would she be able to look at him? There would finally be time to grieve. Time to lament. Time to blame him. A dangerous amount of time.

Was that why she was so desperate to lean into her career?

Busy was a speed she could hide in. Then she wouldn't have to peer behind the curtain of her marriage and the pain that lurked there.

"Miss," the teller said uneasily as she stood in the doorway of the tiny room. "Do you need tissues?"

Leslie snapped the lid of the box closed and wiped at her damp cheeks again. "No. Sorry. I'm sending my youngest off to college, and I needed her birth certificate. I'm a soon-to-be empty-nester, and I'm just not ready."

The teller gave a small understanding smile and nodded. "Been there, done that. My husband and I took a trip to Italy when my youngest went off to college. That helped a little. Having something to look forward to, finally reconnecting with each other as people rather than just parents. You should consider some travel."

The irony was laughable, so that's what Leslie did. She chuckled and nodded as she handed over the box and thanked the teller for her great advice.

It was time to get back to the house and make a decision. She could tell a story about the koi pond that Paul could swallow, bake the cookies, string the popcorn, and wrap the presents. She could get excited to go to Europe and reconnect with Paul. In different ways, she'd done all this before. She was capable of mustering such phony enthusiasm. But she was also tired of having to. Paul had gone behind her back and spoken to her boss. It wasn't the first time he'd stepped over the line. Hell, it wasn't even the first time this year he'd done something like that. Leslie felt too fragile to have to play her part in their usual issues.

Pushing her way out of the bank door, she weighed her options. Completely unsure of what was the right path. Luckily, leaning on the hood of her car was the sounding board she needed. Claudette had her hair wrapped up in a bandana and, though it was overcast and cold, she wore almost comically large sunglasses. Cherry red lipstick and matching high heels made her look glamorous and camera ready.

"What are you wearing?" Leslie laughed out the words, sounding exhausted.

"Hey if we're about to Thelma and Louise out of this town, I want to look the part." She spun and showed off her outfit.

"What are you talking about?" Leslie knew she looked a mess. Her eyes red-rimmed. Her hair wild. It would be hard to explain it all away. Especially to her very astute friend.

"Kerry called me." Claudette rounded the front of the car and sat in the passenger seat, waiting for Leslie to get in.

For a brief second Leslie considered running away. Just turning away from the bank and jogging in the other direction. But that would be silly. And only a temporary solution to a permanent problem. Not to mention, Claudette would kick off those high heels and with her long legs chase her down. So she got in the car.

"What exactly did Kerry have to say?" She tried to hide the

bandages on her fingers but it was useless. Claudette never missed a beat.

"She told me you said you were going to the bank. To her it sounded odd considering you kind of lost your crap and destroyed the koi pond. Are you taking out a loan to replace it?"

She hadn't remembered giving Kerry that detail about the bank. It had been a blur. "The koi pond was stupid." Her voice trailed off and she waved her hands around as if there was more to say but it didn't matter. "I assumed you were clearing out your account, and we were making a break for the Canadian border together. I didn't have time to pack, but we can buy what we need when we get there."

Leslie laughed in spite of the pain. "We're not going anywhere. I'm fine. I just had a moment."

"I didn't know about the trip to Europe," Claudette said apologetically. "He was smart not to ask me first. You know I would have told him to talk to you before booking anything. I'm sure he meant well."

"He did." It pained Leslie to admit it.

"Nothing is really nonrefundable these days. He was probably just being dramatic."

"I threw a bench in a koi pond; I'm not sure Paul's in the running for first place when it comes to being dramatic today."

Claudette's forehead was creased with worry. Something she would normally avoid for fear of encouraging wrinkles. Her sunglasses were off now and the bandana pulled from her head and sitting in her lap. "Is this about work? About your career? I've been thinking about it since you said something at the coffee shop. How did I miss that this was important to you? I feel terrible."

"I'm worried that it's not about work." The tears did come this time. She realized she didn't feel sad but scared as she gripped the steering wheel for stability. Afraid of saying something she couldn't take back. "I'm worried it's more about Paul and me. I can't even picture spending three uninterrupted weeks together. No business trips for him to take off on. No math team state championships for me to take Kerry to. Just the two of us."

"I think that's a normal concern," Claudette began gently, but Leslie cut in sharply.

"Please don't. Not wanting to be around my husband is not normal. Crying for weeks after I had Kerry was not normal. Not getting out of bed when my hormones were unbalanced with menopause. Not normal. Don't excuse this away."

"Leslie," Claudette said warmly, letting all her standard humor melt away, "you can talk to me. Tell me what's going on."

"I'm incredibly angry at Paul." She spoke as if making a vow. A seriousness she couldn't easily take back. "I can't forgive him."

"About Europe?"

"No. This goes back way farther."

"I'm listening." Claudette tapped her red fingernails to the center console of the car. "What did he do?"

"I told you we had a rough time when we were younger. I never really faced it. I just buried it all away and now it's coming back up. I have no excuse but to face it head-on. I think if I start to let it out, even a little bit, it's going to get ugly."

"There's something you aren't telling me," Claudette said, turning to get a good look at Leslie. "And that's perfectly all right. All I need to know is how I can help."

Leslie brought her thumbnail to her mouth and bit nervously at it. "Promise me no matter what you find out about me, it won't change our friendship."

Claudette wasn't quick enough to mask her shock at the request, but she was smart enough to settle her face back to concern. "Nothing you could ever tell me would take away from what I think of you. You have been in my corner through some of the toughest moments of my life. When I lost my dad, you were right by my side. I have watched you care for everyone around you for decades. You have my word, nothing will change."

Leslie understood that promise was a lie. It would be impossible to know what she'd done and not judge her. Judging was Claudette's part-time job. Their friendship wouldn't be enough to protect her from that.

If things were about to fall apart, the best Leslie could hope for was the strength to cling to the wreckage.

CHAPTER 7

Gwen

T he hospital was more intimidating than she had imagined. Gwen had convinced herself she'd march to the labor-and-delivery wing and ask for Lenny Frenzo. She'd insist the nurse go on break and they'd sit over a cup of nasty hospital cafeteria coffee. Lenny would take the time to tell Gwen anything she remembered about her birth mother. It wouldn't be everything, but some pieces of the pictures would come into focus. She'd have notes to scratch down in her journal. Something to hold on to. Something to move forward with.

It didn't work like that. Hospitals, like most places now, were loaded with security measures. Without having a good reason, you couldn't just go up to the maternity wing. Paging a nurse down to the lobby without explanation didn't get you very far either. Especially when they were in the middle of a busy shift. Lenny's profile picture on social media was just a pretty potted plant. There would be no way to spot her in this crowd. It all felt anticlimactic. Like getting stood up for a blind date you'd been excited for.

"This was stupid. What did I think was going to happen? I'd just bump into her outside that little baby zoo room where they line up the newborns in front of the glass window?"

"Baby zoo? You mean the nursery?"

"Call it what you want, unless you plan to pop out a baby anytime soon, they aren't letting us up there." Her voice was sharp, full of nerves and disappointment. If her tone bothered Griff, he didn't show it.

"That's our in." Griff lit with an idea.

"The gift shop? Are we going to buy balloons that say, it's a girl and hope we guess the name of some mom who's up there right now? Any chance there's an Ann Smith?"

Griff shook his head and pointed to the ATM machine outside the gift shop. He marched over without explanation and took out some cash.

"What are you talking about?" Gwen asked in a hushed voice as he passed her on the way back to the front desk. They'd already been turned away from there twice. The woman working the phones had kindly explained she couldn't help them. There was protocol and people needing actual medical attention here at the hospital. Her large-rimmed glasses were almost comically big, making her eyes seem bug-like and cold. But for some reason, Griff was going to take another shot at the woman whose name tag read Benita.

"Ma'am," Griff whispered to the woman. "Benita. We really need to talk to Lenny Frenzo. Maybe when her shift's over and she comes out this way, could you just let us know?"

She pushed her long brown bangs out of her face. It was apparent she loved the power associated with her job as a gate-keeper. Letting people in and turning them away with the full force of the rules behind her. "Why would I tell you when I see Lenny Frenzo?"

He subtly flashed a hundred dollars at her and then tucked it back in his hand. "Because you are really nice and you care deeply about my friend and her search for her biological mother. You, Benita, have a tender heart and a big beautiful smile."

The woman's eyes opened wide. Her lids were heavy with too much blue eye shadow, amplified behind her magnifying glasses. "I do care. But I could care twice as much as that." She jutted her chin toward his hand that held the hundred dollars.

"Twice as much is fine by me." He took another bill out of his pocket and folded them together so she could see.

Benita, now cheerful and receptive again, handed him a clipboard with a pen attached by a chain. "Fill out these papers and then give it back to me. With whatever other *paperwork* you have. Then I'll be sure to let you know when I see Lenny. Her shift ends in an hour."

"Thank you," Griff said victoriously as he took the clipboard and settled into one of the plastic chairs in the corner.

"Seriously? A bribe?" Gwen plopped down next to him with mixed emotions. He'd just solved their problem. That was nice. But he did it in a less than admirable way.

"Sadly the one thing I learned from my career is money talks. It greases the wheels when nothing else will."

"I'll pay you back." She patted her purse. The idea of taking two hundred dollars out of her bank account and handing it over to a stranger like Benita wasn't something she'd normally do. Between her school loans and her apartment, most of the money she made at the lab went to necessities. She'd known that Griff's career was a lucrative one. Hers would be one day as well, but for now two hundred dollars was a good amount to hand out.

"It's fine," Griff said, waving her off. "It's well worth it if this works."

"No seriously. I will." She could always take out a cash advance on her credit card. Griff had done so much for her already. Being in debt to him financially wasn't going to work. She'd spent what she had saved up on the hotel reservation for them.

"Whatever, I'm not worried about it. Just pretend to fill this out and then go give it to cheery Benita up there. Most importantly make sure you know what you want to ask Lenny because I'm guessing you'll only get one shot at this."

She handed back the clipboard with two hundred dollars tucked beneath the papers and watched the woman skillfully pocket it.

"Now what?" Gwen asked, flopping unceremoniously back into the chair next to him. "We just wait?"

"We could play twenty questions like we used to." He put the magazine he was pretending to read down on the table and clapped his hands together in excitement. "I was great at that game."

"No you weren't. All you picked were gross things and silly body parts. Then I'd pick a former president or an island off the coast of Italy, you'd lose and tell me I was cheating."

"You were sort of cheating."

"How?"

"By taking it seriously. Playing twenty questions and making someone guess *butt crack* is never not funny. Picking Abe Lincoln ruins the game. It's cheating me out of a laugh."

They bantered as people around them funneled in through the revolving door and others funneled out. They were all in varying levels of distress or excitement, some physical some emotional. All impatiently waiting to be called.

Watching the second hand on the large lobby clock did little to calm Gwen's mind. It felt like an eternity before Benita finally gave her a strange look and called out loudly.

"Bye, Lenny, I hope you had a good shift." As Benita offered an unnaturally excited wave, Gwen snapped her head around to see which person turned.

An older woman with brown skin and gray streaks in her short black hair stopped in her tracks and eyed Benita curiously. She looked confused by the personalized goodbye and shifted uncomfortably in her white thick-soled shoes as she waved back tentatively.

"Lenny," Gwen said, hopping to her feet and cutting the distance between them. "Can I talk to you for a minute?" There had been nothing natural about her approach and she couldn't blame Lenny for recoiling. Her pace and body language were all wrong for putting Lenny at ease.

The awkward look of confusion on Lenny's face only grew. She clutched her purse tighter and stepped back. "Do I know you?"

"You don't," Gwen said apologetically. She nervously tucked her hair behind her ear, feeling suddenly sheepish.

Griff had stood as well, but kept his distance. With a less frantic tone, Gwen continued. "I wanted to see if I could ask you a couple questions about your time at the West Street Women's Clinic."

"That placed is closed." Lenny had an exhausted bite to her words. "I can't help you with anything. Check the records department on the sixth floor. Some old charts would have been transferred there."

"I don't think the records would help me. This is going back a while. Twenty-five years." Gwen straightened up, trying to be a specimen that Lenny could examine as though she were the embodiment of the story she was about to tell.

"I have to go pick up my grandson. What exactly is this about?" Lenny pursed her lips and set her jaw tightly. Her face was harried by a long shift. Her scrubs were wrinkled and her eyes sagged with exhaustion. Gwen suddenly felt guilty for punctuating this woman's workday with her desperate questions. She'd do best to get to the point before Lenny stormed away.

"It's about an adoption. It took place twenty-five years ago while you were working at the clinic. I have some details that might refresh your memory. The adoption was unconventional and rather quick. It should stand out to you if you were there that day." Gwen gestured at the chairs in the corner of the large lobby, but Lenny didn't make a move toward them.

"Is this about Ivy Chantal?" Lenny shifted her weight from one foot to the other, looking antsy. "I knew this would come back to bite us some day. Are you a journalist? Is this for a podcast? I have no comment."

"No," Gwen said, waving off the idea. "I'm not doing some kind of story about the clinic. This is about me. About my adoption. Ivy was the nurse working the night I was abandoned. My parents knew her."

Lenny let out a humorless laugh. "I've known for years this would eventually come up. That's why I left, to get myself far away from her poor choices."

"Poor choices?" Gwen questioned nervously, glancing toward Griff for backup. He moved in closer, sensing her unease. Sure this was a misunderstanding, she pressed on. "I'm not explaining this right. Ivy was just the person who contacted my adoptive parents. I was born at the clinic. There were no poor choices. She coordinated my adoption."

"Ha," Lenny scoffed loudly enough to draw a few curious glances their way. "Except she wasn't an adoption coordinator. She was a labor and delivery nurse who stepped way outside her role. To me, she was always walking the line of an ethical nightmare. I lost more than one night of sleep over the years about it. There are agencies for adoptions. Laws. Rules. Oversight. Ivy always thought she was above the law. It wasn't just with the

adoptions, but that was the thing that finally got her in trouble."
Lenny made a hasty sign of the cross and whispered an apology
for speaking ill of the dead. She might not have liked Ivy but it
didn't mean she wanted to upset the cosmos either. "She put her
job on the line. All of our jobs."

"Do you have a moment to sit and talk over coffee?" Griff
asked as Lenny made a move to step by them. "It won't take long.
But it's important to Gwen. She's looking for information about
her birth mother."

"The situations with Ivy are not something I want to dig back
up." Lenny dropped her voice to a whisper as if some kind of
danger to her job still loomed. It seemed odd to Gwen since for
her these things were, quite literally, a lifetime ago. How could it
have any implication for Lenny now?

"Wait." Gwen held up a hand as a sharp twinge of worry
stabbed at her side. "There was more than one situation like
mine? How could that be? I was abandoned and Ivy called a
friend in the middle of the night. She went to high school with my
father and thought she could help. Was that a frequent occur-
rence? Did people just leave babies?"

"Was your adoptive father sixty-five years old at the time?
Because if not he didn't go to school with Ivy. That's how old Ivy
was at the time. Trust me, there were a lot of stories told around
those adoptions but none were by the book. Ivy had a stellar reputation as a nurse, and she was well respected in the community in
general. Her husband held a public office, and I know that helped
her get away with what she did. She took liberties well beyond
her job. People loved her, and they used her integrity as collateral
in decision-making. You can't do that. You can't assume because
a good person says this is all right, let's make it all right." Lenny
looked suddenly furious, but beat it back to keep her voice from
drawing more attention.

"Please sit for a few minutes," Gwen pleaded as Lenny's body language grew more rigid. If this woman walked away now, she'd be left with more questions than answers and no avenue forward. This was a tipping point and Gwen needed it to finally tip her way.

"I have five minutes." Lenny moved reluctantly over to the quietest corner in the large lobby and settled her purse into her lap as she sat. Her back was arrow straight as though she was ready to shoot up and run any moment. Not the posture of a skittish wild animal but the readiness of a trained martial artist, completely in control.

Gwen tried to gather her thoughts as she and Griff sat down too. "You're saying I'm not the only child who was delivered in your clinic and adopted under untraditional circumstances?"

"It was not my clinic," Lenny said sharply. "I know of four adoptions involving Ivy that happened while I was on shift. There could be plenty more. Ivy was involved in all of them." Lenny's nostrils flared as though there was a stink associated with this history. A smell she couldn't get rid of no matter how many years had passed.

Griff drew in a deep breath as he tried to explain. "Gwen is twenty-five. Her mother was a Jane Doe. She left the hospital in the middle of the night not long after giving birth. Does that narrow it down for you?"

"Two of the moms were Jane Does who bailed in the dark of the night. I think both were coached by Ivy to do so. One was years before. Maybe closer to thirty years ago." Lenny closed her eyes, either from exhaustion or in an effort to conjure up the right memory.

"Then you remember me?" Gwen asked, leaning in, as though maybe Lenny just needed to get a better look at her. As if her little hours-old face could be the connection to make the memories flood back for Lenny.

"I remember some things about the situation. Your mother

came in when she was deep into labor. She wouldn't provide her name or information but obviously we couldn't turn her away. Being a clinic, we saw all sorts of scenarios that might not turn up at the main hospital. Women felt safer with us. As though a smaller place somehow provided them with more anonymity or less judgment. We'd learned to roll with it. Do our jobs, provide medical care and then call in the folks who could help with the other issues."

"What other issues?" Griff pressed. His questions were productive and moved them closer to the information Lenny might be holding back. As opposed to Gwen's questions which were centered around things that surely Lenny couldn't answer for.

Why? Why did she leave me?

"If a mother came in strung out on drugs, we'd have to involve Child Protective Services. If a father seemed abusive, we'd call in the police. Maybe there wasn't a stable home to release them to. We had resources for that too. There were procedures to follow. Rules. Ivy loved to skirt the rules."

"My mother," Gwen edged the words out slowly. She was finally on the cusp of some answers, and she imagined it was similar to that second before bungee jumping for the first time. A mix of adrenaline-fueled excitement and the flutter of terror. "What was she like? What did she look like?" She bit at her lip, nearly drawing blood. The questions were pointless. If the goal was to find out who her mother was, talking about her facial features as Lenny remembered them twenty-five years later wouldn't help narrow it down.

"I don't remember specifics." Lenny sighed, looking sorry for her lack of memory on that front. "I've helped deliver thousands of babies over the years. I do recall she had long blond hair. Pretty eyes. Green or blue I think. I really can't remember anything else."

Griff wrung his hands nervously, clearly unsure what his role in all of this should be. Finally, he spoke up again. "No one ever got her name? There was no other information on her?"

"What should have happened," Lenny said through pursed lips, "is the police should have been called once she abandoned the baby. Or more should have been done to get her to tell us who she was before she left. There were no safe-haven laws at the time. Unlike today, a mother couldn't walk into your nearest fire station and drop a newborn off with no consequences. The moment we knew that woman wasn't coming back, Child Protective Services should have taken custody of the child. More should have been done to find out who the mother was, and in turn who the father was. Biological family members could have been sought and given the opportunity for custody. But instead, in the dead of the night, Ivy called someone to come get the baby, and then pushed the paperwork through back channels by manipulating her relationships with people in power. It's not supposed to work that way."

Gwen's head spun with the urgency of the time limit Lenny had set. *Had it been five minutes?* She had so many questions, but something told her Griff was right. This would be her one shot. "Why would my adoptive parents tell me they knew Ivy from school? They were barely thirty years old when they adopted me. The story was always told the same way to me. It all just fell into place when I was left behind. This blissful mix of serendipity and destiny."

Lenny cocked a suspicious eyebrow high up her wrinkled forehead. "I don't know about that. Over the years, I've met parents who are desperate for children. They don't ask questions or make waves. They just hold their breath until everything is finalized and they have what they wanted. They're blinded by their desires and don't realize what might be really happening. I don't blame them. They trust the system is there to do its job. That could have been the case for the people who adopted you."

Gwen shook her head. "No. My parents weren't trying to adopt. They had two boys of their own already. I was not part of their plan. They got that call and were just trying to help. That's the kind of people they are."

"Two boys of their own? Maybe they wanted a girl." Lenny shrugged and the dismissive look on her face brought Gwen to the brink of rage. This woman didn't understand who Noel and Millie Fox were. They weren't blinded by desires for another child. It was selflessness that had them opening their home and hearts to her.

"I'm telling you, they just answered the call," Gwen sneered. "They wouldn't lie to me about that. They've been completely open with me over the years about being adopted. They've told me everything they know."

"Good people can be surprisingly bad when they want something. I'm not saying that's the case for you. But I do know you were the final straw that got Ivy flak from the higher-ups. She was reprimanded and forced to retire after whispers made their way to the leadership of the hospital. They didn't want any litigation trouble so they buried it all. Some of us thought the hospital or the state might step in and work to make it right. Instead they made it go away. It always upset me. I just kept thinking of those babies and the families they'd never know."

"Why?" Griff asked, when Gwen sat motionless. There was suddenly a rough edge to his voice and she was relieved to hear it. The tremors of anger had turned to aftershocks of doubt in her mind. Was she hearing this right? Overreacting? But now that Griff sounded put off she knew the idea of her parents lying was ridiculous and insulting. "Gwen ended up with a great family. One of the best families I've ever met. Ivy might not have been traditional in her process, but it worked out. Would you rather

Gwen's mother, who didn't want her, had tried to make it work and failed? Hurt Gwen or done some serious damage to her?"

Gwen leaned into his arm. His strength mattered right now and she was glad for it.

Lenny looked at him with a mix of pity and distain. "Individual people don't get to decide the fate of a child. They don't get to deem a couple worthy or better than others. There are laws in place to make sure this is done appropriately. Safely. Ethically. We don't know who Gwen's birth mother was. If she chose adoption then I respect the difficult choice she faced. But if she was pressured because there was a waiting set of parents and a kind-faced nurse telling her that was the best option, that's wrong. The reason for some of the red tape associated with these situations is to protect the mother and the baby and give her time to consider her options."

"Those laws fail all the time," Gwen shot out, feeling protective of Millie and Noel. They were not the bad guys in this situation. They couldn't be. "How many stories have you heard of children in the foster system who are abused? Children are adopted and then sent back. It can be hell."

Lenny's expression softened slightly. "All of that is true. I'm glad it worked out for you. But there might have been other people you aren't thinking of. Your people, who would have been ready to raise you. Your blood out there who could have waited with open arms for you. A father. A grandmother. Ivy was playing God. She had a way of talking that made people trust her, and I personally think she took advantage of that." Lenny stood, an old anger stirring in her expression. "She was counseling these mothers and promising things she was in no position to promise. And it was done in a way that closed a door. Tightly. Locked it up forever. No records. No finality for anyone."

"What do you mean?" Gwen licked her dry lips and held her breath.

"The anonymity she provided is unprecedented. I believe she told these women to withhold their identities, and I'm sure she helped them leave. There is no paper trail back to your family now. No agency who could provide you with even some basic information and solace. She helped facilitate the closing of that door. It's cruel."

Those had been the parts Gwen had never been able to sort out in her mind. The anger she felt about her abandonment had festered, never properly faced. The way she went from being someone's child one second to being no one, identity stripped away, had been sharp edged and indeed, as Lenny said, cruel.

She'd always thought her mother's actions were selfish and reckless but she had imagined they were hers alone. To know that someone might have been in her ear, encouraging her to leave, was stomach churning. The urge to vomit crawled up her, but she wouldn't waste her five minutes being sick.

"Do you remember anything else about my mother at all?" The words felt thick in her mouth. Gwen had always, even in her own mind, tried to refer to this woman as her birth mother or biological mother. The term *mom* or *mother* was held for Millie alone. It felt like a betrayal to forget the extra terms.

Lenny's gaze dropped to the floor. "I don't like stereotypes. I've had to dodge plenty of them in my own life. But in my experience your mother didn't seem to fit my idea of what someone giving up their baby would be like. It's a stupid thing to even say. There is no one kind of person who chooses adoption." Lenny looked ready to drop the point, regret filling the corners of her downturned mouth.

"Please tell me. In what way was she different?"

"As a clinic we normally served women of modest means. Your mother was clearly well educated. Dressed immaculately. Nails done. Hair done. She came in with a nice purse. Clean shoes. Don't get me wrong." Lenny looked uncomfortable with her own bias as she tried to find the right words. "Women of all socioeconomic situations make the decision to put a child up for adoption, for many reasons. They just tend to do so through agencies and at a more sophisticated or modern hospital. As a clinic our technology was limited at the time. People who could afford better care normally sought it out."

"She never said anything to you about why?" Gwen could feel the crease in her brow deepen.

"In my memory, it stood out to me that we didn't know why she was leaving you. Some moms share their story. Some, the reason is obvious. But I do remember thinking why on earth does this woman, who seems to have it all, and have it all together, want to leave this child behind. And her age."

"What about her age?" Gwen asked, clinging to another piece of data she could possibly use.

"I can't be entirely certain of her age. Women can look older or younger than they are. But I certainly remember thinking she wasn't young. Not a child like we see in some cases."

"She wasn't?" Gwen had an image in her mind, no matter how much she tried to fight it. The easiest scenario to swallow had always been the idea that her mother was too young. Unable to care for herself, let alone a baby. Maybe she'd made a mistake one night and found herself alone and pregnant. Brave in the face of her fear and inexperience, she'd decided to go through labor and give the baby to people who could provide her a better life. Maybe her grandparents were conservative and pressured her to make the choice. All of that would be understandable. This revelation, the idea that a stable grown woman with the means to get a manicure and a decent purse made the choice to give her up was far less digestible.

"I would say she was at least your age." Lenny reported, the wrinkles in her forehead growing deeper as she strained to remember. "Mid-twenties? That stuck with me. I always wondered why. I wondered where you ended up. That information never came out. The reprimanding of Ivy was kept pretty quiet. The only thing that ever did surface was that somehow Mission Crest Agency was involved." She groaned in disgust as she said the name.

"Who is that?" Griff asked, turning to Gwen, checking to see if that information registered with her.

Lenny shook her head and sighed loudly. "I don't have time to get into it all. Just look them up. The story on them went public years ago. I'm sure you can find the information. I need to go pick up my grandson." She paused and looked empathetically at Gwen. "Miguel. He's nine. He lives with me. My daughter, she couldn't take care of him, but I could. He's a blessing in my life, and I'm glad to have the opportunity to raise him. I'd be devastated if what happened to your mother happened to my daughter. My girl was given time, support, and options. While she isn't in a position to raise him, she is in his life. One day, I think they could have a wonderful mother-son relationship."

With that Lenny stood and marched off, turning to join the herd of people moving toward the revolving door that led to the parking lot.

Gwen felt her breath catching in her throat as she stood and clutched her car keys. Their sharp edges felt good digging into her palm, which was tingling with nerves. She wanted to say thank you. Or goodbye but Lenny was gone.

"We should go. I want to go." She gulped out the words.

"You want to take a minute? That was a lot of information." Griff steadied her with his hand on her shoulder, but she shook him off.

"I want to go."

He reached out and gently plucked the keys from her hand. "Where do you want to go?"

"To hide. To drink maybe. I need a drink." It felt good to be decisive about something even if that something was tequila.

He nodded and wrapped his arm around her. The way he had after she skinned her knee coming down Dead Man's Hill on her bike when she was twelve. This time the sting she felt was all over, and she knew it wouldn't be healed with a bandage and kiss from her mother.

CHAPTER 8

Gwen

"I've got a place," Griff assured her. They walked in silence to the car and this time he didn't play upbeat music or make silly gestures. The car was filled with thick and pained silence. Claustrophobia began to set in, as if she'd been buried up to her neck in the sand and the tide was coming in. There would be nothing he could say right now to help her, and luckily he seemed to understand that.

Griff drove with more confidence than she imagined he would for this area, not turning the GPS on. Leading them somewhere he seemed familiar with.

"Where are we going?" Gwen asked finally as the busy streets turned to quiet residential back roads.

"There's a bar not far from here. It's on the water, but it's usually deserted this time of year. We should eat. I'm writing you a prescription for carbs. They make everything better. Greasy onion rings. Cheese fries. They're more powerful than a bottle of pills."

"How do you know this area?"

"I've been around here before," he answered vaguely.

Too lost in her own thoughts, her brain whirred with incessant wondering. "I thought she'd be younger," Gwen said, mostly to herself. "Didn't you think so?"

"I'm not sure I gave that much thought," he admitted. "But I can see why you would."

"Lenny said she might have been around my age. If I got pregnant right now, it wouldn't be easy, but I could make it work. Right? Nothing, I mean nothing at all would make me want to give my child away. I can't even imagine it. That doesn't make sense."

"There are thousands of variables," Griff countered somberly, apologetic to have to be the one making the case against her emotions. "It could have been a complicated situation. Age isn't always a factor in stability. Look at me. My life is in shambles right now, and I'm older than you."

"And if you suddenly found yourself pregnant?" Gwen rolled her eyes at his attempted argument. He couldn't possibly understand. "Or if Laura had gotten pregnant while you guys were in Florida. I know you, and you wouldn't be here right now. Even with all the stuff you had going on, as complicated as it was, you'd have kept your child."

"It's too easy to make those kinds of statements. Hypothetical scenarios are a dangerous rabbit hole to fall down. It would have depended on what Laura wanted too. And she's never wanted children. She just knows that about herself."

"Wait," Gwen held up her hand. "You weren't going to have any children ever?"

"Lots of people decide not to have kids and still live very fulfilled lives. Plus, what kind of father could I possibly be with the upbringing I had? I'm not saying I was as adamant as Laura was about not having children, but I was all right with it."

"All right with it?" she mocked, puffing out a heavy breath. "You would be an amazing father, not because you had some great example but because you're a good man with a big heart. Any kid would be lucky to have you."

"This isn't about me. We were talking about your birth mother and the fact that we don't know why she decided to choose adoption. Jumping to conclusions isn't helpful. It could have been anything. And I was trying to explain that life doesn't always go as planned."

"You're saying she had a good excuse?"

"That's not the point I'm trying to make. I can't imagine that responsibility. Pregnancy was bestowed upon women for a reason. Men couldn't deal. But I am trying to say that my life looks measurably different than I expected it would six months ago. I'd be lying if I said I'm all right. I'm not. And that can happen to anyone at any time. The carpet can be ripped right out from under you. Maybe she'd been going through something."

Gwen examined his profile as he admitted how difficult things had been for him. "This trip can't be helping. I know you have a lot to deal with. It's bad timing."

"Actually it is helping. It's giving me perspective. I understand more now about why I went back to Old Wesley. Home might be miserable and frustrating, but reliably so. I needed to come back to something I knew would be exactly how I left it."

Gwen lowered her voice and regained her composure. "I'm not trying to villainize adoption. It's an important and wonderful thing. I believe, without a doubt, my life was better for it. But Lenny isn't wrong. There might have been people who wanted me. Who should have been given the chance. This whole thing, this going around the system, it's never really been on my radar before. Now my head is spinning about it. All of this searching and the answers were supposed to make me feel better, not worse."

"Honestly, I thought Lenny was a crabby bitch. Maybe she was tired from work. We snuck up on her. I get all that, but still, I don't know that I'd put too much stock in how she said everything. Maybe she and Ivy didn't get along for lots of other reasons. Obviously her own experiences with her grandson color her views. Your story is going to need to be seen from more angles than just one." His words should have resonated, should have quieted the swirl of anger rising in her. But it wasn't enough. "You should try to find out more about Mission Crest Agency. Maybe it'll shed light on how it all went down. Lenny is just one person with a singular perspective."

"She had money?" Gwen asked as though Griff could answer. "My birth mother wasn't living on the streets. No signs of a drug problem. Just a woman who didn't want her baby. Like I was an inconvenience or something."

Griff pulled down a sand-covered asphalt road and parked in front of a shabby building. The awnings sagged and the metal door was more rust than paint. The sign over the door read: Olly's Burgers and Beer. She caught a glimpse of the sea over the small dunes and had the urge, in spite of the cold, to put her feet in. The stinging shock of the ice-cold waves and pull of the sand from under her feet might shock the sadness out of her heart.

He placed his folded sweatshirt in her lap and grabbed his coat. "Come on in and eat."

"I don't think I'm hungry." She hugged the sweatshirt to her chest.

"You'll like this place. I came a few times as a kid. We can sit in a corner booth and drink flat beer, eat stale bar nuts, and talk."

"I bet you've taken loads of girls here." Gwen smirked and slipped his sweatshirt over her head. It was warm and smelled of his cologne. Well-worn and nearly threadbare in some places, she could tell it must be a favorite of his.

"Other ladies? Only if I want them to know I'm a high roller with a sophisticated taste in food. I save it for the fancy girls like you." He stepped out of the car and waited for her to meet him in front. "You might be overdressed in that holey sweatshirt."

"It's that nice of a place?" She laughed and waited as he pulled open the heavy door. It took a moment for her eyes to adjust to the dim smoky room, and she wondered if this new information would be the same way. Would it take time to adjust to every new detail that rocked her previous understanding of herself and her story? How long until it finally came into focus and she could see again?

The long bar ran the length of the room and looked cobbled together from mismatched wood. Behind the bar was a man propped on a stool, who didn't bother looking up from his cross-word puzzle. His white T-shirt was covered in splotches of food and grease. The neon signs on the walls were all half lit, burned out in different corners making the remaining words seem like part of some long-forgotten bar language.

"Whoa," Gwen said, catching herself from tripping on the unnaturally slanted floor. "You came here as a kid?"

"With my dad. He had a buddy from Vietnam he used to meet out here. My mom hated him going, and so she'd send me along to make sure he didn't get himself into trouble."

"Did that work?"

"Not usually, but at least I could report back to her. That's really what she wanted. My parents' anger was a fire and they liked to keep it stoked." Griff slid into a booth, and she, after making sure it was clean enough, did the same. "But I figured you didn't want a crowd and this was the first place I thought of that would work."

"That would work for me falling apart?"

"You can do that if you want, but I don't see it going that way. I think you'll sort it out." He slid the stained paper menu toward her. "Please enjoy their wide selection of processed cheeses on various fried foods."

After they placed their order with the man on the stool and settled back into the booth, Griff pulled his phone out saying simply, "Mission Crest Adoption Agency."

"That doesn't make sense," Gwen cut in. "No agency was used in my adoption. I was just given to the people who some nurse thought were good enough. And then my parents lied to me about knowing Ivy from school."

"You don't have enough information to know the lies from the truth yet. It can be deceiving." His reference to facts and reality was borderline infuriating. Part of her just wanted to lash out at the possibilities.

"Or the truth can be apparent."

"Well, if you asked anyone who tried to take me down at Pipeline Investments, I'm a thieving, lying, white-collar criminal who belongs in jail. You have to get the facts before you jump to conclusions." Griff turned his phone so she could see what popped up when he googled his own name. Words like *scandal* and *Ponzi scheme* caught her eye. "Things aren't always as they appear. But if you dig deep enough before deciding, I'm sure you'll find the truth." He typed away at his phone screen and then made a curious noise.

"What?"

"Mission Crest Adoption Agency has an interesting past. Daniel Sawyer was the owner and operator of the agency, and he served a ten-year sentence for racketeering, fraud, and obstruction. It was an adoption-for-profit ring based here in New England."

"Adoption for profit?" Gwen gasped at the implications. She'd never heard that term before. Visions of her parents swapping a bag full of money with some shady characters in a back alley flooded her mind. Were they handed a baby in return? "You think my parents paid Ivy or this agency to pressure my birth mother to give me up? They've told me all these years that they weren't trying to adopt. They didn't plan to have more children. I was some kind of miracle surprise they never expected. Now that I think about it, who takes a call like that in the middle of the night and just goes to get a baby with no warning? They would have needed to think about it. Discuss it. They must have wanted to know about my mother and the situation."

"Before we decide your whole life is a lie, we should find out more. These guys started operating in the eighties and were busted by the late nineties. I'm only skimming right now, but it seems like they had a religious affiliation and advertised in the newspaper. Their ads targeted unwed pregnant women who might have been seeking help. Then, reports say, through coercion, pressure and sometimes even threats they would get the birth mothers to sign over their legal rights. The children would be essentially sold to the highest bidder. All of that was done without thoroughly vetting the families for adoption."

"How is that even possible?"

"People do horrible things for money."

"Do you think Ivy worked for this place and my parents didn't know? Maybe she pressured my birth mother to give me up all on her own."

"I don't see her name associated with the people who were convicted. Three preachers, four lawyers, and a couple thug enforcers were all put away when the scandal broke. There is nothing about a nurse. Daniel Sawyer was one of the lawyers." He winced as he continued reading.

"What?" Her heart thudded against her ribs. The expression on Griff's face was unsettling.

"One couple who adopted two babies from the MCA said

there was a sea of babies at the office they visited. Beautiful bundled up infants for them to pick from. So many, they claimed, it was hard to choose. Like a department store of perfect children."

"How did they get that many women to work with them and give their children over without going through the proper channels?" Disgust erupted in her stomach.

"It was the sales pitch the birth mothers fell for then they were forced to honor the contract. Initially MCA paid the mother's medical care bills and gave her five hundred dollars cash. After the baby was born and the adoption complete, she was promised another thousand dollars. The adoptive parents paid MCA up to fifteen thousand for a healthy baby. That's a hefty profit margin."

"Thinking of your next career choice?" she asked, raising a judgmental brow. The man from behind the bar carried over the high-caloric dinner, full of fried and processed food. She didn't see how her stomach could handle it but she also craved the comfort.

"I didn't mean it like that. I think it's despicable to prey on people just to make money. Especially vulnerable women who feel like they don't have many options."

Gwen squirted the pile of fries with ketchup and started eating ravenously. "If I puke from all this food it's your fault."

"Fair enough." He grabbed a handful of the onion rings and piled them on his plate. "But I don't recommend doing that here. If I recall, it's less of a bathroom and more of an outhouse."

Gwen grimaced and leaned back in the booth. "Do you really think my birth mother, my parents, and Ivy were involved with the MCA?"

Griff put his phone on the table and began to eat. His eyes moved quickly over his phone screen as he continued to read. "There's a group of children who've been identified as adoptees from the agency. In recent years they've banded together to try to determine who their biological families are. They're calling them-selves the MCA Survivors. Most live in states that block adult adoptees from getting their birth certificates. I didn't know that was a thing states could do."

"It wouldn't matter for me. My birth certificate isn't accurate anyway." She took a long sip of her beer and considered the new layer of questions that had been laid on top of the all the old ones. "I feel like I'm getting farther from the truth, not closer. I don't want more questions. I want answers."

"Hang in there, kid." Griff pulled a paper towel off the roll at the end of the table and handed it to her. "One thing at a time. Start with the ketchup on your face."

Gwen sighed and wiped her cheek. "I guess people in that group probably have more options now that DNA results are so readily available."

"It says here," Griff explained, scrolling with one hand on his phone, "that with the introduction of DNA testing on public sites, people are finding answers. Sounds like you've got a solid plan. Maybe wait until you get those DNA results before you talk to Noel and Millie."

"I want to do more." Gwen leaned back as another tray of food was brought their way. "You're going to have to roll me out of here after we eat all this."

"What more can you do? Ivy is dead. Any kind of document associated with this litigation would be sealed. I didn't get the impression Lenny had more she'd be willing to say. But you accomplished a lot today. Don't feel like you failed."

"What did I accomplish?" She leaned back and eyed him skeptically. She was rebuffing his kind words. Not because she didn't want to hear them, but because she so desperately needed him to be right.

"You just stood with a woman who stood with your mother on the day you were born. You officially met one person who met your mom. That's a big deal." Griff smiled the same smile he had when he was a boy. Innocent. Punctuated by a dimple. As disarming as it was charming.

"I did do that." She let her tight back relax a bit and leaned against the ripped cushion behind her. "We did that."

CHAPTER 9

Leslie

S he didn't want this to be a reckoning. Tossing pots and pans at each other as they screamed their long-buried hurt. She and Paul had never been those people. He was a rational man. Maddeningly so. Calm in the face of challenges and expecting the same from Leslie. It was amazing the power she'd handed over to him in some of her most formative years without ever realizing it.

Looking back, she could see it now. Paul was like water and she was a stone He was always relentlessly flowing over her and smoothing out the rough edges of her personality. Making her smooth, but smaller in the process.

If he'd have done it all at once, she never would have stuck around. She'd seen the after-school specials and knew enough not to hand over her power and control to a man. The slow pace at which it had happened created camouflage he hid behind. Paul was a good man. But a selfish one. A taker who, in Leslie, had found a giver.

Over the years, he'd criticize her emotional reaction to being slighted by friends. Jabbing her with the words *dramatic and emotional* as though they were weapons. It was effective. She began wondering if maybe she had overreacted. Crying over something so trivial hadn't helped the situation. The next time something like that happened, she kept her feelings to herself. Didn't bring it up over dinner. Stayed quiet when they were lying in bed at night. Paul didn't have time to dissect every social relationship she had. He didn't need to hear about how one of the kids had made her feel bad.

One of his favorite lines was that if everything is important, then nothing is. So she wouldn't make a big deal out of nothing. Especially to him.

Surely though, some emotional situations in life required discussion. The big ones. But even in those moments Paul was quick to remind Leslie emotions clouded judgment and good decisions couldn't be made with tears in her eyes. Her pain was always met with the same advice one might give a colleague. A lot of *chin up. Stay focused.* Nothing that wrapped her in empathy or compassion. He would try to coach her through the hard stuff rather than love her through it.

In the last few weeks, self-appraisal and scrutinizing their marriage had become her new pastime. Leslie was sad to admit it didn't land favorably on Paul. She kept finding more ways she was different now than before they met. Kept attributing the changes in herself to his actions. Some days her assessment felt spot on. Other days she knew she was being unreasonably harsh. Today she had no trouble blaming him.

Her sense of humor had been different when they met. Bigger. Animated. She'd been labeled by her friends and acquaintances as quick-witted and sharp. More like Claudette. Open and approachable. Paul had chipped away slowly at that.

After an evening out with their peers, Paul would always

debrief in the car ride home. Taking his time to tell her which puns he felt crossed the line. How someone seemed put off by her jokes. They'd all been laughing, but he was better at seeing the nuances. The small changes in a person's body language he felt compelled to warn her about. According to Paul, it would help her in social settings to *dial it down*. At the time, though there might have been a sting to it, she genuinely felt his advice was well meaning. And after she accepted it once, he must have felt empowered to keep doing it. She wondered now if she'd have told him to worry about himself and let her be, what he would have done.

But she hadn't and as a result, over the years, she'd become noticeably less fun. Not just out on the town, at home too. The disciplinarian to the children. The one to have the serious talks and hold them to curfew. The taker of their electronics. Before she had children, she'd always envisioned herself as the fun mom. The one in the sandbox building epic castles. Hosting ambitious sleepovers with living room forts and no bedtime. But it hadn't turned out that way. Paul had a vision for that too, and it required tough love for the kids. A high expectation of them academically. Rigor in their schedules. He'd decide one of their friends was a bad influence or not a high achiever and expect the kids to move on from them.

Paul was the idea man. The one who set the expectation and made his desires for his family known. It was up to Leslie to find a way to make it happen. Cole was supposed to be in honors classes when he started high school. When he wasn't on track for that, it was up to Leslie to get him to the tutor. Encourage him to work hard. Punish him until he did. That meant yelling more than she wanted to. Punishing, when all she wanted to do was forget the kid's misstep and move on.

Now as she sat on the couch in the formal living room, which like the koi pond went mostly unused, she waited for Paul. She considered the repercussions of this conversation. He'd pulled in the driveway a few minutes earlier and was wrapping up a call. There was enough time to change her mind. She could stuff down these feelings the way her children stuffed down the full waste-basket in an effort to avoid having to take it out. Maybe there was more room in there if she really tried.

When Paul's key turned in the front door, she drew in a deep breath. There would be no way to keep holding on to this anger. There was no more room in her for it. They wouldn't survive if she kept placing so much blame squarely on his shoulders. It would be a disease that would eventually infect them all. It was time to face it and cut it away.

"You look like you're waiting for me." Paul smiled. The heaviness he'd left the house with had since floated away. Assuming by now Leslie would have come over to his side. He had nothing to worry about.

Lucky him.

She eyed him closely, remembering why she fell in love with him. It was easy to still see the man he used to be. He'd aged well. There was still a childish sparkle in his eyes when he smiled. His hairline had moved back an inch but overall he was looking good with very little effort. Men had it easier. Instead of fretting, the family joked about his beard. He grew it out between Christmas and New Year's Day, and it was now speckled with gray. But otherwise he still looked much like the man she'd fallen in love with.

"I didn't want you to see the backyard before we had a chance to talk." She patted the spot on the couch next to her. She wanted him close. She wanted to be able to put a hand on his cheek and draw his eyes to hers. Because she knew he'd want this to go away. Paul would want her to neatly discuss her feelings and then move on. Actually, if he had his way, she wouldn't bring up her feelings at all.

He'd learned enough to at least acknowledge what she had to say, but he never went as far as validating it. In her experience she knew he believed that if he gave an inch, she'd take a mile. If he told her she was right to be angry at the way the PTA meeting had run long because of someone's late arrival, that might spiral into a sea of complaints he'd have to hear. So instead, he'd slow her down, remind her it was no big deal. A silly school meeting. Some sage advice about not sweating the small stuff and a quick change of the subject. Not this time. Her grip was tight on her goals.

"The backyard?" He didn't take the seat near her. Instead in true Paul fashion he sat across from her in the large wingback chair. Reminiscent of a boss, rather than a husband.

"I threw the bench into the koi pond." She folded her bandaged hands in her lap and waited for him to speak. She wouldn't overexplain. Not at first.

"Why?" He chuckled a bit, waiting for the punch line.

"Because it's stupid."

"The bench or the pond?" He was still waiting. Something more had to be coming. Leslie had always been compliant. Somewhere in her mind she'd believed that following the rules would be rewarded someday. As though someone somewhere was keeping score and she'd be in the lead. Paul was accustomed to that now.

"Both. The koi pond and the bench are stupid."

"Are you all right?" He leaned in to appraise her more closely. "Have you been drinking or something?"

She glared back at him. "No, Paul. I haven't been drinking. I've been doing something far more dangerous."

His eyes rounded with shock. "Pills? I know housewives are getting hooked on pills now, but I didn't think you'd fall prey." He smirked and waited for her face to soften. It didn't, so his lips turned down in disappointment.

"No. Thinking. I've been thinking a lot. About us."

"Oh." He put his hand over his chest, sighing with relief. "I thought this was serious. Could you please relax a little?"

"It is serious."

"I understand it feels very severe to you. I'm just glad it's not something worse. I thought you were about to drop a bombshell. You scared the hell out of me."

"I just want to talk." She closed her eyes for a long beat, readying herself, but he cut in.

"I've been thinking too. I sprang that trip on you this morning. Rookie move. I know you hate surprises."

She didn't.

Surprises were wonderful if they were equal parts thoughtful and clandestine. Paul did a great job of keeping her in the dark about a gift but he was far less adept at picking something she actually wanted. It had made for a few awkward anniversaries and birthdays. Thus she was always labeled as being anti-surprise.

He softened his voice and his chin wrinkled a bit as he spoke. "I will call the travel agent today and chat with her about the details. I know we can't change the trip but maybe you can put your spin on it. Make it your own."

She swallowed the gravel in her throat and felt it hit with a thud to the bottom of her stomach. "Paul, the koi pond. You heard what I said right? The bench is floating out there right now."

"You were mad. I didn't know you were throwing-furniture mad. But I get it. I really do. And I hear you about your career. Everything you are feeling right now is very natural. Moms get freaked out when their youngest kid leaves home. It'll pass. You'll get your bearings and the dust will settle. Take it from a guy who has spent a lot of years building his career. You don't want the headache of taking on more." His expression was one of pity. His silly little wife was falling to pieces over this latest change. The rage boiled just below her skin.

"You're minimizing this." She straightened her back and tipped her chin up.

"Please don't get all television psychologist on me. Those shows you watch are so dramatic. It's not real life. No buzzword is going to change what's going on here."

If Paul had a shovel right now, he'd be halfway done digging his own grave.

"Shut up." Her voice was sharp and unwavering. "Could you honestly just shut up? I don't sit at home all day watching some afternoon television trying to sort out what to say to you. It's a fact. You're doing what you always do. Minimizing. Dismissing."

"And you're generalizing. Telling me what I always do. We both have a big vocabulary. Two can play this game." His brows shot up victoriously.

"If you don't watch it, you'll find yourself without anyone around for the games."

"What's that supposed to mean?" Paul's eyes went narrow and the muscles in his jaw clenched. Now she knew he was listening.

Something about his expression brought her pleasure. He was rarely taken aback. Always calculated, working to have the upper hand. Right now, he didn't have a clue where this was going.

Good.

"You can't laugh this off or plan it away, Paul. These are my feelings. You're not going to dismiss them."

He rolled his eyes. "Then what do you want me to do, Leslie? You tell me and I'll do it."

He'd caught her there. She hadn't actually thought that far ahead. But his offer was hollow anyway. "You don't mean that. You're not capable of changing what you want because of what I need. I'm always the one to bend. I'm always the one to sacrifice and change."

"Right. So today you're the martyr. The poor woman who has to go on a three-week trip to Italy with her adoring husband. I don't know how you'll make it through." Paul wasn't petty. He didn't usually make digs like this. But she realized that was because she never put his back to the ropes. Long before this part of an argument, she usually caved. At the first sign of him questioning her stability, she'd have backed down.

Leslie stood and shook her head in disappointment. "No, Paul, I'm not a martyr. I'm the woman you gave an ultimatum to all those years ago. I'm what's left of her."

"Don't go digging that up." His voice was uncharacteristically loud. "That's revisionist history, and it serves no purpose. You're emotional about what's happening now, and so you're looking for ammunition. I don't deserve that."

She checked herself. Was she remembering things wrong?

No.

"Revisionist history? Trust me, the vividness with which I remember is painfully vibrant. Nearly blinding. I remember the day you decided you were leaving. It was a Tuesday. Sunny. Hot. You were wearing that ugly blue tie you always said was lucky. Your seat on the plane to Beijing was twelve-D. I remember how sure you looked of your decision."

He gulped, and she could see the fear in his eyes. She knew what he wanted. Best-case scenario in his opinion was she would neatly pack away her feelings and put them back in the drawer she'd been storing them in all these years. She knew what was next. He'd try a different tactic.

He pumped his palms in the air. "Let's take a breath. It's not going to do either of us any good to go back down that road."

"Please, for the love of everything holy, Paul, stop deciding what's going to do me any good. A trip to Europe. Slowing down my career. Stuffing my feelings down. Don't you see, we've been buried in our lives all these years? Responsible for the children. The jobs. The stupid household projects that took up our weekends, like that useless koi pond. It's ending, Paul. The noise is going away. The hectic time in our lives is done. It's going to be you and me. And we've got a hell of a lot of work to do, if that's the case."

Paul stood and pulled his bottom lip into his mouth contemplatively. An effort to force himself to be measured and thoughtful in his rebuttal. An attribute most people would love in their partner. But in that moment, Leslie would have preferred a boiling over of his emotions. Something less robotic and cold.

Finally, when he spoke his voice was level. "Let's table this." He tucked his hands into his pockets and nodded his own agreement to the idea.

"No." She smirked. "Let's not."

"We aren't talking about this with Kerry upstairs. We always agreed they shouldn't know about this part of our lives."

"First, Kerry went to the library. Second, you decided that."

"You never disagreed with me." His finger shot out in her direction, pointing accusingly.

"What would the point have been? You'd talk in circles and make me feel silly for my opinion. You'd toss in words like selfish and shortsighted and I'd second-guess my gut and eventually agree with you anyway. But Kerry's not here. There's no business trip to run off to. No baseball tournament to pack up for. It's you and me. That's the point I'm trying to make. There are no more reasons to table this now."

"Then we'll wait until you're on solid ground again. You think I'm so critical of you? You're making it out like my assessment of your stability is based on nothing. Rather than the fact that you've had plenty of moments where you truly do overreact. Fall apart. I'm not the one who stayed in bed crying after Kerry was born. I've never been picked up off the floor by my best friend in a heap of tears when my hormones got out of whack."

"By my best friend." Leslie hung the words out like clothes on a line. Flapping in the wind between them.

"What's that supposed to mean?" He was halfway out of the living room but she wasn't going to let this go. If that meant chasing him from room to room she would.

"During the few moments I haven't been able to be completely composed and live up to your standards, Claudette has been the one to help me. Or my mother. Neither one of them have ever once told me to get over it. Or deal with it."

"Neither have I," he asserted.

"Not in those words. But it's exactly what you want. Peace and quiet. No drama. No excessive showing of emotions. No needing too much."

He rolled his eyes and tossed his hands up dramatically. "Who wants all that? Excuse me for hoping for a simple life."

"You don't *want* a simple life, you demand it. And guess what? Life's messy. And people feel things. And need things. I've let you skate by all these years without ever holding you accountable for being my partner. The partner I needed in the darkest moments. The one I wanted to come home and vent to on a normal day. You just couldn't be bothered with that. I had to be some emotional version of a self-cleaning oven."

"Should I sit down while you disparage me? Would that be easier?" He gestured animatedly at the chair but didn't sit. "I can't believe how you're coming at me like this. Blindsiding me. We hit a rough patch years ago. You're telling me you're not over that? All these years you've been faking it?"

"Over it? A rough patch? That is not what we went through. You left. And you're right; it's my fault for how easily I forced it behind us and acted like nothing had happened. I didn't want to think about the fact that you took off. I didn't want to think about all the time you were gone. So instead I gave in to the life you wanted us to have."

"It was a choice. Your choice."

"It was an ultimatum. I had to give up what was important to me, what I wanted, to make you happy. So you would choose me and come back."

"That is not what happened. We decided—"

"You really don't see it, do you? You're a steamroller, Paul. We didn't decide anything. You weren't getting what you wanted out of our lives and you left. Then you considered coming back, dangled it in front of me, and I caved."

"It's a little damn late to be complaining now. Look at everything that life has afforded you and our children. College funds. Vacations. Cars. This house. None of that would have been possible without my career." His face grew red and his nostrils flared.

"And that had to come at the expense of my career?" Her eyes betrayed her and began to leak tears. She wanted to tell him they were not born out of sadness but anger. "I was being promoted. I had an opportunity to be on a fast track at my company. And you couldn't stand that."

"It had nothing to do with my ego. I didn't want a wife who was spending as many hours in the office as I was. Who the hell would be around to run the house? What kind of life would that be? Do you know any couples raising families who are both senior leadership at *Fortune 500* companies? I'd doubt there are many. A family requires different roles. It would have imploded if you and I were out there climbing the corporate ladder, competing rung for rung."

"It didn't have to be a competition. There is plenty of room at the top for both of us. And everything else could have been sorted out. You wanted a big family. You wanted kids close in age. We could have done it differently and all gotten what we wanted."

"Are you saying we should have kept our careers and only had two kids instead of three? I'm glad Kerry isn't home to hear this."

"Don't be stupid," Leslie spat out. It was the meanest thing she'd said to him in their entire marriage. And judging by the look on his face, he knew that. "I'm not saying I wish we had less children. I'm saying we could have made it work for all of us. If you'd have tried instead of taking that job overseas."

"That job, the move to Beijing, launched my career. If I hadn't taken it and diversified my field experience, I wouldn't be where I am today. You should have supported that. You should have come. The fact that you put your career over the good of our future says more about you than about me. I'm done with this conversation. If you don't want to go to Europe, don't. I'm going. I plan to finally reap the benefits of my hard work and enjoy life. I hope it's with my wife, but that's up to you. You have the choice now." Paul stormed out and slammed the front door behind him. He was leaving angry. Something she rarely let him do. Always smoothing things over before he had a chance to go.

Falling onto the couch, she curled her knees to her chest. The doubt crept in. His words were burrowing deep into her brain. With all her might, she recalled that period of their lives. That phone call where he told her he would consider coming back. That he missed his life and what they had built. All she had to do was compromise. In his words, she needed to give a little. In reality she needed to give in.

Paul didn't know in his absence she'd created a bigger dilemma. One Leslie would need to handle. A choice she'd have to make if she wanted Paul back. If she wanted her other life back. An impossible choice. Paul wouldn't come back from Asia if he knew. He wouldn't understand. Her life only had room for Paul or the baby. Not both.

CHAPTER 10

Gwen

The hotel room had turned into a research bunker. The last four days had been spent digging. Reading. Trips to libraries. Searching through newspaper archives. Griff had been a good sport not to call into question why any of this information mattered. He never asked what the point was. Even if the Mission Crest Agency had anything to do with Gwen's adoption, knowing every detail of the scandal didn't bring her closer to finding her birth parents. Plus, the more they learned, the more they realized MCA was a black hole. Other adoptees had been searching unsuccessfully for years to gain access to the documents that had been taken by the FBI. Documents that would easily be able to connect these stolen children to their birth parents. It wasn't going to happen.

"You have the timeline worked out really well." Griff leaned over her shoulder. The desk in the corner of the room where she was sitting was littered with papers. Her handwritten notes. Photocopies of news articles. It had hit the point of obsession now. She recognized that. But she didn't feel concerned enough to stop. They'd done mostly room service and hadn't bothered enjoying any of the holiday festivities in the lobby. Everything centered on finding the next lead. And she'd just gotten another one.

"Look here." She pointed to an article she'd printed at the library. "The nurse, Ivy Chantal, is the wife of Tyson Chantal. Remember Lenny said he held a public office?"

Every time Gwen brought up Lenny, Griff made an unimpressed face. "Yes. She felt that was how Ivy was able to keep skirting the rules." Griff shook off the dismay and perked up the way he always did when they found something of interest. That's what made all of this work. Him. His reaction. Griff didn't judge her or question her. Not yet. He was giving her a lot of rope and hopefully, he'd be there to take it back before she could hang herself with it.

"He was the assistant city manager. That would have given him some serious power. He'd have been connected. I wonder if he was involved in some way."

"In those days, Rhode Island was notoriously corrupt. Providence had plenty of scandals of its own. If he was involved, I'm sure it was buried. People who are in power do a great job of insulating themselves from the fallout. I learned that the hard way."

She put her hand on his knee.

Somehow all this time together didn't feel bizarre. Cohabitating in a cramped hotel room with two full-sized beds didn't bother either of them. Maybe it was all the time they spent together as children. They were picking up where they'd left off. This was just another slumber party. The difference was they were contending with far more intense emotions. She'd never been this dramatic before, even as a teenager. But he was taking that in stride. And in return as often as she could, Gwen was trying to keep it together. Fighting to make sure she wasn't jumping to conclusions or overreacting to things they found.

But her compulsion was real. Any time they were sitting quietly at night, Gwen scrolled through the members of the social media page dedicated to the MCA adoption scandal. People posting information about the children they put up for adoption. Other posts were from people looking for the parents they had little to no information about. Sometimes, like in Gwen's case, the most they could provide was a location and date of birth.

The page highlighted some success stories. But in those cases the parents and the children had been looking for each other.

Was anyone looking for her?

One that brought her hope was a mom longing to find the son she gave up under pressure from her family and the lawyers at MCA. A son searching for answers. When it all came together they made a reunion video and were featured on the local news. It was all tear-filled hugs and joyful conversations about what their lives had been like. Then that was it. The video ended with the two of them sharing a pot of coffee at a local diner. No updates. No *"Where are they now?"* segment. How did he integrate into the rest of her family? Were her parents still living, and if so, what did they have to say about all of that? Did his adoptive family support his search? The small clip of smiles and laughter was only scratching the surface of a reunion. But it tugged at her heartstrings and lent hope to those who came to the page for support.

It didn't show the full picture. Reunions had the makings of a disaster. Potentially devastated rejection. Unearthed secrets. Disruption to both parties' lives. There were no videos of that.

The secrets were what Gwen worried most about. There was a simmering anger just under the surface of her skin. She wasn't sure how she'd deal with finding out her parents had lied to her all these years. If they'd been involved in this MCA adoption scandal with Ivy, she'd be sick. The phone call in the middle of the night with an unexpected bundle of joy waiting for them might have all been a ruse. A silly story they told her at night to make her feel special.

If so, something would shatter. They were supposed to be the control group in this experiment. The stable part that wouldn't change the outcome of whatever she found. Now that was at risk.

Gwen pointed to her notebook. "These were not victimless crimes. There are so many people who don't know where to turn because their adoptions weren't handled properly. Both biological parents and adoptive children were left in the dark. The people they quote in these articles, you can sense their pain. In some cases, the MCA went as far as threatening bodily harm to get the mothers to leave their children. There was no changing their minds once they signed the paperwork. It wasn't even legally binding paperwork, but the mothers didn't know that. MCA employees forced the mothers to say they didn't know who the father was in order to simplify things. Their tactics were cruel."

"It's horrible." Griff handed her a paper cup of coffee he'd gotten from the lobby. The sun had set, but they hadn't gotten much sleep. Coffee this time of night was welcomed.

Griff shuffled back uneasily, clearly reluctant to tell her something.

"What's the matter?" She raised a curious brow at him.

"Your mom called my phone again while I was downstairs for coffee. I told her you were out shopping at the outlets. She wanted to know why you weren't calling her back. I'm starting to worry she might think I murdered you."

"She watches too much true crime television."

"She wants a sign of life. You should give her a call before she sends out a search party for you. Or at least send her a picture of you holding today's newspaper. Take the heat off me."

"We're going back in the morning. My brothers get in early tomorrow. We'll go back, and it'll be fine." She turned back to her papers and tried to pretend she was reading.

"Are you going to ask them?" Griff sat on the edge of the bed and skimmed the article next to him. One of many she had laid out.

"Ask them what?" Gwen understood what Griff was getting at, but she hesitated to go too far down that path. She hadn't sorted out exactly what going home should be like, now that she had more information.

He shrugged. "I don't know. Ask them about MCA. Or about Ivy. They told you they went to school with her. Obviously that's not the case. They may know more than they've said."

"Asking them right now, before I know more, would be a mistake." Gwen stood up and tried to tidy the desk. "I think I should just get through Christmas. We can all have a normal holiday. Maybe I'll go back to school before I bring it up to them. Some distance might make it easier."

"Solid plan. I think you should wait, but I don't know that you'll be able to. And if you can't hold back, it could be very messy with everyone there." Griff had spent most of his young life dealing with conflict. Yelling was not in short supply at his home growing up. She could see why he wouldn't want to be a bystander if she tossed an emotional grenade out by the Christmas tree.

"You don't think I have self-control?" She spun and looked at him with a smug smile.

"You could never keep your hand out of the cookie jar."

"It's been a long time since we were close. There is a lot you don't know about me now."

He shook his head in disagreement. "I know more about you right now than I care to." He ticked the list off on his fingers. "You snore like a broken chainsaw. You never hang up your wet towels. And your messy bun is starting to look like an animal habitat."

She touched her hair and then glared at him. "I washed it yesterday."

"That was two days ago."

"What are you, a calendar?"

"Listen." He took her hand in his and let his smile slip away. "I don't want things to implode for you tomorrow when you get home. We've been here, doing all this research, but we don't know too much more than we did when we left. In the wrong moment you might say something in anger. I don't want you to regret it. I'm worried about what might happen."

"Then come keep me quiet." She squeezed his hand.

"I'm supposed to do that at your parents?" He rolled his eyes. "I think your mom is already upset with me. She probably thinks this road trip was all my idea."

"Think of how happy she'll be to see me alive when we get back."

"It's your family Christmas."

"Griff, we always made room for you before. Everyone understands your house is lacking Christmas cheer. My brothers will be thrilled to catch up with you. Then you'll be perfectly positioned to keep me from saying anything I'll regret."

"Or you have another option."

"I certainly hope it's not some very logical advice suggesting I take the high road and act like an adult."

Griff wrinkled up his chin apologetically. "It is. I don't see why you can't sit them down and tell them what you know. Calm and in control. I think they'll be open to hearing what you have to say."

Gwen pulled her hand back slowly and propped it up on her hip. "I'm not ready. I love my parents. I hope this turns out to be some big misunderstanding. I want what they've always told me to be the truth. I'm not ready to ask them yet."

"Or you're not ready to find out they've been lying?"

"A little of that too. Just do me a favor and keep me quiet."

"Should I bring a cattle prod or something? When you look like you're about to lose it and accuse the people you love of being backstabbing liars, I'll just zap you." He poked at her ribs playfully. "Seriously, Gwen, if you want me there, if it'll help, I'm there."

"The cattle prod will be too obvious. Keep brainstorming."

"Maybe I could pinch you?"

She laughed and dodged his fingers as they came her way. She gave him a curious look. "Why are you doing all this? I know you're going to say your life sucks and you have nothing better to do." She gestured around the room. "This isn't some road trip to a bunch of breweries. This is heavy stuff. Not even remotely glamorous. We're stuck in a room that can't be much better than your parents' house at this point. It smells like turkey clubs and—"

"And your wet towels."

"I hang up my towels," she growled. "Stop besmirching my good name and tell me the truth. Why?"

His eyes closed for a long beat. When they opened he looked content and at ease. "I haven't helped anyone in a while. I thought I was doing okay by people, assisting my clients. But it turns out I wasn't. Lives were ruined. Futures destroyed. For most of that time, in the aftermath, I was still only focused on saving my own ass. Freaking out about what might happen to me. After a couple weeks of living back home, it finally hit me. Whether I knew it or not, I'd contributed to people's pain. A lot of it. If karma exists, I have a pretty big dose of it coming my way."

"Helping me is to even up with the cosmos?"

"No." He shook his head and folded his hands as he gave it more thought. "I just want to do right by people. I've always wanted that. But I'm way off course now. Bumping into you, it was obvious you needed something. It seemed perfect."

"Perfect in what way?" She chuckled as she tried to get to his meaning. "I'm not feeling very perfect."

"You were part of my before."

"Before?" She kicked her head to the side and narrowed her eyes. "Before what?"

"There's the before and after things went wrong for me. And I'm not even talking about the scandal at work. Things weren't right for a while in my life. You were one of the most important people to me for a long time. I always hated seeing you hurt, and you always knew you could count on me. I lost touch with how great both of those feelings were. I stopped paying attention to that. That's why I'm here. That's why if you need me, I'll be around. You look at me the way you remember me. I want to get back to being that guy."

Gwen sat by him on the bed and rested her head on his shoulder. She understood his words deeply. Similarly, Griff looked at her as she once was, not the mess she was now.

Griff's hand planted on her thigh.

"You're a good man, Griff. You don't need to help me out for that to be true. But I'm glad you're here. I don't know what I'd do if you weren't."

"You'd have some soggy-ass towels all over the floor," he groaned, shrugging her off his shoulder playfully. "And get that rat's nest hair off me." He mocked her, brushing his shoulder in disgust.

"I regret all the nice things I said about you." She pointed her finger accusingly at him. "Jerk."

"Go take a shower. Wash your hair. Put on some clean clothes, hang up your towel, and let me take you for a proper dinner.

We've done all we can with this lead. It's time to take a break. I'm going to be pretty disappointed if I don't get to see those gingerbread houses on display."

This was how it kept happening. If anything remotely like romantic tension crept up, one of them would pop it like a bubble. Humor. Levity. It always worked at breaking up the brewing moment. Gwen could see that clearly. What wasn't as clear was whether she was relieved or disappointed every time it happened.

"Let's get out of this room," he insisted, hopping to his feet and slapping his hands together. That childish excitement was like medicine for her soul. Everything had felt so serious lately. Since her breakup last year, laughter had become infrequent. It was a slow process, but she'd managed to pull away from the few friends she had at school. Canceling plans enough times to get them to stop asking.

This week was different. For the first time in over a year she leaned in instead of running away. Laughed instead of giving in to the ache of her broken heart. The way Griff smiled and rocked from his heels to his toes trying to get her energized for his plan made the difference. It was the thing tugging her back to happiness.

"I love you." She blurted the words in a serious way and then winced. It would have been easier if she'd delivered it with a laugh. A lighthearted *you're the best and I love you*. Gwen cleared her throat and avoided looking at him straight on. "Like in the sense that—"

Griff tilted his head to the side. "Love?"

"Yeah, that was stupid. Shutting up now." She zipped her lips closed, which only added to the ridiculousness of the moment. The pretend motion was not effective. She couldn't help herself. "It's just that I wanted you to know that you are loved. Even in this crappy part of your life. Even when things aren't right with your parents. I love you. Just sort of—"

The bubble was floating by once again. He could easily reach his finger out and pop the growing intensity with a witty comeback.

"Thank you." Griff beamed. "I needed to hear that." There was the slightest rise of his brow. A flicker of gratitude. She glimpsed the sweet boy she used to know. The one she could tell was hurting even when they were laughing. The boy who was grateful when her father tossed the football with him. And endlessly smiling when there was a present under their tree for him. Unlike her and her brothers, he was never put off by Noel's and Millie's unfunny jokes or attempts to embarrass them. He embraced it all, thirsty for the love and attention. "I would probably love you too, if you washed your hair. I guess we'll never know."

Stomping a foot, she reached for the pillow off her bed and launched it at him.

"Gross, this touched your hair." Griff swatted it away. "We're leaving for dinner in half an hour. We need fresh air. We're getting out of here."

She slipped into the bathroom and closed the door. Spinning the knobs on the shower she chastised herself silently. At every turn Gwen was making this situation more complicated than it needed to be. She just told him she loved him without even knowing exactly what she meant. Like a brother? Like a best friend? They didn't know each other as adults. Only occasionally chatting over social media about something having to do with the family. How could she possibly know how she felt about him now?

No matter how close they were as kids, she'd never told him she loved him. The questions swirled in her mind. Did he mean regular dinner? Like sustenance and fresh air so they could get out of the hotel. Or was he asking her to dinner, like a date?

The answer wasn't clear even as they left the hotel and got

into the car. He had a fresh collared shirt on and cologne, but that didn't mean anything. It wasn't as if he were dressing up for her all of a sudden.

"Where do you want to eat?" she asked, fishing for more clues. "Back to the bar? Those onion rings were amazing."

"I think we can do better than that dive. That's the place you go to wallow and complain. We need a place to celebrate."

"And what are we celebrating? You better not make another crack about my hair being washed."

"Your hair looks beautiful," he commented casually. She tried dissecting his tone but it was hopeless. He checked his watch and put the car in gear. "We're celebrating you. I think what you're doing is amazing. You have this dogged attitude about finding answers. I'm in awe, and you should be proud of yourself. That deserves a decent steak dinner."

"I might be about to plummet two or more families into complete disaster. I'm not sure I should get a pat on the back for that."

"Or maybe it'll turn out amazing. I've seen stories of adoption reunions that go great."

"Everyone has. Those are the ones they make videos about. But that's half an hour of people's lives, not the aftermath. I think I'm being selfish, and you shouldn't celebrate that."

"Knowing who you are and why you are on the path you're on is not selfish. For some people it's a basic human need. One way or another you'll get to the other side of this, and the people who love you will be there."

"You're pretty optimistic for a guy who lost his girlfriend, his career, and his lifestyle."

"I'm living proof that people on the other side love me still." He laced his fingers into hers, and she welcomed the touch. An anchor to keep her from floating toward uncertainty.

"Is this a date?" She stared straight ahead and pretended to be fascinated by the streetlights. "Or just dinner?"

"I don't know," he admitted with a shrug. "I think neither one of us is in a good place to start a relationship."

"I agree," she said, with disproportionate enthusiasm. "That's smart."

"But on the other hand—"

"What other hand?" She leaned in a bit.

"I've really liked reconnecting, and I'd be lying if I said you've been awful to spend time with."

"I haven't been awful? That's flattering?" Holding hands should have been strange. It should have required more definition and intent. Hand-holding was just a gateway drug to a first kiss.

"I don't know where I'm going next. I'm not staying in Old Wesley and neither are you. It would be irresponsible of me to start something with you when we are both in the middle of some kind of quarter-life crisis."

"It's my quarter-life crisis. You're practically thirty." She watched as he grimaced at her dig.

"Maybe I'll live longer than you."

"Statistically the odds aren't in your favor. Women live longer."

"The point is," he said, dragging out the words in a silly way, "if all of this wasn't going on, and I ran into you at home under normal circumstances, I'd be hard pressed not to fall for you."

Butterflies filled her stomach. She'd made herself forget how much she'd pined over Griff all those years ago. Written it off as puppy love. But she'd be lying if she said his words weren't resonating with the part of her heart she'd quieted. It didn't mean she couldn't face reality. "These are not normal circumstances."

"So I say we keep doing what we're doing right now. Be there for each other the way we can. I've found timing is a big part of life. If it's off and you try to ignore that, you get kicked in the ass with the consequences. Well you know, look what happened to you and Ryan."

"Timing wasn't our problem." She licked her dry lips and let a few painful memories flash in. Ryan was the love of her life. That linear kind of love that follows a plan. Always moves forward to the next milestone. Coy friendship and common interests blossomed into exclusive dating. Then it made more sense to live together. Why pay two rents? Things were going so well; it was a natural progression. Their relationship was different than all their friends. Stable. No drama. Two people with drive and ambition who knew what they wanted out of life. The envy of all her friends.

There were well-planned picnics. Romantic hikes with smiling photos to document their achievements. Day trips. A sharing of the household responsibilities. Meals made together as music played in their tiny apartment kitchen. What she liked most about Ryan was his respect for her time. School mattered to her so he didn't complain when she was studying instead of paying attention to him. And in turn they made sure their quality time was fulfilling. It was a mature relationship for their age, and she loved that. In quantity, the good times outweighed the bad.

Unfortunately, she learned a relationship was mostly made of metal. There was no way to know how it would stand up until it was put through fire. Ryan was an honest, dependable man who loved her and would have kept loving her if she had let him. But she couldn't let him.

"I blew it with Ryan because things got hard, and I realized he wasn't the person I wanted to go through hard times with." It seemed like a simple explanation, but she saw Griff react strongly. A nod of his head, a rise of his shoulders, like an arrow had just pierced him.

"Yes. That's exactly it. Anyone can have a good relationship when nothing is going wrong. I wish I'd known that earlier. I wish I'd understood what a partner was before things went bad."

Gwen considered what her life would be like right now if she would've stayed with Ryan. He wouldn't have let her fall apart and isolate herself. With cool logic and unwavering support, he'd have insisted she get better. But that pressure would have kept her from feeling. The dark place she'd found herself in wasn't a hole to climb out of, it was a place to pass through. And if she'd avoided it, she'd have spent her whole life knowing it was right around the corner. It was better this way. She'd face this and be ready for someone on the other side.

"You broke up with him then?" Griff turned the car into a parking spot outside of a small intimate looking restaurant.

"I did. But I think the way things were going he'd have done it soon enough anyway. I wasn't the person he started dating all those years before."

"Why? What changed?"

She gulped back the answer she couldn't bear to speak and replaced it with a half-truth. "I screwed up and it started a domino effect I couldn't stop. You've seen how things affect me lately. I'd been a pretty normal girlfriend for years; Ryan wasn't ready, nor did he deserve me falling apart."

"You don't think he could have handled it?"

She thought for a moment of her sweet ex-boyfriend and his kind eyes. "No. He'd had a very good life up to that point. Not many challenges or heartaches. He couldn't have understood what I needed."

"I know what you need." He let her hand go and turned the car off. "I'll make sure you get it."

Her chest flooded with warmth. Not because he spoke flowery words, but because he meant them, and she believed him. "So this is not a date. Because we are not in a position to date. Our futures are completely unsettled and we'd be selfish irresponsible friends to date right now."

"For sure." He laughed as he looked up, seeming to consider a memory. "This is the second time I almost took you on a date but didn't."

"Um, no. I can assure you, if we almost dated I'd have known about it. I was obsessed with you."

"I know you were." With that, he got out of the car and left her sitting with her own admission. He rounded the front of the car and opened her door. "I saw the notebooks with my name written all over them. I overheard the slumber party chatter about me with your friends."

Her cheeks warmed but she battled away the embarrassment. It was a lifetime ago. Silly kid's stuff. "Then you would know that any potential date between us would be something I knew about."

"Want to bet?"

"Sure, loser buys dinner." She felt abundantly confident she was right.

He shot his hand out for them to shake on it. "Your senior prom. You were dating that kid with the stupid name."

She snapped her fingers together as the memory came into focus. "Wookie Smith. It was a nickname. He could make the noise from the movie. Pretty cool stuff at the time."

"The name was stupid, and so was he because he broke up with you two days before prom."

She dropped her head into her hands. "I'd completely forgotten about that. He was mad because I wouldn't wear flats and I was almost as tall as him."

"Your mom called me that night. She knew I was home from college already, and she asked if I'd take you."

"She didn't." Gwen stepped back and slapped a hand to her chest. "She wouldn't dare!"

"She did. And all I could think was how bad it would be if

you had to go alone. Or if you decided to skip it all together because of some jerk. You had just turned eighteen. You weren't a little kid anymore. I thought finally it wouldn't be weird for us to really hang out. I went as far as putting a deposit on a tux."

"You didn't."

He pursed his lips and nodded.

"That afternoon Wookie asked me to be his girlfriend again. He said I could wear whatever shoes I wanted, as long as I slouched in the pictures." She giggled at the thought of it but then fell serious. "You were going to take me to prom?"

"I was." Griff looked disappointed, as though the failed plans had happened yesterday. "But it didn't work out. Bad timing."

"Just like now."

"At least I didn't lose a deposit on a tux this time."

"You only lost a week of your life on this road trip. The tux was a better deal."

"I haven't lost a thing." He draped his arm over her shoulder and pulled her in tight. "I'd have been a great prom date."

"Wookie wasn't too bad. He behaved himself better than I expected."

"That might be because I ran into him at the gas station that morning once I knew he was your date again."

"You did?"

"It happens in a small town."

"What did you say to him?" She glanced at his face and breathed in his cologne.

"I told him you were like family to me, and if he tried anything with you, I'd make him even shorter than he already was. I might have crushed his bag of chips too."

"You crushed his chips?"

"Yeah. You were my girl. I wanted him to know I was serious. I'm not proud of it now, but I'm also not sure I'd change a thing if I had the chance. I'm glad to hear he behaved."

Shock washed over her face as she imagined Griff and Wookie in the gas station parking lot talking about preserving her honor. "I guess you win the bet. I'll buy dinner tonight."

"Not a chance. I'm buying. This might not be a date, but you're still my girl."

CHAPTER 11

Leslie

Nothing had been done. Holiday cheer had shriveled off her to-do list and died away. Leslie didn't bake the cookies or wrap the presents. It was bad enough, that for the first time ever her boys weren't coming home. Kerry seemed wholly uninterested in the holiday spirit too. To top it all off, she and Paul hadn't spoken more than a few cursory words to each other in days. There seemed no point to force the old traditions.

Instead she sat. Read. Stewed and pondered. All while wearing her sweatpants and an oversized sweatshirt. Gripping a warm mug of coffee or binging on a bag of chips. She wasn't due back at work until the day after Christmas, and so she could go full cocoon-mode for at least three more days.

Flipping open her laptop, Leslie did something she hadn't in over a decade. She searched for the visual aids that accompanied her fuzzy memories, hoping to bring them back into focus. First, she examined online images of the MCA office. Dozens popped up. It was a small single level, nondescript brick building. The glass door had a decal of white letters that told people what it was. Without that, it could easily be dismissed as an office building with no clear purpose.

Her other senses kicked in as she looked at more pictures. There was an inauthentic smell of pine in the lobby. The welcoming plush chairs and bright splashes of art had initially put Leslie at ease. Some back-alley business wouldn't bother with these small details. It was too beautiful to be dangerous.

It didn't take long for that reassurance to dissolve. The plan she thought she'd put together had fallen apart. Reba Burns, her coordinator at MCA, had betrayed her. The promises she'd made about finding the perfect family for Leslie's child were lies.

Lies she would not sit by and ignore. Leslie was not some sixteen-year-old kid, lost and ready to take the first solution she stumbled upon. Discretion was key, which is why she'd narrowed her options down to MCA adoption. But the more she pushed for answers the clearer it became that the company she'd picked had a dark secret. Reba, initially a gentle spirit with kind eyes and plump over-blushed cheeks had morphed quickly into a vehement witch when challenged by Leslie.

Pulling up a picture of Reba took her back to one of their last in-person exchanges. A moment scratched into her memory like a fleeing animal's claws into the bark of a tree. The photograph above the newspaper article showed Reba's sweeter side. Pinned-up curls and a gapped-tooth smile. A face that likely had most young women feeling at ease. As though they were meeting an understanding aunt with judgment-free advice. Leslie knew it was probably why Reba was hired in the first place. A gatekeeper to hell who wore a halo.

Her lacey collared dress was buttoned tightly, and in the frame of the picture a familiar brooch could be seen pinned to her chest. A metal outline of the manger scene. As Reba had explained it, the birth of Jesus was held close to her heart all year long. The pin and its shiny symbolism transported Leslie back in time.

"You've already signed the contract," Reba bit out as she stood and closed the door to her large, beautifully decorated office. Leslie kicked herself as she recounted how that beautiful office had given her the sense that this was a reputable business. She'd foolishly fallen for the façade MCA was selling. Clearly pregnancy hormones had clouded her judgment.

"People are saying this is an adoption-for-profit situation," Leslie cut back, one hand protectively over her full pregnant belly. Her words were cut up by a breathlessness that had taken over in her last month of pregnancy. Everything, including her lungs, compressed in her body. "I'm not selling my baby to the highest bidder. I want a thorough screening process. A family who takes this child for the right reasons."

Reba scoffed, her sour cigarette breath undercutting her clean-cut image. "And what reasons are those?"

"Because they can't have children of their own. Because they want to complete their family and have an abundance of love to give."

"You are a woman of means." Reba circled the room like a vulture stalking roadkill. "Don't you want to afford this child at least as good of a lifestyle as you are leading? The clients we work with can provide that."

"I want the baby to be loved. I'm not comfortable with your practices, and I'm not moving forward with this adoption." Leslie gulped, an eerie blanket of worry falling over her whole body. It had been in this building two weeks ago that a woman sitting by her in the waiting room had first alerted her to the situation. The young girl was not pregnant but had the body of someone who had recently delivered a baby. She cried silently in the corner of the waiting room until Leslie finally asked if she was all right. In brief cryptic sentences she told Leslie her son had been taken

from her at the hospital before the state-imposed waiting period for her to decide had run out. She'd changed her mind, but Reba had told her it was too late. The contract she'd signed with MCA was binding. When she inquired about where her son had ended up she'd been ignored. Stonewalled. Even the money she'd been promised had only partially been paid.

Leslie had tried to explain that away. The girl was young. Emotional. Postpartum. Surely she was mixed up by what had actually happened. But the conversation gnawed at her for days until she decided to dig deeper. There were no big news headlines to alert her. But some small articles in the paper had been published with interviews from women who claimed they'd been pressured or duped by MCA.

"Leslie, you came to us because you needed this to be discreet, correct?" Reba folded her arms over her ample bosom and scowled.

"I'm hoping for a closed adoption." Leslie edged out the words, but she knew that wasn't what Reba was alluding to.

"No, what you want is for this to disappear. Poof." Reba made a magician motion with her hands. "This inconvenience to you should just go away. You want the paper trail gone and any record of this to vanish. Your husband doesn't know, does he?" Reba raised her thinly penciled eyebrows and declared victory. "We can provide that anonymity. Other agencies cannot. They may tell you they can, but they will keep the records. They will abide by the laws that could someday get you found out."

A dagger of fear plunged into her heart. Paul couldn't know. Everything between them, what they were trying to build back up was a house of cards. She believed one day they would stand on solid ground again. Their marriage would survive and be strong, but at this stage it was fragile. This news would be a wrecking ball. "I may take my chances with a more reputable agency," Leslie gulped out, shifting uncomfortably in her seat.

"Then I'll be the one to call your husband myself." Reba gestured to her phone. "I'm sure he'll be easy enough to track down. He's not the father is he? That'll be hard to swallow." As if she knew she'd won this argument, Reba settled into her chair and leaned back casaully.

"You're threatening me?" This was where Leslie believed she was different than the usual clients at MCA. "You've admitted you won't abide by the law in this process. Now threats. You're opening yourself up to some serious litigation. I imagine it wouldn't be difficult for me to track down some of your former clients. They likely have stories too. Can you say class action lawsuit?" She leaned forward over her bulging belly and slapped a hand to her desk. The thought of Paul finding out about this pregnancy took a temporary backseat to getting threatened. Maybe it wasn't practical but she didn't cower to bullies.

The grin on Reba's face was devilishly big. "Bring it on. Those other clients are running from the same kinds of secrets you are. No way they're going to crawl out from the darkness to shine a light on us. That's what makes all of this work. Money talks and, when push comes to shove, people are selfish cowards. I've been doing this a long time. Trust me."

The words echoed in Leslie's mind as she slammed her laptop closed, crushing the memories down.

There had been so many mistakes, mountains of regret. But trusting Reba in the first place was a misstep that flattened her still today.

It wasn't until her last few days of pregnancy that she decided she couldn't be blackmailed and threatened. Her child didn't deserve to be punished for her cowardice. Driving three states away and finding the clinic instead of calling Reba might have meant she'd destroy her life with Paul. But how could she live a life with anyone knowing she'd left her baby with that monster and her associates?

When labor pains began, the clinic in Rhode Island was an oasis in the desert. A random find in the yellow pages. Ivy, her nurse, had been her angel. She'd given her a solution when Leslie felt completely out of options. It hadn't fixed her problems with MCA. Reba, upon realizing she'd broken her contract, could still have told Paul. She could have continued to threaten Leslie throughout the years. A looming dread, but at least her child, her daughter, would be in loving arms.

After giving birth, Leslie changed her phone number. Moved out of the sublet apartment and into one that would suit Paul better on his return. She'd already been out of work for months. It meant Reba had limited ways to find her. When Leslie walked back into MCA five weeks later with her head held high and her belly shrunk down, she told them she'd delivered a stillborn baby. There was nothing left for them to take, nothing to threaten her with. It would end there or she would divulge everything she knew about the company and their practices.

Maybe it was the way her chin was tipped back or how her rehearsed speech flowed so confidently, but Reba backed down. Shredded the contract right in front of her and said there was no point in pursuing this any further.

With that Leslie snipped the last loose end of this frayed situation. Paul would be back in a few weeks. She'd made peace with knowing her career might not advance. The detour she'd taken had somehow routed her back to something familiar. Something she could work with. If only she could keep the shards of her broken heart from cutting her open.

"Mom," Kerry's voice felt like a far-off echo. Leslie had curled up in the oversized recliner in the shadowy media room, pretending to be able to read a book in the dark.

"In here, honey," she called, shooting up unnaturally and trying to look busy at fluffing the cushions of the couch.

"Do you want to bake some cookies?" Kerry asked, poking just her head into the dark room. "I already took the butter out to get soft."

"You don't have to do that. I know you're studying. Don't feel bad about it. I hate that I've been giving you a hard time. I'm proud of how hard you work."

"Tomorrow is Christmas Eve; it'll be strange not having those cookies to sneak before bed." Kerry disappeared down the long hallway and Leslie followed, her eyes taking time to adjust to the light. She'd nearly forgotten it was still daytime.

Walking by the front window she saw Paul's car was not in the driveway. He'd likely found some excuse to duck into the office and hide from her. "Kerry, I know things have been tense here between your father and me the last couple of days. But don't let that change your plans. We don't need to bake."

"I want to bake with you." Kerry's light hair was pulled into the high ponytail she preferred when she studied. She was doing a hell of a job looking genuine about this new enthusiasm, and Leslie was thankful for that. She needed a win. "Whose recipe was this?" Kerry ran her fingers over the worn-out recipe card and began gathering the ingredients.

"It's your great grandmother Laudon's recipe. She made these little elves every Christmas for her own children."

"When did you start baking them?" If she was feigning interest, it was hard to spot.

"The first Christmas I spent with your father, his mother, Grandma Laudon gave me the recipe and told me the story of how her mother came to have it. She showed me how to make them. Your father talked about them so much leading up to the holiday I knew they were special. I've been making them ever since."

"Sounds like Dad," Kerry's chipper voice dulled.

"Don't be so hard on your dad. We're having a rough couple of days, but that doesn't mean you should think poorly of him in any way."

Kerry rolled her eyes and put the wooden spoon down firmly enough on the counter to make a loud noise. "Mom, this has nothing to do with the last couple of days. You have to know that, right?"

"Know what?"

"Never mind," Kerry drew in a deep breath and turned her attention back to the recipe. "Why don't you and Grandma Laudon get along?"

"Of course we get along." This lie was harder to get out with a straight face. Leslie had made it a point to never let her relationship with her mother-in-law impact her children. There was no reason they shouldn't be close with their grandmother just because the woman hated her.

"Grandma comes out here for two weeks every year around Easter, and your blood pressure goes through the roof. We all have to walk around in our nice clothes all day and you take out the fancy china as if we use it all the time. Her entire trip is like some bizarre play we put on for her benefit. With all that, she still doesn't seem pleased."

Damn, her daughter was astute.

"Your grandmother loves you all very much. You know that."

"But she doesn't like you?"

"Some relationships are more complex than others. You'll see it when you get older."

Kerry's pitch grew unnaturally high. "I am older, Mom. I'll be eighteen in a couple months. And I don't want that kind of relationship with you. I don't want to put on some fake act when I see you. I want to be completely myself."

There is an alarm system a mother hones over the years. An alert that messages the brain right before something big happens.

Leslie's was loudly sounding now. "Kerry, you and I are never going to have that relationship. You can be yourself with me. I don't need the good china, and I never will. Grandma grew up in a different time in a much different way. That'll never be us." Leslie took the spoon from her daughter's hand and guided her over to the table in the breakfast nook. "Tell me what this is really about."

"I want you to come to California with me." Kerry's lashes were wet with tears as she nervously bit her lip. She was not Leslie's emotional child. Kerry was levelheaded. Cole was usually the one worked up over things.

"It's all right to be scared to go off to school. It's far away and you're nervous. But I promise when you get settled out there the last thing you'll want is me around."

Kerry shook her head and gathered herself. "I'm not scared to go to school, Mom. I can't wait to get there. But I don't want to leave you here. I want you to get the same fresh start I'm getting."

A knot tightened in Leslie's stomach. That was what she was worried about. The moment of honesty she'd shared with Kerry after she'd tossed the bench in the pond. It must have planted an acorn of concern that Kerry, and her active mind, cultivated into an oak tree of full-on worry. "I don't need a fresh start, honey. My whole life is here, and I'm very happy. Your father and I should have done a better job of keeping this nonsense from you. It's silly and not at all something you need to concern yourself with."

"Please don't do that. Don't excuse this away for him. It's not about the trip to Europe or the argument you're having right now. It's so much bigger than that."

"Kerry, your father is a good man. Don't let something I said the other day color your opinion of him. I'll never forgive myself if I thought I contributed to that."

"Mom, you understand that he's the reason I'm going to college on the other side of the country, right? He's the reason the boys aren't coming home for Christmas." A few rogue tears ran down her cheeks, and Leslie instinctively brushed them away.

"What are you talking about?"

"Cole never wanted to be a dentist. He hates it. Coming back here to talk to Dad about growing his practice and how to market better to his patients is his nightmare."

"Cole went to dental school; of course he wanted to be a dentist." Leslie felt as though she'd accidentally changed the channel in the middle of her favorite show and now nothing made sense.

"He wanted to go into animation. Cole wanted to get an art degree. You do remember that, right? Dad drove that dream into the ground. He pressured him into something more practical."

"Animation isn't that practical," Leslie argued, though she didn't really know anything about the field.

"And you can't actually think Stephen wants to follow in Dad's footsteps. Being on the fast track to leadership at some trading company was never his passion, but Dad had him pigeon-holed since his first lemonade stand in the driveway when he was twelve. He'd been chanting the praises of his business acumen and making connections for him all along. Stephen is miserable. He's thinking about quitting and selling cars so he can get out from under Dad's grip. How could you not know any of this?"

Leslie slid into the chair next to Kerry and gripped the table. Her words came more out of habit than thought. "Your father wants what's best for all of you."

"And what does he think is best for me?" Kerry laughed out the words as though the answer would be ridiculous.

Leslie opened her mouth and then closed it quickly. Not because she wasn't sure, but because she was, and she was embarrassed by how right Kerry had been.

"A teacher. He wants you to be a teacher."

"If I'm lucky a professor maybe. He's been saying it since I was twelve. How blessed I'd be to get a job at a university and still be able to raise a family. He talks about the flexibility of my schedule. How great of an example you've set for me. Dad wants me to be a mom and have a good adaptable job."

"And that's not what you want." Leslie didn't need to pose it as a question. She knew her daughter well enough to know the answer.

"I'm going to go to med school. I'll work an obscene amount of hours. So many that I can hardly manage a relationship. Then, I'll travel the world with Doctors Without Borders. I don't ever want to settle down. I don't want your life." She looked suddenly apologetic, but Leslie wouldn't allow her to say sorry.

"And that's fine," Leslie said, grabbing her daughter's hand.

"You don't want your life either. So come with me. You can get a job in California. A little condo on the beach. You can live whatever life you want to."

"This doesn't have to be about me. If you know what you want then you know we'll support it."

Kerry looked disgusted in that way only a teenager could. "I've known I've wanted this for three years. Don't you think it's strange I never told you about it?"

"Why haven't you?" Leslie put her hand over her heart, bracing for a verbal dagger she was sure was coming.

"Because before I saw you throw that bench in the pond, I didn't know if I could trust you. I thought up until that moment, you'd be on his side. Now I know you see it. You understand how he does it."

"How he does what?" Leslie wasn't ready to accept that her daughter could see as clearly as she could now.

"He gets his way without ever looking like the bully. The way he gets people to do things and somehow make them think it was their idea. You know how it would start with me. If I'd have stayed around here like the boys did, he'd start with my first summer. Setting up internships. Making calls. Pressuring me to meet up with people who could guide me on the career path he wants for me. It's all this strategic chess game for him."

"So tell him you want to be a doctor." Leslie knew her point wasn't strong, but she felt compelled to make it.

"Right, so he could start dismantling it. Telling me every con on the list associated with being a doctor. Reminding me he pays for my college. Then, like he did to Cole, inevitably threatening to cut me off if I didn't bend to what he thought was best for me. These college funds aren't gifts; they are puppet strings. I'm cutting mine. In a couple of months, I'm going to tell Dad I am choosing pre-med, and I don't need a dime of his money. I have a full ride on academic scholarships. I'll get a job and pay for all of my incidentals. I can do this on my own." Witnessing Kerry's long-held secret come to life was like watching a hatchling burst free of its shell. Leslie was all at once proud of her daughter and pained at how blind she'd been.

"Honey, I don't know what to say. I had no idea you felt this way. I think if we talked to your father—"

"He'd listen." Kerry nodded her head. "Maybe even agree for a little while. But only long enough to formulate his own master plan. I'm not going to be a teacher. I don't need the summers off for my kids. That's an awesome life for someone, but not for me. I'm sure about this. I know what I want, and he's not taking it from me."

Leslie's instincts of loyalty began to kick in. "You're making him sound far worse than he is. He loves you. He loves us all."

"Mom, he can love us and still make mistakes. I hope that he and I don't turn into the same thing you and Grandma Laudon are. I want him to visit me in California and be proud of what I'm doing. To show off pictures of me traveling the world and practicing medicine. I hope that happens. But I'm not waiting around to find out. You shouldn't wait around either."

"I'm not leaving your father." Leslie sneered at the absurdity. "I'm a middle-aged woman with a comfortable marriage. You don't walk away from that just because the other person is strong-willed. We can go to counseling. Communicate better. I'm so sorry you've had to even think about this. We're not going to split up."

"Just do me one favor?" Kerry's face crumpled as she leaned her head on her mother's shoulder. "Some people stay together for their kids. Don't do that. I speak for all your kids when I say you deserve to have whatever life you want, and Dad deserves to have his own life too. Something he can control all on his own. You don't have to stick it out for us."

Leslie dropped her mouth open and searched for the right words. Her instinct was to defend her marriage. To build her husband back up. But what good would that do? She wasn't talking to some child who didn't understand. Kerry seemed to comprehend perfectly what had been going on. Maybe better than anyone else in the house had. "I love you, Kerry. I've made mistakes too. But I promise you can always be yourself with me. I'll support whatever dream you have. I don't know what will happen with your father and I, but I do know you can count on me. I think you'll make one hell of a doctor someday. I'll be proud to brag about you."

Kerry's shoulders began to tremble as she cried. "I'm sorry, Mom. I didn't mean to dump all this on you."

"I'm your mother. Anytime. Anywhere. Anything. You can come to me. You are more important to me than anything in the world. I don't have the answers right now, but I can promise you, we'll figure this out together."

Kerry snuggled into Leslie's arms like she hadn't since she was a child. It had been so long since any of her children had needed her this way. Her mind wandered to her boys. How out of touch she'd become with their needs. There was a time they ran to her with everything. Now she realized they saw her as just a pole propping up Paul and his agendas. Of course they wouldn't come to her with their frustrations. All she'd do was remind them of how lucky they were to have their father's support. But that support came with enough strings attached to hang a person.

Leslie squeezed Kerry tightly and made a vow to herself. She was going to reclaim her children. Hear their needs. Support their dreams. The way she had when they were small. She didn't want to be her mother-in-law. She didn't want to fall into those patterns of visiting only to see a façade. Paper doll cutouts of her own flesh and blood propped up on stage for her benefit.

This was her wake-up call. Her children needed her. Their nest might be empty soon, but this mama bird was still able to tend to her chicks.

CHAPTER 12

Gwen

The Fox family house was warm. No, it was downright hot. Simple science could explain it. When you turned on the tiny oven all day and stuffed the place with so many people, the temperature was bound to rise. Even with the windows open on a December day, the tiny house was toasty.

Every holiday hosted there was the same. It was a tapestry of card tables against their kitchen table that took up most of the room. The heights were never quite right but when the red Santa tablecloths went over everything, it made it look all right. Mismatched chairs from all over the house were wedged so tightly it took strategy to maneuver into your seat. There was no getting up once you were in unless your neighbor planned to move first.

Millie didn't put much stock in matching dishes or expensive centerpieces. There wouldn't even be room in the middle of the table for a small bunch of flowers or a clever arrangement of holiday décor. What did make an appearance every year was a handed down set of crystal salt and pepper shakers and an antique dish for mixed nuts.

The entire setup was a cobbled together mess that somehow ended up looking perfectly beautiful to everyone in attendance. Over the years there had been a few cousins and aunts and uncles in attendance. But as families do, they grew and moved on to their own branches of the tree. Began their own traditions with new spouses and children. This was by far the smallest group to gather for a Fox Christmas as far as Gwen could remember. But still it was cramped. Maybe ten fewer bodies than years past.

The math perplexed Gwen enough to look around the room and finally pose the question to her mother. "How in the world did we fit here when Uncle Smitty and Aunt Linda and their three kids would come? And Great Uncle Rob. Dad, the year your second cousin came with her two kids. I don't remember how you made it work."

Her mother grinned as the fond memories seemed to play out in her mind. "Anything is possible, if you want it bad enough."

The words, intended to be a ringing endorsement of perseverance, gave Gwen a fleeting sense of a sinister meaning.

Had that been how she came to be adopted? Did the Fox family want her bad enough to break the law?

Her father, wearing his traditional Christmas sweater, strolled out the few feet from the galley kitchen and into the small dining area. "You were all still small at the time. Grown-ups sat at this table and you kids sat in the living room on a blanket like a picnic. You loved it. You actually complained the first year we tried to move you to a table." She noticed for the first time how her father's frame had changed. His shoulders came to a point under the well-loved, well-worn Christmas sweater. His belly, usually a little bigger from holiday indulgence, normally stretched the material. Now there was extra room. His back injury had taken a lot out of him and finally she was seeing it first-hand.

The clamor of all the company rose and fell as conversations began about Christmases from years earlier.

Gwen tried to blame the queasy feeling she had on the heat in the house instead of the rush of emotions she was battling. The urge to blurt her questions was nearly overwhelming. The temptation was akin to holding a dandelion and trying not to blow the seeds into the wind. She bounced with nervous energy as she tried to find ways to keep busy. Setting the table. Pulling the serving trays out from the back of the cabinets.

When her mother had called her out on the odd behavior, her cheeks had pinked. But as time ticked by, everyone had a reason to be a little rosy in the face.

"Limoncello is my favorite," Nick announced as he raised his glass a little higher. "Dave, next time you go to Italy, bring back ten bottles of this for me."

"We've all had a bit, haven't we?" Millie clutched her pearls and grinned widely at her children. "I better feed everyone before you pass out. The turkey is ready."

Christmas Eve-Eve had become the Fox family night. Millie had been smart in changing the tradition a couple of years back. At some point her children would have kids of their own. Naturally, they'd want to spend Christmas morning at their own houses. So she claimed the day before Christmas Eve instead.

Like a blueprint that had been thoroughly examined, everything was exactly where it was meant to be. The holiday details put in the same spot every year.

There was only one area in the living room big enough for the Christmas tree. The mantel had exactly the same trinkets it had since Gwen was a girl. Tinsel wrapped around the banisters and ornaments dangled from the stockings. The consistency was comforting.

"Don't fall in the oven, Mom," Dave called, following his mother to the kitchen. His hairline had started to recede a bit and his face was rounder than the last time Gwen had seen him. He was looking more like their father every day. "I'll take the turkey out."

Noel grunted and took a seat by Gwen and Griff at the table. "This damn back is such a pain. I can't even take the turkey out of the oven anymore. You know I hate sitting still, and it's about the only damn thing I can do now."

The salt-and-pepper gray at his temples had climbed upward and now covered most of his head. Even his calloused hands were looking idle and smooth lately.

"You'll be back to normal before you know it, Dad," Gwen said, handing him a beer and shifting to try to give him more room.

"Who drank my beers by the way?" Noel knit his overgrown brows together and eyed her closely. "The recycling bin was full of them."

"There were four in there," Gwen corrected with a roll of her eyes. "Griff and I had some."

"In the tree house," Griff commented casually. "That thing still holds us. A real testament to your craftsmanship, Noel. It was a great night's sleep."

Gwen looked for an inconspicuous way to kick Griff, but she knew it would rattle the table.

Noel kept his stern expression. "You slept up there? Together? Didn't I make a rule about co-ed sleepovers in the tree house?"

"Oh, Noel," Millie sang from the kitchen. The double-edged sword of a small house was everyone could hear everything in any room. "The statute of limitations has run out on your rules. I'm glad they slept up there. It's cute."

"Cute," Noel said, his watery blue eyes looking unimpressed

by his wife's assessment. "And this road trip you two took, what was that about?"

Dave and Nick were back in the small dining room, looking suddenly very interested in the conversation.

"I told you already," Gwen reported uncomfortably. "We just wanted to hang out and see some sights. Who wants to stay in Old Wesley for a week? You guys know there is nothing here."

Dave, with his bright blue eyes and constantly quizzical face jumped in. "But when is the last time you two even saw each other?"

Gwen's voice rose a few octaves. "Why does that matter?"

Nick cleared his throat and ran a hand over the back of his thick neck as though he were mulling over the right thought. He was shorter and stockier than Dave but they shared enough features to easily be spotted as brothers. "It matters because people who just bump into each other after a long time, don't go away for a week together."

"Oh please," Gwen said, swatting at the accusation. "We spent every waking minute together when we were kids. All of us. It's no different than if I went away for the week with one of you guys."

Nick laughed and whacked Dave's shoulder. "Right."

"I want you all to stop that this instant," Millie said, her hands still stuffed into oven mitts. "Whatever is going on between Gwen and Griff is their business."

"Nothing is going on," Gwen cut back with a huff. "Honestly, you guys love to stir things up."

Dave slapped a hand to Griff's shoulder and squeezed. "You wouldn't make a move on my little sister, right? Not while she's going through something."

Griff opened his mouth to answer but Gwen cut him off.

"Going through something? What the hell does that mean? I'm not going through anything, and who I choose to spend my time with is none of your business." Gwen hopped to her feet, bumping the table, and propped a hand up on her hip. She blocked Dave from moving toward the dinner table.

"Now, now," Millie tried, but Nick was too fast. He cut back in the way only a big brother could.

"Going to the hospital because you have a breakdown is a thing. You don't want to just jump into a relationship because you're feeling bad."

Griff raised a hand. "Uh, we're not in a relationship."

Nick groaned. "Well, you don't go hooking up for that reason either."

"Nicholas," Millie scolded, "stop that this instant. No one is *hooking up at anyone.*"

With that misuse of the hip vernacular, the tension broke. All the kids gave sideways glances at each other and stifled laughs.

"Thank you, Mom," Gwen grinned. "You are right. We are not hooking up at each other. We were merely burning a week, and we decided we should hang out. End of story. Now can we eat and enjoy the night?"

"Good idea, sweetheart. Dave, when is Cynthia getting here?" Millie checked her watch and glanced at the turkey.

"She said not to wait for her," Dave reported with a quick glance away toward his lap. It could have been nothing, but Gwen wondered if the happy couple was having problems. Cynthia was different than them in almost every way. Maybe that was why Dave had started dating her in the first place. The allure of opposites. She'd grown up in a large house. An only child. Two parents in the hustle and bustle of the business world. By the time Cynthia hit high school she'd traveled to far corners of the planet. The farthest the Fox family had ventured was into Maine for swimming in frigid waters and camping in leaky tents. But that trip had left them with lasting memories of mishaps that led to endless laughs. Cynthia never seemed to have the same kinds of stories to tell about her trips.

Most of her recounting consisted of fancy places they'd eaten or museums they'd visited. The Fox family would coo and nod and listen intently before breaking back in to talk about the time they accidently left Nick at the gas station because they didn't know he'd gotten out of the back of the station wagon. Cynthia's eyes would go wide and a look of horror would overtake her. She seemed constantly worried for the Fox family and their odd idea of what was funny versus what was dangerous.

She and Dave had been dating for over three years. But it was clear she was a part of his other life. The part that involved international travel and sales conventions. Cynthia was accustomed to him wearing business suits and carrying his briefcase. Coming back to this tiny house and cramming in with everyone, she never looked particularly comfortable. Her pinched features and quiet voice didn't match the Fox family, and it always made Gwen wonder how it would ever match her brother.

Dave shifted in his seat. "She's stuck on work calls at the hotel. They're working on a major acquisition. She's going to try to pop in after dessert, but you know how it goes." It had been that way the last couple times they'd come home. The argument was, it just made more sense for them to stay in a hotel. They couldn't very well sleep comfortably in his old room on his twin bunk beds. Even if Nick took the couch. It was easier for everyone. Millie would hum a reluctant agreement and offer a few other sleeping arrangement options, but it never worked. He'd remind her that he had loads of travel points and the hotel was basically free for him. Finally, Millie would give up.

"We'll miss her," Millie replied, trying to sound more disappointed than she was.

Noel closed his eyes and dropped his head, indicating it was time to say grace. They weren't an overly religious family, but

Millie had always described herself as spiritual. Not bound to any one set of rules but quick to do what's right.

As Gwen watched her family bow their heads and pray, she wondered if her parents had truly done what was right over the years. Were they as good as they always appeared to be? If that was an illusion she'd have a hard time believing anything was real.

Like a synchronized dance, they passed food around the table. Scooping, slicing, and buttering with precision. When the last drop of gravy was doled out, the stories began. They usually went back to the same pile of memories, the way people veer back to the streets they drive every day. Muscle memory leads you back more than conscious thought.

With Griff there, there was an added layer of joy associated with the reminiscing. But around the edges, there was something Gwen had never noticed before. A dark rim around every smile he flashed when he talked about the past. She knew now why Griff showed up at their doorstep so often. Why Noel had been the one to teach him things his father hadn't. Why Millie put the bandages on his skinned knees and sent him home with the leftovers.

"Why did you put that steak on Griff's eye that night?" Gwen asked suddenly as the memory flashed through her mind. "It was so late. I remember you came to the door and Dad slapped this huge steak to your eye. It was supposed to be our dinner the next night."

Her fear that everyone knew something she didn't grew and spread like a plague through her bloodstream. The look on their faces made it obvious. Things had been kept from her. Now it made her wonder how many things? How often did they all get together and decide she didn't need to be informed?

Griff, seeming to read the expression of doubt on her face, fessed up. "My father had a lot to drink that night. He was going after my mom about the mess and I got in the way. He tossed me out, and I didn't know where else to go." His hand went instinctively to his eye and then slipped down his cheek. "Your old man knew a good steak was the solution to keep the swelling down."

Millie's eyes were wet with the threat of tears. "It still turned into a bad shiner though."

Dave took a sip of his drink and put his glass down gingerly. "Mom made me get out of the top bunk and give it to you that night. Once I got a look at you, I stopped bitching about it."

"Did that happen a lot?" Gwen asked, anger in her voice. Angry that she'd not known. That she'd been left to sleep that night and only stumbled upon the scene when she walked out for a drink of water.

"Not after that night," Griff said, swapping knowing looks with Noel. "Your dad made sure of that."

"How?" Gwen leaned back in her chair and put her fork down by her plate. "What did you do?"

Nick chuckled. "He went down there and kicked his ass."

Millie huffed. "He didn't. That's not what happened."

Gwen looked at Griff. "How did I know nothing about this? You guys kept this from me?"

"You were younger," Millie said. "We didn't want you worrying."

"I'm not that much younger than Nick. I don't see why that would keep me from knowing what was happening." She turned toward her dad. "You beat him up?"

Millie had a pained expression on her sweet face. "Is this really what we're going to talk about over Christmas dinner?"

"I want to know what happened," Gwen insisted. "I'm part of this family, aren't I? Since when do we keep secrets?" She shot a look to Griff, who met her gaze with an expression of caution. If he had the cattle prod he might use it now.

Noel shrugged. "It wasn't much of a fight. Your mom put Griff to bed, and I grabbed Dave's baseball bat and went over there. He was sloshed. I didn't have to do much but threaten him. I blackened his eye just so he knew what it felt like. Times were different then. Most guys felt like what happened in people's houses was their business. We tried to stay out of it but I'd be damned if he was going to go that far."

"And he never did again," Griff said, raising his glass as a sign of thanks to Noel. "I don't know what I would have done without you two."

Millie smiled and waved off his praise. "You've said thank you plenty of times. No need at all."

"No," Griff said, tipping his head down. "There aren't enough thank-yous in the world to be even with you. Noel, you took the time to teach me everything a kid should know. It's not just that I can change my own oil and fix a flat tire. Or that I can swing a hammer. There are plenty of places I could have learned that stuff. You treated me like your own. Held me to a high standard when no one else cared what I was getting into. You could have let me go down the wrong path and turn out just like my father. You never did. And Millie"—Griff choked on the emotion—"it actually felt strange to me the first time you hugged me and packed me a lunch for school. You'd put the same little notes in my bag as you did your own boys. You'd kiss my forehead at the sleepovers when it was time for bed. You'd forgive me when I screwed up. It's not an easy thing to admit, but I don't think I ever felt love until you loved me. I didn't know what it was right away, I just knew I needed it and you were giving it to me."

Gwen felt her eyes well with tears as Griff leaned back in his chair and raised his glass higher. Everyone else did the same, and said a quiet "Cheers," as they clanked their glasses together. Millie was a heap of tears now and even Noel seemed to be biting at his quivering lip.

"Griffy," Millie mustered through the emotion, "you are very loved here. You always will be."

That was the hard part about being a grown-up on the inner circle of things now. You saw behind the curtain, and it was never as good as you imagined it would be. She'd wanted to know what had really happened, and now that she had, it was bittersweet. It meant peeling back the pain Griff had packed away. Guilt gnawed at her.

"How's work, Griff?" Dave asked, pouring himself another drink of icy limoncello. Now that the emotion had seeped into dinner, the drink was flowing fast and the silly laughs were spilling over the table to prove it. Gwen had never been drunk with her parents, but she could tell tonight might be the night.

"Work sucks," Griff said animatedly. "As in I'm not working right now because the company went under for bad business practices."

A silence swam like a school of minnows darting in a circle around the table, trapping them in the middle.

"I didn't know," Dave replied, looking to his mother as though she should have told him. "I've been so caught up in my own stuff I haven't checked in with you in so long. I'm sorry about that, man."

Nick grumbled something as he took another roll from the breadbasket. "Can we add unemployment to the list of reasons not to date my sister right now?"

"Don't start this again," Gwen groaned. "Griff is going through enough right now. He doesn't need you guys criminalizing the idea of him being nice to me."

"That's a big college word," Noel teased, tossing his napkin down onto his empty plate as though he'd been victorious over the dish of food. "Any new job prospects, Griff? What's next for you?"

"I don't know," Griff shrugged, bobbling his glass a bit as he went in for another sip. They were all feeling the buzz now. "I'm going to see what comes."

"Oh," Noel said, through pursed lips. "You're in that stage. I've been there."

"What stage?" Griff asked, narrowing his eyes. It was clear he didn't feel like he was in any particular place at all.

Noel moved his chair back a bit and crossed one leg over the other. "The *too afraid to make a move* stage. You wait for life to happen for you instead of making something happen. It's not a good place to be. Trust me."

"I'm not afraid," Griff argued, but his voice was hollow and ineffectual. Not even Gwen bought it.

"Call it what you like," Noel folded his arms, looking unimpressed. "Have I told you about this house?" He gestured up at the ceiling.

"What about it, Dad?" Nick asked, sounding worried that his father might be losing it. "We know it's a house."

"I mean, who built it and the story behind it?" Noel clarified.

Dave nodded. "Grandad Fox built it." David loved being right and being first. He sat up a little straighter. "You've told us."

"I told you he built it, but I didn't tell you the story behind it." Noel looked suddenly smug, ready to give them all a bit of history whether they wanted it or not. Wedged so tightly around the table, they were trapped. "I was the youngest of six children, and when I came along my dad was already an old man. At least by the standards in that day. My dad grew up just after the depression. He knew tough times when he was small. He hurt his foot after I was born and was out of work a while. It eventually healed but his job wasn't there anymore. We lived with my mother's parents and my dad wanted out. It wasn't easy finding a place to move with your family of eight."

"I'm sure you've told this story," Millie said, waving off Dave who filled her glass anyway. They were all going to feel it in the morning, but at this point it was better to finish the bottles he'd brought. Or at least that's what he kept saying.

179

"Well, my dad decided he'd buy a little plot of land and build a house. It's not an easy thing to do, but when you're determined you can make anything happen. Living with your mother-in-law can be a good motivator. This area was not built up at all. Just woods. He went down and bought the land and found out two weeks later they wouldn't let him put in an access road. So it was useless land."

"Oh," Nick said with a devilish grin. "That's where Gwen gets her planning skills."

"Yes," Gwen shot back quickly. "It must be genetic." Adoption jokes were fair game over the years. They never bothered her. Only Millie used to huff about them, but now even she smirked.

Noel continued, staring up at the ceiling to make sure he recalled all the right details. "My father wasn't going to give up. He wanted out of the in-laws' house, and so he camped out at the county commissioner's office every day until someone took a meeting with him. Then he showed them the blueprints he had and where he wanted the access road. Still they told him no."

"But," Millie said, sipping gingerly on her drink, "that obviously isn't where the story ends or we wouldn't be here."

"Right," Noel agreed. "He was persistent. He started bringing a chair with him. Packing a lunch. A stack of books he could read. Finally, when they realized he wouldn't go away they gave him the rights to the land and the ability to make an access road. There were only two conditions. One, if he had any further requests from the office, he'd have to have his wife come in instead. And two, the man who spent the most time dealing with my father insisted on naming the road."

"Redwood Road?" Gwen asked, glancing to her mother as if she'd missed something. "That's what they called it? Why?"

"Carl Sterling." Noel announced the name as though it held some meaning to the rest of them. He stared off and smiled. His pause was too long to be natural.

"Dad?" Gwen asked, sounding impatient. "Who the heck is Carl Sterling? He dealt with Grandpa in the office there?"

"Yes," he said proudly. "My father was the most determined man Carl ever met. He died before you kids were born. He and my father actually became friends and years later Carl told us the story of the house and why he named the road. In his later years he told us again and again, but I never grew tired of hearing it. When Carl was in the Army he spent time on the West Coast. Upon seeing the Redwood Forest he was awestruck. He'd been drinking too much. Gambling. Throwing his life away. Seeing those trees changed him. It was apparently the most humbling experience of his life. Sitting my sibling and I down, Carl went into detail about the trees. I remember his gritty voice as he told us the redwoods make the Statue of Liberty look like a measly garden gnome. Even the tallest man in the world could walk next to them and feel like an ant. Nature's skyscrapers. Far sturdier and more beautiful than anything man could make. He wanted us to know exactly how it had all come to pass. He said God must have used a little of the redwood tree when he built my father."

"Are those beams in the attic made of redwood?" Dave asked.

"They sure are. All part of the story. Carl believed the house my father built would stand the test of time. So the road it was built on should represent that sentiment. I grew up knowing the Fox family and the house he built would be sturdy, timeless, and unshakable. Just like those trees. Just like my father."

"That's really neat, Dad," Nick said, patting his dad's shoulder. "He was right. The house is still as good as ever. You've seen to that."

"I can't keep it up though," Noel admitted, dropping his eyes down to this plate.

"Not tonight, Noel," Millie scolded. "We're celebrating, and we're all a little drunk, I think. We can talk about it tomorrow."

"What's going on?" Dave asked, his brows rising with worry. "The house has long since been paid off. If it's money—"

Noel grunted. "It's not money."

"What's wrong with the house?" Dave looked around as if something might become apparent. A loose board. A leaky pipe.

"A lot is wrong," Noel explained somberly. "That's how old houses are. With my back being the way it is, your mother and I think maybe we should make other arrangements for ourselves."

Gwen felt her pulse quicken at the thought of change. Some epic shifting away from what she'd always known. Her parents were too young to throw in the towel and end up at some retirement community. "What kind of arrangements are you talking about?"

"Your father would do better somewhere with a bedroom on the main floor. Going up and down the stairs most days is fine, but when his back is really bad it's too much. Then sleeping on the couch just makes it even worse." Millie stood and began clearing dishes. Everyone else would normally offer to help, but she would only tell them no. There was no room in the kitchen for all of them and something would end up breaking. After she took a load to the sink, she returned and continued. "Plus, a place that offers maintenance would be great. This way he doesn't have to do quite so much handyman work."

"You're selling our house?" Nick asked, his concern sounding more like anger than he probably intended. "You can't do that. This is where we grew up. What about the story you just told us? The timelessness of the redwood trees."

"We don't want to sell the house," Noel said, the corners of his mouth rising a bit. "But we don't want it sitting empty either. Dave you're in North Carolina, and Cynthia wouldn't want to come live here anyway. Nick, you're about to start a new job in New York. It doesn't make sense for you either."

Everyone at the table looked over at Gwen and her cheeks

burned with a mix of drunkenness and embarrassment. "What? I can't live here. I'm going to be graduating and working at a lab by the campus. That's two hours from here."

"There are a few labs here in the state," Millie offered in a much too chipper voice. "You could at least look into them. Your father and I would be delighted to know you were here, looking in on the place and it could be good for you. We're looking to move right down the road into those condos they just put up by the fire station."

"You'd be neighbors," Griff said, his eyes lit with some kind of dubious mischief. "Fun."

"You don't need to be in the city," Dave said, nodding his agreement as he let the information set in. "Who needs all that commotion? You're graduating with a great degree; a small lab here would be very lucky to have you."

Things came clearly into focus for her suddenly. "Oh this is because you all think I'm losing my mind. Having a breakdown. Somehow moving back here would be good for me?"

Millie cut her hands through the air much more animatedly than she would have if it had not been for the drinks. "That's not it at all. We've had this in the works long before you—"

Nick scratched his chin. "Yes, what are we calling this? Before you lost your marbles?"

"Nicholas," Millie scolded. "She's not lost anything."

"I'm really fine," Gwen sighed, her eyes catching Griff's. She could tell them. Right now. She could tell them about the DNA test and how mailing it off had scared her. She could let them know about the nurse they saw in Rhode Island. Or what she'd found out about Ivy. Without a word, Griff offered a knowing look. It wasn't the right time.

Gwen softened her defensive posture. "I don't appreciate everyone pretending this scheme is spontaneous."

Millie grabbed another handful of dishes and smiled. "We

wouldn't do that to you, Gwen. The Fox family doesn't keep secrets. You know that."

As a child that sentiment actually brought Gwen peace. It made her feel a part of something unique. An unbreakable bond. But now, she could feel how those words made everyone's skin prickle. Of course there were secrets. Gwen had gotten wind of a few of them, but knew for sure her parents were completely in the dark.

Dave was living a completely different life than his parents knew. He reported a fraction of his adventures to them. He told her and Nick much more about the details of his trips. They'd never understand the things he was doing in the city. The parties. The late nights. The gray area of ethics he frequently skated into.

They definitely didn't know about Nick's recreational drug use, something Gwen and Dave loved teasing him about. He was not just going to Colorado for the great ski conditions. They also believed the job he was about to take at the corporate office of a big box store was far more glamorous than it was. In truth his cubical would be one of hundreds, and he'd mostly answer phone calls from disgruntled customers. The apartment he'd lined up was barely a livable size.

Gwen had done the same about her breakup with Ryan. But the illusion was what brought peace and comfort to Noel and Millie, and all the kids felt they deserved that. It was better for everyone this way. Why worry them over things that they couldn't change or control.

But Millie's mantra of a secret-free family fell awkwardly around the table. Even more so now that Gwen wondered about the truth behind her own adoption. "It's fine, Mom, I understand that you all think you are helping me."

Millie came back with a sheet of paper in her hand and waved it. "This is the quote they gave us when your father and I went down there to look at the places and get more information. It's dated. Months before you went to the hospital."

Gwen didn't want to look. She didn't want to hurt her mother by checking the evidence. Yet, she wanted to know the integrity of their relationship still stood. Maybe she should extend this truth to the questions weighing on her.

Taking the paper, she raised her brows skeptically and read it over. The date was indeed from months earlier. Relief flooded her, followed closely by guilt about her accusation.

Maybe it was the haze of the alcohol but Gwen wasn't mad about the offer. She didn't even hate the idea. When she got to the other side of whatever this journey was, she hoped this house would still be a part of that. That her parents would be the angels she always knew they were. Maybe Griff would stick around too?

Yes, she was drunk. Those were fairy tales.

"Sweetheart." Noel gave her a soft-eyed look. The same he'd offered when he explained she couldn't strap wings on and fly off the roof. "We always want you to do what you want. What you think is best in your life. I'm not putting any pressure on you. The house, we can keep it and rent it if we want to. But if there's a chance you'd want to be here, we'd love to make that work."

How? How could that sweetness and loving support be fake? It couldn't. That was the point. Millie and Noel were the real deal. Any paperwork she dug up or possible lead she thought she found couldn't change that. Maybe they simplified the story about Ivy to make it easy for her to understand as a child. Or maybe she'd dreamt up the part of the story about how they knew each other. There had to be an explanation that didn't involve making Millie and Noel into evil villains in her story.

This was her house. Around this table was her family. Nothing she found out was going to change that.

"We really weren't going to bring it up tonight," Millie said, sounding apologetic.

"But we all got tipsy," Noel admitted. "And stuff comes out when the booze starts flowing. Like maybe you two will tell us what's actually going on with you?" He pointed playfully at Gwen and Griff. "Sleeping in the tree house like a couple of kids. Probably playing spin the bottle with my beers."

"I tried," Griff replied with a shrug. "You raised her right. She wouldn't play."

"Don't encourage them," Gwen complained, her heart feeling lighter suddenly, though she wasn't sure why. The drinks? The idea that her family home wasn't going on the market? Or that the jokes had begun again. "They are trying to get a rise out of us."

Noel hummed. "And it's working, which means we're right." He puckered up his face and looked at them skeptically. "I know what new love looks like. You forget your mother and I were real people before you kids came along and turned us into old trolls who only know how to yell about dirty socks and missing curfew. We had our share of fun. Your mom didn't get her nickname for no reason."

"What nickname?" Griff asked, glancing around the table to a bunch of groaning and complaining people.

"Don't ask that, man," Dave begged. "I don't want to know her nickname. Dad, don't you dare tell us."

"Fine," Millie said, flopping back into her chair. "Just think of us as old cranky tired people who only knew how to parent."

"Thank you," Nick said, sighing with relief. "Let's not change the subject. What's going on with Gwen and Griff isn't any kind of new love."

"We know that," Millie giggled. "Gwen's been pining over Griffy since they were little. I caught her kissing her teddy bear once and calling it Griff."

"Mom!" Gwen slapped the table and then covered her face in embarrassment.

Griff leaned back in his chair and put one arm over Gwen's

shoulder, pulling her in as she kept her face covered. "Would it really be so bad if Gwen and I started seeing each other? It's better than her dating that teddy bear."

"Yes." The word rang out in unison around the table. It would have been laughable if not so well coordinated.

"Why?" Griff looked suddenly insulted as Gwen emerged slowly from her cocoon of humiliation. "She could do worse than me. What if she got caught up with some biker gang? Some dude named Aces with a face tattoo who tends bar? I'm better than that."

Dave shrugged, laughing the words out. "That's arguable. At least Aces is employed."

Gwen picked up a dinner roll and launched it at her brother. "You guys are terrible. I wouldn't even bring Aces around here. You don't deserve him."

Millie caught her breath first. "You are both perfect, just not perfect for each other. That's all we're saying."

Gwen's laughter evaporated and was replaced with real curiosity. "Why? Griff and I have plenty in common."

"And what happens when it doesn't work out?" Nick folded his arms over his chest. "There certainly wouldn't be any more nights like this. We're finally getting Griff back. You guys will ruin it and make it weird. Then we'll have to pick sides."

"Pick sides?" Gwen reached for another dinner roll. "Would that be a hard choice?"

Nick had a pained expression. "Griff might get a really cool job next and go work in some awesome city. Maybe a new sports car. Don't put us in a position to choose."

Noel nodded. "He always helps me out when he's in town. Chops wood. Last week he cleaned the gutters. Gwen, you don't even know where we keep the axe."

Gwen reached sloppily for her glass. "I'm thinking I might go find it and start whacking you guys."

Millie came around and put a hand on each of their shoulders. Griff used his free hand to cover hers and the gesture warmed Gwen's heart. He really was family here. Loved. He belonged. "Whatever you two decide to do"—she leaned in and lowered her voice—"know that we love you and want what's best for you both. And please be safe."

"Safe?" Gwen asked, kicking her head to the side.

"I can buy you some you-know-whats if you're both too embarrassed. I did it for Dave when he was younger. Better safe than sorry."

Dave's laughter burst across the table. "She really did. From Costco. A box of one hundred fifty. A variety pack if I recall. I wasn't sure how to feel about the quantity. I would have preferred she bought them when I wasn't there in the checkout line with her."

Nick looked confused. "Wait, you didn't buy me any?"

"Oh honey," Millie said, wiping laugh-induced tears from her cheeks. "You didn't have any need for them. No need to lock the bedroom window when no one is there to throw pebbles at it."

A solid burn from Millie was just too much. They doubled over. Moving back from the table, spilling into the living room. Holding on to each other. Gasping for breath. When everything settled a bit and they fell onto the couches, full stomachs, swelling hearts, Gwen looked around and felt enormous remorse. Her family was a well-built engine. For years running clean. Powerful. Her recent actions may have been about to yank the spark plugs right out.

All because she felt she deserved to know. Did she deserve this truth more than her father deserved to focus on his health? More than her mother deserved to enjoy this phase of her life? The time that should be relaxing and set aside to rediscover herself after mothering constantly for decades. What would it do to her brothers? To nights like this. More than some pretend breakup with Griff, she could implode the fragile inner workings of the Fox clan.

That power was frightening. The dichotomy of her desire to preserve what she had but to know more was polarizing her soul. There would come a point in the near future when she'd have to choose. A moment she was dreading.

CHAPTER 13

Leslie

Leslie wanted her children. It was a deep, innate need that as a mother she'd felt many times in her life. The idea that they weren't coming home for Christmas had become unbearable. It was reminiscent of Stephen's first night in his own crib after spending three months of his life right by her in the bassinet. She missed the parts of them that were hers. The freckle she'd kissed on Cole's cheek every night at bedtime, like it was a bullseye for her lips. Stephen's funny snort-laughs when they all sat around and watched a movie on a Friday night. These were the parts of her children she'd cultivated and grown in her own little garden.

Somehow she knew she needed to see them up close. To watch their faces change as she spoke to them about her future. Leslie would know what a raised brow or the little nibble of a bottom lip would mean.

She couldn't blame them for the nervous reaction they had on the phone. The entire exchange to get them here had been dramatic. They were met with phone calls that involved very little information. Just her begging them with a swell of tears and ending with pleas for them to come home for Christmas.

It was logistically possible. Each of them could get in their car and get there that night. Cole had peppered her with questions she wouldn't answer. Stephen had been less quizzical and more stoic. But both boys agreed pretty quickly to come.

Cole had recently broken up with his girlfriend, Beth. They'd dated for a year and she'd gotten a job that had her working day and night. He hadn't told Leslie they broke up, but Kerry had mentioned it casually one day. Stephen was never one to settle down. Judging from his social media posts, there was a different beautiful girl in his life every few months. She never pried into their romantic lives but suddenly there seemed to be a canyon between what she knew about them and what she wanted to know.

Why had she given them so much space? Why had she allowed them to slip so far away? To keep their bedroom doors shut? Their hearts so closed off? For years she'd just written it off that they were closer to Paul. More like him. Could they have been mama's boys if she'd pushed harder?

"The boys are on their way," Leslie reported to Paul as she leaned against the door frame of his study. He'd built a fire and already put the ice cubes in his glass of scotch. But his hand froze as he reached for the bottle.

"They are?"

"Yes. I called them both and told them to come. I want to see them on Christmas."

"They had plans didn't they? Stephen had to make an appearance at the office party. Dinner with his direct reports who have transferred to his office and don't have family locally. Those things are important for morale. He needs to think about his career. About keeping his employees motivated. For Cole his practice is closed for the holiday but he can make big bucks with after-hours emergencies."

"I want them here." Leslie's cold stare was unwavering. "They are our children. Getting together on Christmas isn't an inconvenience. It's Kerry's last year at home. We should be together."

Paul rubbed at his eyebrow. "Yeah, okay. So are we having dinner?"

"I'll make something. They'll stay tonight and be here in the morning to open presents."

"Did we get them something?" Paul finally reached for his bottle and filled his glass.

"Yes, Paul, I bought our children Christmas presents. It wasn't easy, considering we're barely a part of their lives."

Paul groaned. "What's that supposed to mean? I talk to the boys every week."

"About what? Their careers? I find out more about their lives from pictures they post online than things they actually tell us. That has to change."

"Here we go." Paul took a long sip of his drink. "It's amazing how suddenly everything has to change. If you want a better relationship with the boys, do it. But they aren't boys. They are men. With lives and careers, and they don't want to tell Mom every detail of what's going on. And as hard as it's going to be, neither will Kerry. I hate to be the one to tell you."

"And yet you're smiling."

"Leslie, it's the holidays. Everything is changing. I get it. But you can't just stand back and pull a pin on the grenade right now. Enjoy the time you have with Kerry. Don't ruin it by panicking."

"I don't want you here when the boys get here." She hadn't planned that part. Somewhere in her mind she imagined they'd sit for dinner all together. Hash things out. Be open with each other. But then she realized Paul wouldn't let that happen. He'd be a roadblock. He'd dominate and be a broken record about how Leslie was just struggling with change and being emotional.

"Uh, what do you mean?"

"I want some time alone with the kids tonight. I'm sure you can get a room for the night in town."

"You want me to stay in a hotel on Christmas Eve so you can be alone with the kids? Why?"

"Because I want to talk to them, and I think they'll be more open with me if you aren't here."

"Open about what?" He put his glass down hard on the table. "You really need allies in this argument? That's not appropriate."

"I'm not looking for allies, Paul; I'm looking to know our sons. To know what's happening in their lives and to see if they are all right. They didn't want to come home for Christmas. They'd rather be somewhere else."

"I'm not leaving my house so you can prove a point. Not on Christmas Eve. It's not a reasonable thing to ask of me. They are my sons."

"That didn't stop you the first time you walked out." The old rage she'd pushed down clawed its way out of the deep grave she'd buried it in. "You had no problem leaving me with two children back then. But now, when I'm asking you for space, for time to figure this all out, now you dig in." Here was the punch she'd never thrown before. On the rare occasion she or Paul mentioned his leaving her, she'd never made it about the children. That was too deep a wound to poke at. But the reality was, he'd not just left her when he went to Beijing, he'd left his two boys. He'd missed nearly two years of their lives. Milestones he hadn't been there to witness. Stephen and Cole were too young to remember his absence but to this day she still couldn't believe he could look down at his young children and walk out. All on principle. On demanding the life he imagined going the way he wanted it. How could they be a bargaining chip he was willing to play?

She knew, by the look on his face, the remorse he felt for that time in his life was a rubbed raw nerve he tried to cover up.

Paul clutched his glass so tightly it looked as though it might shatter under his grip. "You are not a cruel person, Leslie, but you are certainly acting like one right now. The choices we made back then were not easy for either of us. You are the one who insisted the boys should not leave their routines. It was the hardest period of my life being away from them. You have no idea what that felt like. I came back as often as I could to visit, and I took them with me the last two months I was there so you could get things ready for us back home."

"You visited twice that whole time. Stayed no more than a long weekend." This was petty. She knew that slicing up how long Paul was gone didn't matter. It was that he could look into the faces of his baby and his toddler and make the choice to leave in the first place. Not how long he left for, just that he could leave at all. But she knew that pain too. She left a baby behind. The difference was she couldn't come back for her.

She wanted to reassure him. "I don't intend to say anything disparaging to the boys. I just want some time to talk things over with them."

"Do whatever you want," Paul hissed out, standing and blowing by her out the study door. "I don't even recognize you right now, Leslie. It's scary. You want me to go, then I'll go. Just like last time I'll wait until you come to your senses, and then I'll come back. Don't be stubborn for so long this time. I might not wait around."

She stood alone in the study and listened to the stomping and banging that followed as Paul gathered up his things and finally slammed the front door on his way out.

Kerry wasn't far behind the sound of tires squealing out of the driveway. "What's going on?" She flipped the light on in the study and looked around as though something might jump out.

"Your brothers will be here soon. I called them."

"You did?"

"I asked your father to give us some space tonight. He'll be back in the morning. I don't want you to say anything to your brothers. Let me explain things to them."

Kerry came and wrapped her arms around Leslie's waist. "We should make some dinner then?"

Leslie nodded and let her daughter lead her to the kitchen. When they'd pulled open the fridge doors and looked through the pantry they talked themselves out of every option. The ham would take too long. Neither one of them wanted to peel potatoes. A salad would be fine but it wouldn't feel like holiday dinner.

"Chinese food," Kerry said, reaching in the junk drawer and grabbing the menu. "The boys used to love this place. I still remember their order."

"Me too. Remember when Dad was traveling and we'd get enough to last three days?"

Kerry had a bemused look on her face. "And you'd let us eat it in the living room. Dad hated that."

When her sons texted that they'd be there soon, Leslie felt a wave of nerves. An odd reaction to seeing her own children. Perhaps she'd been overly dramatic in calling them home.

"Cole's here," Kerry sang out, peering from behind the curtain in the front window. "Stephen said he'd be here in five minutes."

The clamoring of their entrance, shrugging off their snow dampened coats, and Kerry's excitement temporarily calmed Leslie's nerves.

It wasn't until they were sitting around the kitchen counter that she felt sick again.

"We ordered some Chinese food," Kerry reported, waving the menu at them. "We can even eat it in the living room."

"Where's Dad?" Cole's glasses looked smudged, and Leslie fought the urge to wipe them clean like she used to when he was a boy. If your adult children wanted to run around with smudged glasses or hair so long it was in their eyes, you had to let them. That wasn't something she'd learned all at once. It was the way they rolled their eyes. Or jerked their heads away. The sighs and the groans that replaced their other language skills. That's how she knew to let go. But those grumpy teenagers were gone. Now she was standing with the men they'd turned into. The men she wanted to get to know again.

Stephen bit nervously at his lip. "What's going on? Are you sick? Is Dad?"

"No," Leslie cut back quickly. "No one is sick. I'm sorry if I made you worry. It's nothing like that at all."

"Yeah," Kerry said, tightening her ponytail and spinning casually back and forth on her bar stool. "Everyone is fine, but Mom is coming to California with me."

"What?" Stephen drew his brows together the way he used to while doing math homework. "Why would she do that?"

Cole drew in a sharp breath. "Are you leaving Dad?"

"No." Leslie stood and shot Kerry a stern look. "I'm not going with Kerry to California, and I'm not leaving your father. I asked you both to come home so I could talk to you."

Cole kicked his sneakers off and looked to Kerry for the truth as if his mom would sugarcoat it all too much. "Did Dad leave? Did he cheat or something?"

Leslie was shocked by how easily they'd jumped to that assumption. "Your father is not here right now because I told him I wanted a chance to talk to you on my own."

"About what?" Cole picked nervously at his thumbnail. He looked too thin and Leslie made a note in her mind to worry about that later.

"Your father and I are having a hard time," Leslie admitted cautiously. "I've come to a place in my life where I've taken the opportunity to really evaluate what I want. What I need."

Kerry scoffed. "She gets it, guys. Dad went behind her back and talked to her boss to get her three weeks off work and planned an entire trip without talking to her about it. He wants her to slow down at work. It's exactly the opposite of what Mom wants."

Leslie tipped her head to the side, assuming the boys would want more explanation, but they looked completely up to speed.

"Nice. That's classic Dad." Cole sighed. "So what does that have to do with us coming back here? You made it sound urgent."

"It feels urgent," Leslie said, her voice breaking with emotion. "It made me realize I hadn't been paying attention to what was going on. I'd resigned myself for many years to how our marriage worked. But I didn't look at how it would affect you kids and my relationship with you. Kerry has been very open with me about how she feels and has given me some insight into what I might have been missing. It scared me."

"Scared you?" Kerry asked with concern. Of course they couldn't understand. There were things Leslie never realized before she was a parent. A layer of emotions she hadn't known existed.

"One of the worst things for a mother to realize is that she's missed time. Time she can't get back. I am missing your lives. And I think it's because you're worried about being open with me. I've given you good reason to worry; I never took your side on anything. I think parenting, when your kids are young, requires a united front but when you start talking about life decisions, what you want for yourselves as adults, I should have stood up for you more. Now I feel like I've lost you and will lose Kerry too if I don't fix this."

Stephen looked at his siblings in disbelief. As though they'd had this conversation dozens of times before and couldn't believe they were finally hearing it from their mother. "Mom, you did a lot for us. I don't think this is something you can fix. Dad's not going to suddenly be open to your opinion. Or ours. He's a pretty old dog who's been getting his way a long time. I don't see him learning any new tricks. The only thing we've found that works is space. Physical miles. Trying to have some boundaries, even though he tends to crash them down."

"I don't want to worry you all about your father and me or how we will work through this. That's not what I called you here for. I just needed to see you, look you in the eye, and let you know that I'm sorry. And that you can trust me with whatever is going on in your lives. I know I have to earn that trust again, but I hope you give me the chance. I'm not looking to smother you or be involved in every detail of what you have going on. I just want to make progress."

Cole stood and put his arms around his mother. "I'm sorry, Mom, if we made you feel like you aren't a part of our lives. I think we've been trying to navigate all the stuff with Dad, just like you have."

"It's going to get better," Leslie asserted as she pulled him in tightly. "You don't have to worry about us breaking up."

"That doesn't worry us," Stephen said coolly. "We're all adults here. People split up, and if that's what you wanted, we'd support that."

Leslie had a strange feeling of disappointment. Part of her expected them to be distraught. Disappointed in her. They weren't even remotely surprised. "You're all being very calm about this."

"You deserve to be happy, Mom," Kerry said as though it was the most obvious thing in the world. "If that's with Dad, great. If it has to come from being alone, that's fine too."

Stephen stood and moved toward the fridge, turning his back to them and searching for something to drink. "It's not like it's the first time you two separated."

Leslie's stomach dropped to the floor. Stephen was two years old the year Paul left. There would be no way he'd remember.

She'd hidden her pregnancy behind baggy clothes and the boys were off with Paul by the time she delivered.

"What do you mean?" she asked, pursing her lips and holding her breath.

"When we were kids, before Kerry was born, Dad left. I know you think that's some secret but it's not. He went off for some job and left us. I don't know how someone can leave their kids like that."

"You're oversimplifying the situation," Leslie said, the back of her neck tingling with fear. "It was a very difficult time, and your father did what he thought was best. How do you even know that? You were two years old. Cole was a baby." If he remembered Paul leaving, had he also remembered anything else? He was almost four by the time it was all over but still, he'd never said anything.

"We used to look through your stuff," Cole admitted casually. "Kids do that. We found a box of letters you and Dad sent back and forth to each other. He was gone for like eighteen months or something. That's crazy."

"He was. You spent a couple of months in Beijing with him. Do you remember that?"

Stephen shook his head. "No. I don't remember any of it."

Leslie had imagined that someday her children would know about this period of her life, though she thought it would be years from now. She'd be sitting in a nursing home, they'd come with their children for a visit and she'd finally bare her secrets to them. Finding out they'd known this secret all along felt anticlimactic. "Your father leaving was not a reflection of his love for you boys. It was something he and I were working out. We needed time."

Stephen shook his head. "We read the letters, Mom. Every one of them. I read them quite a few times."

"Why?" She thought about the letters and where they'd been kept. The top shelf of her closet in a shoebox under out-of-style sweaters she never planned to wear again. But kids snooped. She knew that. It would have been best to throw the letters out but for some reason she'd kept them. A physical record of that time. Something Paul couldn't twist around or convince her didn't happen.

Stephen looked uneasy suddenly. "Those letters from Dad were harsh. He drew a hard line about what he wanted and what you needed to do. I can understand why you were upset. It was just strange to think of you guys as being separated. As being people who didn't know what they were doing. Most of the time parents seem to have their crap together."

"We didn't then," Leslie admitted. "And maybe we don't right now either."

The doorbell rang and Kerry scurried off to get the food delivery, leaving Leslie with an opportunity she was hoping to get. "Your sister is not in the same position as you boys. She is here for another five months. And you know how your father is with the college funds. She's angry, but I don't want her to burn a bridge on my account. So please keep that in mind."

Kerry had two large bags of takeout food and a giant smile when she returned. Stephen and Cole nodded discretely, looking as though they understood.

"Mom," Kerry began quizzically, "why did you let Dad come back? In those letters he seemed totally resigned being out there and telling you that you were wrong not to come. Then he just wakes up and decides he wants to come back? Why let him?"

The question landed hard on her chest. It was bizarre to discuss these things with her children. Especially the one who hadn't even been born at the time. "I loved your father, and the life we could have together with our children could be good. I knew that."

Kerry looked unimpressed with her answer. "But only if you did what he wanted. Took steps back in your career. Raised the boys. Became a housewife with a job rather than a working mom. Why do all that?"

Stephen, likely because of Leslie's warning, spoke up. "You should be glad Mom did that or you wouldn't exist. Dad came back, and they worked things out and eventually had you."

"Worked things out? I don't think we'd all be here talking about this if they'd worked things out." Kerry had an annoyed tone.

"Kerry," Leslie said gently, taking the bags from her hands. "I have had a lot of great years with your father. So have all of you. I have no intention of leaving him, but I do think now that we are all on the same page we can work through this together. Running away to California isn't going to make me happy either. Your father might not like to hear what I have to say, but I think in time he can change. In his defense, I've never asked him to before."

Kerry looked to her brothers, trying to measure their reactions. Both looked stoic and resigned to the idea. Her shoulders stooped a bit, the drive to fight back melting away. "If you think that's best then that's fine. I just want you to be happy, Mom. I want you to be higher up on your own list now that we're all out doing what we want to."

"I love you for that. I love you all for coming here when I called. It's going to be better. The Laudon's are strong people, but we need to be a strong family too. That's what's top on my list. Now everyone get your food and let's go watch Christmas movies, and you guys can fill me in on what's new in your lives. The good stuff."

Her worry was big. Skyscraper high. Would Paul really change? Was everything she'd worked on for the last few decades going to splinter into pieces and fly away?

Their chatter grew funnier and the kids took pleasure in spilling each other's business to Leslie. Kerry blabbing about Stephen's trip to Amsterdam and nearly getting arrested. Stephen outing Cole and his new girlfriend with the purple hair and nose ring. Leslie took it all in stride. Packing away the urge to judge and taking comfort in the fact that her children had found in each other what they couldn't in her. She knew they were close but didn't realize they were this involved with each other. It was a club she wanted to be in.

As she examined their now adult faces, she wondered how her other daughter would fit in. Older than Kerry. Younger than Cole. Would she have their light eyes? Some mannerisms that were unique to the Laudon children? No. Of course not. Because she would not be a Laudon. She was not Paul's and the children looked most like him.

So maybe she would look like Mark. Leslie ached at the thought of Mark. She could hardly remember what he looked like. But she remembered how he made her feel. That was something she'd never forget.

CHAPTER 14

Back Then

L eslie knew it would be tough. But that had never stopped her before. Going from far below the poverty line to graduating first in her class had been tough. Scraping up enough decent clothing to go to her first internship in a corporate office was difficult, but she'd made it work. Challenges never worried Leslie. She'd persevered. Excelled at work. Married. Had children. And she'd nearly held it all together. Nearly.

Motherhood had been the ultimate challenge. Giving of yourself when you had nothing left to give. Middle of the night feedings of an infant followed by the wake-up call from a grumpy toddler, all followed by difficult days at work.

Paul had been gone for a few months with no sign of coming back. The frequency of his phone calls had become less. The lengths of the calls he did bother making were laughably short.

She was ready to face that now. Her marriage was not going to work. She'd be a single mother of two boys. A working mom. It would be tough, but she'd do her best, like she always did. Paul would make sure she and the boys were financially sound. That was something at least.

Now all she had to do was find a way to keep from going mad. Not give into the overwhelming feeling that she was a failure. Should she have just given in and gone across the world with Paul? Been the wife and mother he wanted her to be?

New goal: Shake that feeling.

"I'm sorry, Mrs. Laudon, but he can't stay here with a fever. You'll need to make arrangements to pick Stephen up." The nasal woman from the daycare tried to sound empathetic but Leslie knew they didn't like her there. She was always running in for the quick drop-off and doing the late pick-up. Never remembering it was dress-up day. Never sending in the extra art supplies she was supposed to.

"Barb, I have an important meeting with a client in thirty minutes. I can finish that by lunch and come get him. He was fine when I dropped him off. And you said the fever is very low."

"You are risking infecting the other children here. You need to come get him this morning. It's our policy. If you aren't able to today, then I'm afraid we won't be able to support you and your boys going forward. You'll have to make other arrangements for Cole and Stephen while you work."

The words, *while you work*, had a sharp edge to them. "I am doing the best I can. My husband is abroad. My job is demanding, and I cannot just leave every time something comes up. Last week you called because Stephen had a rash which upon further inspection turned out to be jelly from his sandwich he dropped on his lap. How many fathers are you calling at work and asking them to run in every two minutes? How many letters home are you sending them about pajama day and bringing extra construction paper? But because I am a working mom you have no problem giving me hell."

"Be here in an hour or we'll terminate your contract. I'll be sure to prorate your monthly payment and refund the rest." The line went dead and Leslie wanted to scream.

Instead she slammed her desk phone down into the cradle hard. Then lifted it and did it over and over again, muttering curse words under her breath.

"Did that phone run over your dog or something?" A man stood in her office doorway looking concerned but amused. His dark hair was slicked back and his eyes were coal black but glittering under the office lights.

Leslie shot to her feet and tried to look natural as she adjusted the phone on her desk to the perfect position as though that had been what she was doing. Suddenly self-conscious, she remembered she'd pulled this dress from the floor this morning. It was well past needing a trip to the dry cleaner.

"Can I help you with something?" She tried unsuccessfully to brush the wrinkles away.

"I'm Mark from Biologic Unlimited." He patted his bright blue tie flat against his chest and jutted his hand out as he walked toward her desk. Too disheveled and shocked, she didn't extend her hand for a shake, and he awkwardly dropped his back to his side. His clothes were overly starched and crisp. Nothing on him was out of sorts, while everything about her was.

She checked her watch and forgot it had been dead and in need of a battery for a week. Leaning over, she looked at the clock on the wall instead. "Um, no we aren't meeting for a half hour. How did you get by Janice, my receptionist? She didn't tell me you were here."

"I'm early. I had an easier commute in than I expected. I'm used to the traffic in Los Angeles. Also, Janice isn't at her desk. In her defense, she did leave a note taped to her chair that said she'd be back after her manicure." Mark flashed a whimsical smile when she'd expected a scowl of disappointment.

"Dammit, Janice," Leslie thundered, hitting her fist into her palm. "I am so sorry you had to deal with that. And that you had to see me . . ." She hesitated as she thought of the right explanation. "My phone didn't deserve that beating. It was a tough call and a tougher morning. Can we maybe reschedule our meeting? Or maybe you're already considering going to my boss and asking for a different consultant."

"I don't want a different consultant," Mark confessed. "I specifically requested you. I was actually a bit of a pain in the ass about it. I'd have to eat some crow if I ask for someone else now."

"You requested me?" she exclaimed with a laughable amount of doubt. "I'm sure you must have me confused with someone else. I'm Leslie Laudon. Did you mean Les? He's been here for more than ten years."

"I didn't mean Les. I know about Les. I do my research before I bring on a consultant. Les is a dinosaur. Totally out of touch with technology. Rick is a knucklehead who thinks the best part of his job is taking clients to strip clubs. Regina is high maintenance. Loves attention. Throws a fit when she doesn't get her way."

Leslie looked around the room, her head on a swivel. There had to be a hidden camera in here. Mark had nailed her coworkers exactly. He was saying things she never had the courage to say herself.

"Well, still. You just saw that little show, and now you know my assistant is a bit of a free spirit. Have you changed your mind?" Leslie drifted back to her seat and settled in. It was hard to look at Mark without staring or smiling. He was the kind of handsome you had to look at long enough to tell if you were seeing a real person. Flawless features. Herculean in size, but his voice was raspy and quiet. Unassuming, when he could have easily been obnoxious and full of himself. Loud enough to dominate a room just because he could be. She saw none of that in him.

"I'm not worried, just curious. Why is your day going so bad? Why did you get in a fist fight with your poor defenseless phone?" He gestured toward her desk. She nodded with her chin for him to sit. If she hadn't scared him off yet she might as well make the most of it.

Mark strolled across the rest of her office with a quiet confidence, sinking into the chair as if he had nowhere else in the world to be right now.

"You know how this industry is," she noted dismissively. "Always a fire to put out. Just a conference call gone wrong."

His mouth twitched with a smile as he flashed a dimple. "It sounded like your kid's daycare was trying to kick you out if you don't get there in an hour." Watching her shocked reaction, Mark looked abundantly proud of his accurate observation.

Leslie impulsively looked for a sufficient excuse she thought he might believe. Mark was an important client, and his account had recently been assigned to her. The last thing she needed was to get a reputation as one of those women who couldn't balance it all. When she couldn't think of a colorful tale to spin, she changed the subject. "We don't need to reschedule," she asserted, folding her hands together and putting them on her desk. "This is our first meeting. I don't want you to think it's not important to our company. I have copies of my presentation here for you."

"Our meeting is not more important than your children right?" He folded his hands just as she had and placed them on her desk the same way. He wasn't trying to mock her in a demeaning way. Leslie could tell he was trying to make her smile. But her face hardly flexed in that direction anymore. She was out of practice for happiness.

Mark didn't look swayed by her reluctance. Instead he leaned in even closer and lowered his voice. "My mother had four children and raised us on her own. All while working two or three jobs at a time. I've seen what it takes to do it all. That's the kind of person I want to work with. A superwoman."

She dropped her head in defeat. "I'm no superwoman. I wish. Ask around, I'm a super failure most days."

"You're trying. I like that. People don't try anymore. Everyone just settles for what they have. I bet you have options easier than all this work?"

Leslie blinked slowly as she looked at him and wondered how he could read her so well. "I do have easier options. I don't intend to take them. Not if it means giving up what I want."

Feverishly agreeing, Mark nodded and clapped his hands together. "What were we going to do today in our meeting?"

"I've had time to evaluate your company's current business practices and procedures. With that information I drafted a proposal for a new process update that might streamline your production as well as a trainer pitch that could help get your techs up to speed faster."

"I don't get car sick." Mark hopped to his feet and pivoted toward the door.

"Um, all right?" Still trying to stay professional, she avoided letting her face show how bizarre she found him. "That's good for you."

"Let's take these files and go pick up your kid at daycare. I'm guessing you know this stuff front to back. You can fill me in on your proposal while you drive."

"I do know it front to back but"—she shook her head, warning bells sounding in her mind—"we can't do that. That's very unprofessional. Too much for me to ask of you."

"You didn't ask, I offered. Also, as your client, I'm saying it's not unprofessional. Professionalism is dictated by the core audience you have to deal with. If I think it's fine, doesn't that make it fine?" He grinned smugly.

"My boss will not think it's fine." Leslie hadn't stood up to join him even though he was already at the door, waiting with a comical expression.

"Your boss and your coworkers won't be in the car will they? You couldn't fit all of us. Do you drive one of those circus cars that like fifteen clowns climb out of?"

With that she offered a fleeting smile that morphed quickly back into a straight-lipped explanation. "My station wagon could fit a football team. But luckily my boss is traveling this week. He wasn't scheduled to be in our meeting anyway. It was just going to be you and me."

"Then it's settled." Mark gestured over at the stack of papers with his company's name on the top. "We'll talk on the way to daycare and on the way back, and then you can drop me back off here."

"Why would you do this?" Leslie asked, trying to read the peculiar look on his face. She stood and grabbed the paperwork she'd poured hours of time and energy into. "Wouldn't it be a lot easier to just talk to someone here and ask for a different consultant?"

"It might be easier, but you have a reputation." The twinkle had returned to his eyes. It had been so long since she'd seen a grown person with this much mischief looming around the edges of everything he did.

The thought of her reputation made her stomach intensely sick. Though she hadn't told anyone directly, people must be talking about how Paul had left her. About how she had two small children and was still delusional enough to believe she could move up in the company. "I have a reputation? I can't imagine what people say about me."

"It's all good stuff. I told you I do my research. My job is to go around the country and improve every one of my company's facilities without making a large investment. All while increasing profits. You have a reputation for making people in my position look very good at our jobs. Apparently, you come in, do all the work, redesign the processes, and I just have to implement them and look like a hero. Word on the street is you don't even have an ego about it. I think it's probably because you don't know how good you are yet. At some point you'll realize that and be a smug powerhouse consultant. I'm trying to get in before you hit that point and won't even take a call from a company as small as mine."

"That's very flattering," Leslie interjected before he could go on. Right now, sitting solidly at rock bottom, compliments felt more like gravel raining down on her head, burying her, little by little. She didn't feel worthy of any praise, so as soon as it went in her ear, her brain would wrap it in a layer of guilt and failure. "I try to make sure my clients get their money's worth. But I still think maybe we should reschedule. It seems like a lot to ask of you." She also hated the idea of him seeing the floor of her station wagon, filled with toys and dry cereal.

Mark waved at her a lot like a man trying to coax a nervous animal from under a house. "The work/home balance isn't easy to manage. I'm relatively new at my company, and I'd like to start off with a win. Grab your bag; let's go."

She checked her watch, again remembered it was dead, and weighed her options. The idea of Stephen feeling sick and her not being with him was killing her. She wanted to get to him as quickly as possible. Mark's sentiment was nice, but could she trust him? Would he use this against her at some point and get her fired?

"I'm going to your station wagon," he said over his shoulder as he headed out of her office. "It's not like Janice is going to miss you."

He was gone before she could protest any further. With the stack of documents in her arms she darted down the hall. She needed to get out of the building before anyone asked where she and Mark were headed. She needed this to work out.

Unfortunately, the car was as bad as she'd remembered. Before she unlocked the passenger-side door for him she quickly swung open her door and cleared off his seat. Snatching at fast food napkins and random receipts. No one had been her passenger since Paul had left, so the seat had become a trash heap.

"You're not living in your car are you?" Mark snickered, his large chest rumbling with laughter he tried to keep in.

It was impossible not to compare him to Paul. Her mind wandered there. Mark was a couple inches taller. His jaw was boxy where Paul's came to a point. Their physical differences were many, but it was most obvious in the way Mark moved. A bounce in his step. A playfulness. Paul had a streak of humor but most days he had that setting turned off. Mark seemed unable to be serious for too long.

"This was a terrible idea." When she slid into the driver's seat she clapped her hands to her eyes and rested her head on the steering wheel, accidently hitting the horn.

"I'm kidding," Mark insisted, reaching over and taking one of her hands from her face when she sat back up. It was intimate. His feathery touch so much lighter than his massive hand was capable of. His hand didn't linger on her skin, but she felt the warmth there long after he let go. "Tell me about this new assembly upgrade." He glanced at one of the proposals she'd drafted that were now in his lap. "Can we really reduce production waste and shave three minutes off per product? That seems impossible."

She drew in a deep breath and sat up straighter, fighting off the hysterical fit she wanted to throw. Like always, she knew there was no time in her life for such indulgence. Falling apart was a luxury saved for people with free time. Instead she thought of the assembly line she'd visited at their local factory. "You can accomplish those improvements if you upgrade to the newer computer software that came out earlier this year. When I toured your facility, your employees were lacking some work space upgrades that would help not only morale but, in turn, efficiency. I included two studies that show data supporting how ergonomic mats and upgraded seating can improve output."

He flipped through the pages as she quickly turned off the CD playing the *Wheels on the Bus* song in a chipmunk voice.

"This is great. And the cost investment is minimal?"

"Overall you'll be in the black three months after you invest in these changes. It's a no-brainer. There have been very few changes and upgrades in the last two years. It is ripe for improvements."

"I'll take this to the CEO and end up looking like the hero. What do you get? You did all the work."

She put the car in drive and headed toward the daycare. She never asked herself what was in it for her. Being a consultant often meant being behind the scenes. Being a woman in this field added to the need to keep her ego in check. Work had never been about praise for her. It was about laying her head down at night and knowing she'd accomplished whatever she'd set out to do. "I'll probably go pick up my son and get the flu. Then I'll work through it as if I'm not sick and move on to the next client."

"If I'm not being too forward do you mind if I ask, where's your husband?" Mark kept his eyes on the papers in his lap as though the question was as casual as asking about rain in the forecast.

At this point it seemed silly to keep anything from him. He hadn't been scared off yet. "Paul's in Asia. He took a job with a new company some months ago."

"Long distance relationships can be hard. Especially with children." Mark nodded, his gentle eyes shimmering in the sunlight. His cologne was sweet and earthy, luckily overpowering the smell of her musty car.

"It's just long distance. No relationship." Leslie hadn't admitted that to anyone yet. She and Paul had a small circle of acquaintances who all believed they were somehow making this situation work. Few people knew about their decision to separate.

"Oh, I'm sorry to hear that. And the kids? How are they doing with it? My dad left when I was small, and I always knew we were better off without him." Mark's voice was kind, and even though she knew it was foolish to share this information with him, she was desperate to talk. It had been building up like a pinched-off firehose. If she didn't connect with someone soon, she was going to burst.

"The kids are too small to know what's going on. Stephen just turned two. Cole is nine months. Paul always wanted to have the kids close in age. He felt like it was more efficient."

"A baby? Your husband left you with a baby?" Mark didn't bother hiding his look of disgust. Leslie felt a rising tide in her. She should cut this off. Tell Mark he's out of line. That he doesn't know Paul or their situation. But deep in her heart she agreed with his disgust.

"It's complicated." That was the mantra she uttered to herself in the quiet moments of her life. Because if she admitted it was simple, that he'd just decided to leave for something better, she would be crushed. Calling it complicated gave him an out and her some peace.

"No it isn't. That's messed up. Are you sure he's not just seeing someone else? Men don't leave good women for a job. It's usually some screwed-up idea about the grass being greener in the next relationship."

It had crossed her mind that maybe there was another woman. If it hadn't been the reason he left, it could be the reason he was still gone.

"Paul's not like other men I've known. He has a vision for his life, and he's focused on trying to achieve it. Laser focused. He has an enormous amount of ambition. I knew that when I married him, and I should have known at some point we'd be at odds about the direction we should go. Maybe this was inevitable."

"Ambition is fine. Blind ambition with collateral damage is not okay. His family got in the way of some five-year plan? That's no excuse."

"I got in the way. The boys were part of the plan. But me working so much was not. I think he always assumed I'd quit my job and raise our family. He certainly didn't expect me to go back to work after I had Cole. I think that was the final straw for him. He hates the idea that I love what I do and want to keep doing it. It doesn't mean I don't love my children. I do. I just believe my life has room for both. Or I used to think so."

Mark's eyes went wide as he turned to look at her. She kept her gaze fixed on the road but felt his stare. "Are you screwing with me right now? Because that is seriously one of the worst things I've ever heard. Your husband wanted to keep you at home with the kids, and when you didn't comply, he left?"

"It's not all him. I'm being stubborn." She'd been saying this in her head for months. Chastising herself for digging in and not compromising. So caught up with the idea of proving she could successfully work at a very high level and have a family. But at what cost?

"No"—he pointed to the papers in his lap—"I've spent five minutes looking at your work, and I can tell you are brilliant. If you want a career and a family, then good for you. Any man who wants to keep you from that isn't worth it. I've done some selfish stuff in my life, but that's really bad."

The tightness in her chest never went away, but it ebbed and flowed in severity depending on the situation. Right now, it was painfully constricted. Leslie was about to admit what she'd been too afraid to. "The problem is, he was right. I can't have it all. Look at me." She waved around her messy station wagon. "You know when I wrote that report about the ergonomic chairs in that folder you are holding? It was two in the morning, and I was pumping breast milk for Cole so he'd be able to have it at daycare." This was overly familiar. Sharing too much, but Mark didn't flinch. "I don't have things in balance. I don't even know where to find the damn scale."

"Breast milk? Is that what is splashed on this paper?" He wiped at the sheet and laughed.

"No," she called back quickly, looking down at the paper in his lap. "I wrote it on my computer and printed it at the office. If anything is splashed on there, it's my tears."

"That's very sad." Mark gave a half grin and winked at her. He didn't look like he was pitying her. More like he was working hard to get her to smile.

"I'm exhausted and I'm failing. I might be mad at Paul's tactics, but he was right."

"I don't know the guy but Paul is an idiot." Mark's tone was serious suddenly. "You aren't failing because you can't do it. You're failing because you are trying to do it alone. A marriage is about sharing the load. Figuring out how to make sure everyone gets what they need. He sounds like a selfish dickhead. You should be glad he's gone."

"But I'm not," she admitted with a hiccup of emotions. "I miss him. I miss our life. If I'd have just gone with him to Asia, I wouldn't be going through all this. We'd have settled in, and I'd be spending all my time with the boys. They wouldn't have to go to daycare and catch every flu or cold floating around. I could sleep at night instead of working."

"This is a masterpiece." He waved the papers at her. "You're exceptional at what you do. Following your husband to Asia and doing what he wants would have eventually crushed you. And it could have set a very dangerous precedence in your marriage. What would he have expected you to do next? I have a feeling you know that. You deserve more than to be someone's carry-on luggage."

Mark came into focus as something more. A good-looking man in an impressive position with kind words and a gentle voice. He wasn't just her ten o'clock meeting anymore. He was a whole person. Three-dimensional. And it stirred something in her. She felt suddenly compelled to know more about him. "You must have a very lucky wife." She hadn't found a way to casually look at his ring finger yet to see if he was married. Plus, she knew that wasn't a perfect indicator of someone's status. She was still wearing hers.

"I'm not married." Mark closed one of the folders as if he'd seen enough. "But if I were, I wouldn't make her give up everything to make me happy. You're not being stubborn. I think you're being fierce."

Fierce.

Leslie let the word sit in her heart for a few beats. She loved it. Lately she'd felt guilty, pathetic, a complete mess. But there was something fierce about what she was doing. Even if some days she wasn't doing it all that well. She wasn't a robot. There was no requirement to be successful every second of every day. But she was trying.

"Thank you for saying all that." A tear rolled down her cheek and she didn't bother wiping it away. This conversation had already crossed every professional line. What did it matter if he saw her cry? He'd just called Paul a selfish dickhead. She was pretty sure he was sitting on a receipt from Stephen's happy meal dinner last night. Lines had been crossed. No going back now.

"Here's what we're going to do," Mark asserted, sitting up straighter. "You're mine for a few weeks right?"

"What?" A flash of heat rolled up her back at the idea of being his in any capacity.

"You're assigned to me for a few weeks. Completely at my disposal. I should know, I drafted the contract myself." He looked proud.

"Technically, I'm your liaison, and I'll be overseeing the launch of any of the changes you decide to move forward with. I am here for whatever you need."

"Right. And I need all the help I can get for that. Your time would be priceless. How would you feel if I asked your boss to let you stay on-site with me for the next three weeks? And we can do this." He gestured with his hand at her and then back at himself.

"Do what? Go pick my sick kids up?"

"If they're sick." Mark looked completely at ease with this possibility. "Or if you need to run out for something else. You can do this work from anywhere. You are probably more productive than anyone I have on staff because you're creative with your time. Moms multitask at a champion level. This will work. You help me, and in return you get a few flexible weeks to just take a breath. No one looking over your shoulder. No one checking your time card. No business clothes. Just be at my disposal for calls and questions. All that brain power without the pressure of the office."

"But—"

"Does that sound like something you'd want? That's all I'm asking. Does that sound good?"

She considered what three weeks without having to worry about every eye in the office checking on how frazzled she was would feel like. Or asking what that stain on her shirt was. Didn't they realize it was always milk or spit-up or her own salad dressing from lunch? They could stop playing *guess what Leslie spilled today.*

"I would love that," she admitted. When she opened her mouth to make a point about why this wouldn't work, he cut in.

"Then it's settled. As of today, you are starting your working vacation. You've already given me a complete blueprint to success. I've got you covered with your office. I'll demand what I want from them and they'll hear nothing but glowing reports about you from me."

"You'll demand what you want?" she breathed out a laugh.

"Yes." He banged his chest lightly with his fist. "I'm a man in corporate America. I can do that."

"Must be nice. I feel bad when I get extra pens from the supply room."

"It's only nice if I use my powers for good. I'll get you as many pens as you need."

"You can't honestly be this nice. What's the catch?" She pursed her lips and waited to hear what he really wanted out of this.

"There's no catch," he promised, tossing his hands up disarmingly. "There is only one thing I haven't sorted out yet."

"What's that?" She felt as though she should be guarded but he didn't stir that in her. It was like talking to an old friend.

"It'll be hard for me to ask you out to dinner, because you'll think it's some kind of quid pro quo. I'll have to find a way to convince you the two offers are completely separate."

Leslie blushed and gripped the steering wheel tighter as she turned into the parking lot of the daycare.

"You want to give me three weeks of cover at my office while I work remotely or on-site. Sing my praises to my boss. And you want to take me to dinner?"

"Yes. But in a mutually exclusive kind of way. Probably you don't believe that. I'll have to take time to prove it to you."

"You're damn right I don't believe you. Was it the dried cereal crunching under your feet or my wrinkly dress that won you over and made you think I'd be a nice companion for dinner?" She laughed off the absurdity. The idea of dating had fallen so far to the wayside she couldn't even see it anymore. When would she date? How would she even find time? Her mother lived hundreds of miles away and she didn't have a good support system right now. The few friends she did have she certainly wouldn't use as babysitters while she went out on the town with some man.

"Leslie, you'd be a lovely dinner date. I bet you have more interesting stories than anyone else in the office. A day in your life would be something I'd like to hear about. I think I'll keep taking you out until you see it for yourself."

"That might take a while." A silly childlike giggle escaped from her mouth.

"I'm a patient man. You seem very worth the wait."

CHAPTER 15

Leslie

Nothing had happened. Nothing really changed. The way a storm blows in, blows out, and the sea eventually settles back to normal. That was how the Laudon household was right then. Her boys came and went. Christmas came and went. Paul came back. Their stiff conversations softened by the day. Old routines came back into play. Kerry lost herself in schoolwork as the holiday break ended. Leslie began a new project at work that required nearly all her attention. Paul was always good at finding some business trip to attach himself to. The smoke choking their household eventually dissipated.

Even in spite of the routines returning, there was no ignoring how bad things were. That week Paul was in Georgia, playing golf with some of his largest customers. The second his suitcase zipped closed and his car pulled out of the driveway she felt relieved. But for now, they were just treading water.

"Mom," Kerry said, her laptop open and balancing on her

hands as she came into the kitchen. "I have to talk to you about something."

There was some marked progress on that front at least. All of her kids, since their long talk at Christmas, had begun making an effort to let her back in. They didn't have a plan yet for how to make it all work, but she appreciated the tidbits of information they shared with her. Maybe Kerry had a bit more for her.

"Need me to read one of your assignments? I'm sure it's perfect." She turned her barstool toward her daughter, and in an instant knew something was terribly wrong. Kerry was wrought with emotion, her expression so apologetic and worried Leslie was instantly enveloped by fear. "What is it?"

Kerry handed over the laptop and stammered out the explanation. "You remember last year when I did that group project for the state science fair?"

"Yes," Leslie said tentatively. She remembered the group had come in third place and Kerry was distraught for a week. But what it could mean now, she couldn't guess.

"We were trying to prove a theory that certain ethnic backgrounds have more access to genealogy information and therefore can trace their roots back farther. We cited how religion and record-keeping practices played a part."

"Right," Leslie said, looking at the computer screen to try to make sense of what was going on.

"All three of us in the group had different ethnic backgrounds. We sent our own DNA off to use as data points."

"You did?" Leslie had a hard time communicating with Kerry when it came to schoolwork. It usually ended in an argument of some kind so she'd stopped asking too many questions by the end of Kerry's sophomore year. She had a rough understanding of what their project was but didn't know all the details.

"Yes, Brenda's mom opened me an account and ordered us the tests. It helped with our theory, but then I just sort of forgot about it. Today I got an email alert." She pointed to the screen as her chin quivered.

The subject line of the email read: You've got a match!

"I don't know what you're showing me." Leslie gulped, searching her daughter's face for something that would quell the rising terror she was feeling.

"I got a DNA match with someone else who's sent their DNA in. It's a public database. I mean I've gotten other ones but only like third and fourth cousins. This is a closer match."

"How close?"

"Half sibling," Kerry whimpered. "I know it's crazy. But I spent a little time trying to look at the profile and the family tree associated with it."

Leslie made a confused, muffled kind of noise but it didn't slow Kerry down.

"At first I thought it was a glitch or something. The problem is this girl . . ." She paused and checked her mother's face closely. "It's a girl that I'm matched with. The problem is she's twenty-five. Older than I am, but younger than the boys. I figured that couldn't be right, but then I realized from all of us talking at Christmas, opening up about things that had happened, this is when Dad was in Asia."

"Yes," Leslie croaked. "That's when your father was in Asia." Her whole body shook and trembled, even her teeth chattered slightly.

"I'm so sorry, Mom," Kerry cried. "I think Dad maybe got someone pregnant while he was there." She brightened up for a second, forcing herself to sound hopeful. "But there's a chance he never knew. Maybe the woman never told him and he came back here. It's not like he has a whole second family or anything. These things happen." She took Leslie's hand in hers and squeezed.

"Kerry, come sit down." Leslie patted the stool next to her. "I know you think you understand the situation, but you don't."

"You knew?" Kerry practically fell off the stool as she tried to sit, gasping with disbelief. "You knew Dad had another kid out there?"

"No." Leslie shook her head and closed her eyes tightly, praying when she opened them she would wake from this nightmare.

"So you didn't know?"

"Your father didn't have a child while he was away. I did." A thousand needles pricked out from her skin and her hands went numb. There was a place in the far corners of her mind where she imagined this revelation happening someday, but it wasn't meant to be like this. Her children would be older with kids of their own, so they could have some perspective. She would be frail, too skinny and weathered for them to hurl anger at.

"What?" Kerry didn't look hurt, she looked annoyed. Like Leslie was playing a trick on her. As though what she said was so implausible it was insulting. "I don't think you understand."

"Kerry, when your father and I separated, I got pregnant. I know that must be very difficult for you to hear. It's not something I find easy to talk about."

"You got pregnant and gave the baby up?"

"Yes." She whispered the word as if it might lessen the blow. "I can't imagine how that makes you feel."

"You had Stephen and Cole already. Then you just gave away a baby? No one does that. You wouldn't do that." She pointed a finger at her mother, still waiting for the part of the story that would make sense. The part that excused Leslie's choices. There wasn't anything that she could say that would accomplish that.

"It was a very difficult time and an impossible decision. If you think I'm at peace with it, you're wrong. Not a day goes by that I don't struggle with what I did. But it's the truth."

"What does Dad think? I get that you were separated for

almost two years. Maybe you'd date or whatever. But you gave a baby up for adoption. He was all right with that?"

"He doesn't know. No one knows. You're the only person I've ever told this to." Kerry let go of her mother's hand and lost her breath.

"Dad doesn't know? Claudette?"

"No one."

"How did you carry a baby, be nine months pregnant, and no one knew? That's not even possible. What about Grandma?"

"Grandma and I weren't speaking much. She didn't agree with my choice not to go to Asia with your father. She lived so far away. The boys were too young to remember. I left work when I started to show. No one knew. I hadn't met Claudette yet and I didn't have any friends. It was a very isolating time."

"But Dad? How did he not know?"

"He only came back twice and that was early after he left. After I was pregnant he didn't visit. It just worked out that way."

"And what exactly happened; who is the father?"

"Kerry, I don't want to shut you out of this, but please understand this is very sensitive to me. It's been twenty-five years since I've faced this. I wasn't expecting you to come downstairs today and have this information. I need some time to figure out what to say."

"You've had twenty-five years to figure out what to say; the problem is you haven't said anything to anyone. And this girl, I mean, she's obviously looking for you. Why else would she upload her DNA for genealogy? What are you going to tell her?"

"I don't know." She stammered. "I really don't know what I'd say."

"That's not good enough, Mom. I need to understand this. I need to know how you did this. Why you did this. You couldn't take care of another baby? Grandma would have come to help you. You weren't poor either. Why didn't you try?"

"Kerry, it hasn't been easy but I don't regret the choice I made. I had very limited options. By the time I found out I was pregnant, the very brief relationship I was in was over. Some months later your father had started calling again. Started implying he wanted to come back. Talked about opportunities he had for work that would bring him home."

"You could have told him then." Kerry sobbed out her words. "You could have told Dad then and found a way to make it work."

"If your father knew I was pregnant he wouldn't have come back. I wanted your brothers to have a father. To have a good life with both of us. The situation, the baby, he wouldn't have come back." Leslie was trying to keep her emotions in check but there was a hint of anger in her voice. She felt attacked and even though she might deserve it her instinct was to push back.

"You don't know that," Kerry cried out.

"Oh, sweetheart. I know it more now than I knew it back then. And I was damn sure of it back then. I wanted all my children to have love. As much love as they could have. And that would not have come from me doing what my heart was telling me. Of course I wanted to keep my baby. Of course it killed me to leave without her. But I knew she'd have a life full of love. As would my boys. I couldn't have everything I wanted, but if I sacrificed, they all could. And you—"

"What about me?" Kerry bit out her words angrily.

"Your father and I got back together. We moved past that pain and the time apart and had you. None of that would have been possible if—"

"Don't." Kerry pointed a finger at her mother in a way she never had before. "Don't tell me that I got this life because you were willing to give up on hers. I don't want to carry that around."

"That's not what I meant." Leslie's hands shook wildly as she reached for her daughter. Kerry stood and stepped away.

"What are you going to do?" Kerry transformed back into the small child Leslie remembered. The one who sought direction at every turn.

"I don't know what I'm going to do."

"You're supposed to know. You're the mom. Are you going to tell Dad?" Kerry wiped at her cheeks with the sleeves of her sweatshirt.

"Yes."

"And the boys?"

"Yes." She wouldn't ask her daughter to carry the secret like she had for decades. "I don't know how, but I'll find a way."

Kerry grabbed the keys from the hook by the fridge and stumbled around the kitchen. She pushed her hair off her wet cheeks. "I have to get out of here. I'm going to pack a bag and go to Claudette's. She knows stuff's been going on with you and Dad. She'll let me stay there."

"I know she will." Leslie gulped. The image of her daughter being pulled out to sea flashed in her mind. As though she'd be lost to her forever if she let her go now. "But I don't want to see you go. Not angry like this. Maybe we can talk. I'll try to answer your questions."

Kerry took a notebook from the drawer and scratched something down as she sniffled. Leslie always assumed the worst pain for a mother was watching your children hurt and not being able to help them. High school had been full of those moments for all her children. Broken hearts. Lost friendships. Failed classes. What she didn't know, and hadn't experienced until this moment was, being the one to cause the pain was far worse.

Kerry slid the paper over to her mom. "This is my username and password for the website. You should message her. Don't make her wait around wondering. She knows now that we're matched this closely. Maybe I'll have more questions. Maybe I'll feel differently about this at some point. Right now, I just want to go."

Leslie nodded and bit at her lip hard, the physical pain offsetting the fact that her soul was currently being pushed through a wood chipper.

When Kerry stepped out the front door with her duffle bag over her shoulder, Leslie waved her off, pretending it was like any other goodbye. A sleepover or a college visit that would keep her away a few days.

The house wasn't crooked. Things weren't sliding off their shelves and smashing to the floor, which shocked Leslie. She was sure the Earth had slipped off its axis. A seismic shift. There was a lopsidedness to her life she'd never be able to correct. And now she knew that would become her new normal. This wasn't the end of the jolt, only the beginning.

CHAPTER 16

Gwen

"Just open your laptop." Griff sat at the edge of Gwen's couch and gestured to her computer. He'd gotten in the car the second she called. Once he knew she'd received results on her DNA there had been no question. He'd driven the two hours to her apartment.

"I can't open it." She slid the computer on the coffee table over to him. "You open it."

"How do you even know you got the results? Or that there is anything to see?"

"I got an email that said, *your results are in*. I think that's pretty clear. Just open the computer and tell me what you see. I can't." Her hands shook as she brought them up to her hot cheeks. Not a small tremble. A shake that instantly made a look of concern crawl across Griff's face.

"Are you all right? I don't think we should do this if you're upset. I don't want you ending up back at the hospital. Not on my watch." He held the top of the laptop closed as if something inside might jump out and bite her.

"I'm okay." Her voice rattled like a maraca.

"You aren't." Griff pulled the computer into his lap, but still held it closed. "We need reinforcements. We need to call your parents."

"No. We don't need to call them."

"Actually"—Griff put one finger up in the air—"I was an avid viewer of every cheesy after-school special. This situation is too big. We're out of our depth. We need an adult."

"We are adults." She hugged her arms around herself.

Griff grimaced. "But are we? I don't feel like an adult. I never have. I keep waiting for someone to tell me I have to go back to sixth grade. I know you don't feel like a grown-up. You ate Froot Loops for dinner three times this week."

It dawned on her that they'd been talking so much he knew what she was eating for dinner every night. This was not a normal friendship anymore. It had become so much more.

"Your parents will know what to say. They'll know what to do."

"Griff, open the computer. I'm okay." She blinked hard and drew in a deep breath. "Really. You're here now. I am ready."

Griff looked reluctant but finally obliged. He took what seemed like an eternity to say something. "There is a pie chart here." He leaned in and looked closely. "I knew it. You're one hundred percent awesome."

"How are you making jokes right now?"

"Because I can. I'm in no distress at all. I know who my parents are and they suck." She reached over and slapped his ribs. "Okay, fine, here we go. You are forty-three percent Spanish. Nineteen percent French. Twelve percent Portuguese. The rest are small categories. Oh."

"Oh what?" She thought her body was as tense as it could get until it ratcheted even tighter suddenly.

"You're matched with lots of people on DNA. But one is a really close match."

"How close? First cousins?"

Griff licked his lips and hesitated. "Uh, half sibling."

"We share a parent?"

"Yes."

She yanked the computer from his lap and pulled it onto her own. "Half sibling. A sister. Oh no. Oh hell no."

"What?" His faced crumpled with concern as tears formed in her eyes. "What is it?"

"I knew it. I knew I was going to regret this. Look at her profile. She's seventeen, Griff. I can see their family tree. The person I'm matched with is a kid. And she's gotten the same notification as me. Right now she's sitting somewhere trying to figure out which of her parents have this deep dark secret."

"Or," Griff said, raising a hand like a caution flag, "maybe she's always known. Maybe her parents were open with her like yours were. Maybe getting this alert is good news. It could be why she added her DNA in the first place."

"No!" Gwen slammed the laptop closed and practically threw it at Griff. "Oh my gosh. No, this can't be."

"What?" He reopened the computer and tried to make sense of what she'd seen.

"They have two boys."

"Your half brothers?"

"Yes. But look at their dates of birth on the family tree." Gwen held her breath as she watched his face contort, trying to find a reason for something that couldn't be explained away easily.

"They are older than you?"

"And according to their tree, all three have the same father. How do you explain that? Besides the fact that they're going to be looking at their dad trying to figure out when he betrayed their mother. What was he doing twenty-five years ago? That girl, that seventeen-year-old child has just stepped on the landmine I put in the ground."

"You did nothing." He reached out and placed a firm hand on her shoulder. "This is not your doing. Existing is not some crime."

"The odds are they'll never be the same after this." She gulped for air.

He studied the results more closely as if maybe she were wrong. His face twisted up, looking fully perplexed. "Yikes."

"What now?"

"It's not the father that matches with you. It's the mother. The father's family line is all Irish and Scottish. A few other traces of nationalities but he's got no Spanish. No French. The French and Portuguese comes from the mother on this chart. She's the connection between you and the kids. Not the father."

"Impossible." Gwen's brain moved at lightning speed, trying to imagine scenarios that would make sense.

"You don't know what might have been going on. Or how it came to be."

"I'm going to be sick." Gwen shot to her feet and charged to the bathroom, barreling through the door and landing hard against the cold porcelain of her toilet. She wretched until her last meal spilled out of her.

Froot Loops. He was right. She was a child.

"Gwen," Griff pleaded, kneeling by her side. She was embarrassed, but this wasn't the first time he'd seen her sick. She'd gotten the flu when she was little and had a few hangovers he'd been privy to over the years. This was different. The cause was sheer overwhelming emotions. A lack of strength.

He sounded far off and worried as he spoke. "I'm in over my head here, Gwen. If you won't call your parents, let me call Dave or Nick. Please. I can't let you end up hurt over this. I won't be able to forgive myself."

"I can't," she cried, resting her sweat-covered forehead on her arm. "I can't tell them yet."

"Then who? There has to be someone who can help."

"The therapist. Her number is on the fridge." She waved her arm wildly as another wave of nausea overcame her.

"I'm going to call. If she can see you now, I'll drive you. If not, I'm calling your mom. You can be pissed at me later. I can deal with you being mad; I can't deal with you being down and not getting back up."

Griff disappeared out of the bathroom. The sudden silence was like a permission slip for her tear ducts. Her cheeks were soaked seconds later. Hiccups and sobs escaped her as she leaned against the tub. The news should have come with some sense of relief, but instead she was filled with turmoil and despair.

Much like the day in her classroom, she couldn't recall how she'd ended up going from one place to the next. Griff had driven her to Dr. Charmrose's office. She'd started feeling a bit better and walked in on her own. She was suddenly sitting in the chair she hadn't wanted to be in the first two times she came. But this time she knew she needed to be here.

Griff had offered to come in with her, but she'd declined. Dr. Charmrose would have too many questions about their relationship, and Gwen didn't have the energy to explain it.

"Gwen, are you all right?" Dr. Charmrose handed her a glass of ice water and sat down across from her. "Are you having trouble breathing?"

She shook her head no as she drank half the glass of water straight down. "I don't need to go to the hospital."

"What do you need?" Dr. Charmrose looked ready to act. To fix. To help. It was comforting. All the strange assumptions and emotions Gwen had last time she was here were gone now. There wasn't any room in her mind for those.

"I need a time machine." She placed the glass on a coaster and hugged her arms around herself.

"What would you change?" Dr. Charmrose didn't have her notebook out this time. As Gwen inspected her closer, she realized she didn't have her makeup on either. Unlike last time her hair wasn't teased quite so high.

"Did you have to come in here just for me?" Gwen asked, deciding one more layer of guilt might smother her completely.

"When your friend called it sounded urgent. It's not uncommon for me to come into the office unexpectedly if a patient is in crisis."

Gwen nearly asserted she wasn't in crisis. *But maybe she was.*

"You said you'd like to go back and change things. Tell me what you would change?"

"I'd never have done the DNA testing. It was selfish. I started something I can't stop now."

"What do you think you started?"

"I got the results today. I'm matched with three half siblings. One is a seventeen-year-old girl. But there are two older brothers as well. Somehow I fall right in the middle of them. Now they know that too."

Even Dr. Charmrose hesitated, moving her mouth to the side as she gave it more thoughts. "People's lives don't move in a straight line. There are dozens of paths we can follow. Things that throw us off course completely. Without more information it would be hard to speculate how your particular journey of adoption came to be."

"I don't care about my journey or my feelings. I care about

these people. What they are dealing with right now. All because I decided knowing the truth was more important than the consequences to other people. Who does that?"

"It's not a measurable quantity. People's pain is relative. People's needs are different. You can't put it on both sides of a scale and decide which one has more value. This was important to you. You were clearly struggling with your identity and your history. Enough to end up in the hospital. I'd argue that if you hadn't moved forward with this you would've been at significant risk for your mental health to decline."

Gwen sat with that assessment. Where would she be now if she hadn't sent the results off? If she hadn't prioritized her need to know?

Dr. Charmrose went on. "You said in our last appointment that you didn't spend a lot of your youth curious about this."

Defensiveness rose like a tide in her chest. "I didn't. You might not believe me, but I didn't grow up with this empty space in me."

"It's not about my belief in your feelings. They are yours to own. The point I am making is that I believe it's important to try to understand what changed. If you have a grasp on your reasons and motivations, you may find peace, some level of comfort, in knowing that you did the right thing for yourself."

This was the locked box Gwen shoved so far down in her soul she couldn't see it anymore. The part of the story she wasn't ready to face. "I just decided. That's all."

Dr. Charmrose nodded in that unconvinced way. "You still haven't talked to your parents about this?"

"No. I don't know if I can trust them." The words came out laced with anger, and she tried to soften them. "I mean I don't know if they've been telling me the truth all this time. I'm afraid to find out they lied. Then I'll truly come out of this with far less than I started. And what was the point?"

"What makes you think your parents haven't been honest?" Dr. Charmrose looked mildly alarmed by Gwen's change in stance since their last appointment when she'd spent her time defending her parents as perfect.

"I found reason to believe the story they've told me about my adoption isn't all true. Now that I've spent time trying to figure out things about my life, I'm flushing out parts that I might not like."

"Looking into things can often present a challenge of not liking what you find."

"I'm not going to talk to my parents yet." Gwen couldn't imagine sitting Millie and Noel down to unload everything she'd done. Everything she was feeling. "I need to know where things go next with my birth mother. Will she message me? Will this turn into anything?"

"I hear you, Gwen. My main focus is keeping you healthy while things progress. I'm concerned that you don't have enough support to weather the inevitable ups and downs of what is to come. If sending the DNA test out in the mail put you in the hospital, what might happen if you get a message from your birth mother? What might happen if you don't?"

"I have Griff." Gwen gestured with her chin in the direction of the lobby where she'd left Griff. "He's here to help me."

"He's a friend?"

"He's my oldest friend. I've known him most of my life."

"And you feel he's prepared to support you through this, no matter what is to come?"

Gwen hesitated. Griff understood his own limitations and had already let her know he was concerned about being enough. Or knowing enough to really help. "I think so."

"Then maybe he is the right person to talk to about how this all started for you last year. What made you buy the DNA kit? You've been working and learning in the field of genetics for years. You've been old enough to take advantage of the science well before now. But there was a catalyst. A change. It's important you face what that was."

She didn't bother arguing. "Maybe."

"I'm going to write out a plan for you. Some ideas for how to cope with the situation as well as when to seek more help immediately. I think you and I should meet at least twice a week until you have more clarity."

"Okay."

"I can help in other ways as well. If you want me to facilitate a conversation with your parents, I can. If you want support penning a letter to your birth mother, I'll be happy to assist. I'm here for you, Gwen. Impartial support. The only motive I have is ensuring your mental health is strong."

Gwen felt a warmth of gratitude spread across her chest. "Thank you."

"Would you like Griff to step in with us as we discuss the next steps?"

She nodded her agreement as she used her sleeves to hastily dry her cheeks. "Sure."

It was well over the hour appointment before Gwen and Griff were heading back to his car.

"You're going to be okay, kid," Griff proclaimed confidently. "You've got this."

"I do." She knew this was only for his benefit but he'd earned it. He deserved a bit of reassurance too.

For the first time since their road trip, they held hands in the car again. Gwen stopped crying, but admittedly it took a lot of effort to ward off the tears. And maybe that was better. If being around Griff made her want to keep it all together right then, as long as he was offering it, she'd take his support.

Pulling her phone from her pocket, she didn't look up her

email to see if there were any new notifications from the genealogy site. Instead she pressed the button to turn it off completely. She couldn't read a message if her phone wasn't on. She couldn't count all the minutes that no message came either.

If only her heart had the same off switch.

CHAPTER 17

Leslie

Leslie had considered many venues. She could take Paul out to dinner at a public place when she broke the news. He was always concerned with looking proper, so she could at least know he wouldn't blow up right away. He'd keep it together long enough for them to get in the car.

The car was another option. They could go for a long drive like they used to before the kids were born. Back then they'd done it for fun. Today if she did it, he'd be trapped, forced to hear her points.

Instead, she opted for the back porch. After Kerry left for Claudette's, Leslie made Paul's favorite sandwiches and home-made French fries. Juiced some fruits and poured it into a crystal pitcher. Finally, she sent the text message asking him to come home.

"It looks nice out here." Paul had his hands in his pockets and a light smile on his face. He was feeling better. Time worked that way for Paul. He didn't need issues resolved, or feelings dealt with. He needed them in the rearview mirror. And the farther behind him they got, the better he felt. "What's the occasion?"

She pulled out a chair and waited for him to sit by her. "I have something to talk to you about."

His smile slid off his face. "Oh boy. I'm in trouble again?"

"No." She filled his glass with juice and slid it closer to him. "This is about something I did. Not something you did."

Paul looked mildly pleased by this. "Let's hear it."

"When we were separated—"

Paul held his hand up. "I thought we were moving forward on this. Not backward."

"This isn't about me trying to put the blame on your shoulders, Paul. It's about how I acted during that time. I think it's why I've been so angry with you. Why it feels so unresolved to me. We need to talk about it."

"How could that help? When I came back home, we didn't bring it up. We didn't hash out what we'd done during that time. Why all these years later should we?"

"You'll just have to trust me that it's suddenly relevant again." She bit at her lip. "I need to tell you what I did."

"I don't want to know." His voice was sharp. "I didn't then and I don't now. Trust me, I was not an angel while we were apart either. I didn't know if we had a future. I went on some dates. I made some choices I wish I hadn't. But digging that up isn't going to help us now."

"Paul, I got pregnant while we were apart." It was as blunt and stinging as a punch to the face. But she knew it would be the only way to get him to listen.

"What?" His protests evaporated and his face puckered in confusion. "No you didn't. I mean, you did?"

"I'm very sorry, Paul. I'm sorry to have kept this from you all these years. I understand you must be in shock."

"You had an abortion?"

She gulped nervously. "I had a baby."

"No you didn't." He laughed nervously, looking at her as if to say this joke was not funny at all. "I would have known if you had a baby. Don't you think I'd know?"

"I did. I had a daughter. She was adopted."

He slid his chair back abruptly, rattling the table like an earthquake. "You are telling me you slept with someone, got pregnant, and gave the baby up for adoption? You never told me this? You've kept this from me our entire marriage?"

He paced the patio in an angry stride.

"Yes."

"Okay." He ran his hand over his head, his eyes wide and wild. "Okay, why didn't you tell me?"

"I wasn't sure what I was going to do. Then you called and said you might be coming back. I looked at the boys, at our life, and I knew I had to choose. You wouldn't have come back if you knew. You wouldn't have been able to have this baby in your life. Which meant we wouldn't have had you."

He thought on that for a long minute. "You're right about that." He grunted out some confused noises before finding his words again. "Okay, we can deal with this. We can figure this out."

"We can?" The wrinkles in her forehead deepened as she tried to think of how they would move forward. It was not the reaction she'd expected. Kerry had been angrier than Paul seemed.

Paul took his seat again and held her hand. "Leslie, I have been trying to tell you over and over again that I want to move forward with the next phase of our life. I want you by my side. I want to enjoy everything we worked for. That hasn't changed. I'm processing this. I'm trying to get my head around it. But I also hear you saying that you did this so we could have this life. I'm sure it wasn't easy for you. But it actually makes more sense now.

How hard it was for you when Kerry was born. When you go into these dark places. You've been carrying this alone for so long."

"I have been," Leslie agreed. She couldn't believe Paul's response. The guilt of lying to him shifted to guilt over doubting his love for her. Any man who could hear this news and find a way to take it so calmly must have deep love in his heart. She'd misjudged him.

"You said it's suddenly relevant?" His face showed worry rather than anger. "Why?"

"Kerry came to me this morning and told me the genealogy project she did last year included uploading her DNA. I didn't know that. Apparently she got a notification that she was matched very closely with someone. As a half sibling."

"Kerry knows?" Paul looked wounded by this. More than the initial news. "How did she take it?"

"She went to Claudette's. She was upset. Confused. I think maybe if she takes some time she'll be able to get past it eventually."

"And how about the girl? Has she reached out or anything?"

The way he said, *the girl,* pained Leslie but she tried to remind herself what a bombshell this was. Paul was responding much better than she imagined.

"She hasn't sent a message or anything yet."

Paul pulled out his phone. "I'm going to send an email to Lucien."

"Our lawyer? Why?"

"Leslie, I've had a handful of colleagues over the years who have been through this type of thing. Men who find out many years later they have children they didn't know about. What do you think is going to happen when this girl finds out we are people of means? Lucien can help ensure we protect ourselves."

"Protect ourselves?"

"You think she's not out there right now looking at our kids' social media? Looking us up on professional websites, realizing what we have? Looking at our vacation photographs? I am not going to leave us open to blackmail or extortion. We can get ahead of this."

Leslie tried to string his words together in a way that would make sense, but ultimately she was still confused. "Paul, we don't even know her or what her life is like right now."

"And we won't. I'll explain to Kerry why it's important that she not tell anyone about this. Does anyone else know? Claudette? The boys?"

"No, no one knows but the three of us."

"That's manageable."

"Paul, I'm not going to make Kerry keep this secret. Trust me, I know how damaging it can be. She's supposed to lie to her brothers?"

Paul pursed his lips as he thought it over. "If you feel passionately about the boys knowing, I can support that. They'll understand how important it is for us to keep this quiet."

"What are we keeping quiet?"

"Leslie, please don't play dumb. We aren't going to announce to the world that we have a new middle child. How do you think that will look?"

"Is that all you're worried about? What people will think?" She didn't expect she'd be snapping at him.

"Isn't that what you were worried about all those years you kept it quiet? Why suddenly do we need to shout your infidelity from the rooftops? You really think people will understand how a woman with two children could give away her third?" His words were cutting and emotionless now. Matter of fact.

"It's different now, because I know who she is. I know how to find her. I never had that information before. I'm not going to lawyer-up and act like she doesn't exist. I don't know exactly how to move forward or what she might want, but I do know I'm going to try hard to make sure she gets it. She deserves that much."

"You think I'm going to tell my colleagues this? You think I'm telling my mother this? You have two choices here, Leslie. We keep this to our immediate family and reach out to Lucien for legal protection, or you do this without me."

"Choices." She breathed the words out and tipped her head back. "Twenty-five years later, and we're right back in the same place. It's life with you, doing things your way, or life without you."

"You could have chosen not to get pregnant." Paul had a sour look on his face that matched the taste in her mouth. Her stomach had churned up a sick feeling. "I didn't put you in this position. I'm only trying to get all of us out of it with the least amount of damage to our family."

"I was right."

"About what?"

"I knew you wouldn't have come back twenty-five years ago, if you knew. You weren't a big enough man to love a child who wasn't yours. You'd have made things hell for all of us if you knew."

"She's not my family."

"She's mine. And I'm yours. That should have been enough. We should have had what it took to get through it together. But I knew, even then, you didn't have it in you."

"How you could spin something like this around on me is amazing. You did this. You chose this. I haven't even asked you who it was. I haven't asked you how long it went on. All I'm asking of you is that you don't let it destroy our lives."

"It doesn't have to." She smiled as an odd peace filled her chest. "You're the only one who thinks it will. I'm not the person I was when this happened. I know better now. Situations don't dictate your happiness or your life. What you do with them does. I don't regret the choice I made. At the time I knew it was the only thing I could do to protect and provide the best life for all three children. I just regret being with a man who ever made me have to choose. Who left in the first place."

"You know what you're doing here, right? You know this will be it for us? I'm not going to leave and bother coming back this time. There are no kids here for me to miss."

"Yes, Paul, I know what I'm doing. I feel sorry you can't see what you're doing. What you're losing out on, all because you can't see the forest through the trees. Maybe people will judge us. Maybe we'll have some explaining to do. Some tough questions to answer. How could that short-term discomfort ever be worth more to you than what could be waiting on the other side?"

"I'm tired of fighting for this marriage, Leslie. I'm exhausted. I'm going to get my stuff and go. You can have fun telling people about how you had a baby and gave it up." Paul stormed back into the house and slammed the sliding door behind him so hard it knocked a potted plant off the deck.

Leslie sat in the wake of the argument, emotionally bobbing up and down in the waves left behind. There should have been a sinking feeling at the thought of ending her marriage. A worry that came with having to face the people in her life and explain her deepest secrets to them. But all she could feel was relief. A secret revealed. A pressure valve in her heart released, steam flooding out into the atmosphere. She wasn't foolish enough to believe it would always feel like this. There would be hard moments. Reality checks. Pain inflicted on more people she loved. But right now, she sat in the sense of liberation, and ate her damn sandwich. If she was hungry enough, she'd eat his too.

CHAPTER 18

Gwen

Griff had been sleeping on her couch all weekend. She knew he was supposed to go to a job interview tomorrow morning. If she didn't show him she was all right soon, he'd skip it. That was the last thing she wanted. Lying in bed that morning, she made a plan. She'd cook a big breakfast. Smile. Even get dressed in real clothes. Maybe study a little. Normal was the goal.

A goal totally in reach until the email arrived. She'd only begun checking the night before. And until this morning there had been nothing. Now the email icon on the genealogy website was blinking. Who else could it be?

"Griff?" She called his name out long and loud. "I got an email."

He came to her bedroom door, and she didn't bother being modest. Her skimpy pajamas didn't matter now. And he was kind enough not to stare at her body too long.

"Is it from her?"

"It must be." She pulled her computer into her lap and slid onto her bed, propping pillows up for both of them. He crawled in and she realized he was only in his shorts. Under any other circumstances this would be intimate and require lots of questions about what it meant. Right now all it meant was *stay with me until I know I'm all right.*

"Want me to read it first?" Griff offered. "Or maybe don't read it until tomorrow when you go to see Dr. Charmrose?"

"I can't wait that long. I want to read it. I'll be okay."

"How can you say that if you don't know what it is? What if she's telling you she doesn't want any contact?"

"At least I'll know."

"Want coffee first?"

"No. I'm ready." She wiped the sleep out of her eyes and let the mouse hover over the email icon. Drawing in a deep breath, she clicked.

Dear Gwen,

I've written many emails in my life but nothing quite like this. There is no template for it. No suggestions for proper etiquette. (I checked.)

It's problematic to know what to write because I don't know you. What a difficult thing to admit to your daughter.

"It's not the girl," Gwen gasped out. "It's from my birth mother."

I don't know where to begin. Mostly, because I don't know what you want to hear. Which parts of the story I should fill in. What will bring you any kind of peace. It feels trite and selfish to give you my reasoning or excuses for choosing adoption. I couldn't possibly fit in a note to you all I was feeling or experiencing at the time.

What I feel right now is a mix of things. First is shame. Never before in her life has my daughter, Kerry, looked at me with such horror and disgust. It's my own doing for keeping this a secret. I am filled to the brim with shame. My choice to put you up for adoption always seemed complex and wrought with internal conflict. Yet I held out hope that you had a good life. The shame I feel now comes from keeping it a secret for so long. So many people in my life deserved to know.

Secondly I feel joy. The chance, if you choose, to hear from you, or meet you fills me with happiness. I don't know if the rest of my family, who is of course your family too, will be ready right away but know that I am. Just say the word. Tell me when and where. I would love to meet. But only when you are ready.

I could write for days. Fill hundreds of pages. If you want me to, rather than meeting, I will. Just ask me whatever you like, and I'll answer. I won't keep anything from you.

Warm wishes,
    Leslie Laudon

Gwen hesitated as she let her eyes hover over the words. "That was pretty good." She looked to Griff.

"I think that's great."

"She wants to meet with me."

"Do you want to meet with her?"

Gwen keyed up the reply screen and smiled. She could bullet-point a hundred questions. Get responses to things she always wanted to know. Instead she keyed in two words and hit send.

I'm ready.

"That answers that," Griff said, nudging her with his shoulder. Now that the email was read and one sent back, they were lying in bed together for no reason. "Now you know what you need to do."

"What's that?" She wondered if he would kiss her. He was close enough to lean over and do it.

"You need to call your parents. It's one thing to reach out to your birth family and want to keep that part of the process from them. Now you've heard back. You're going to make plans to meet her. You have to tell Millie and Noel what's going on."

"I have a lot to tell them. A lot to ask them. But I don't know if I'm ready to hear what they have to say. What if I find out they lied?"

"They may have lied, but they still love you. They may be imperfect and still need to know about this."

"If what they told me about my adoption isn't true, my whole life is based on a lie."

Griff made an empathetic face, but it melted away to a smile. "No. It means they told you a story. It doesn't change every single part of your life that they made amazing. Everything they gave you and taught you over the years. That means more than a mistake they made. It won't change who they are to you. But not telling them this, that'll change things for sure."

Gwen rested her head on his shoulder. "I know. The problem is the things I'm keeping from them, are attached to other secrets. Things I haven't told anyone."

"Things you haven't told me? What do you mean?"

"Dr. Charmrose says facing the reason I started this journey to begin with is going to help me. But I don't think I agree. The reason all this started, that's a dark place. I don't want to go back there. I don't want to have to tell my parents about it."

"Why not? They'd be there for you. We all would be."

"Last year was hard. No. It was devastating. And it's like having an emotional flu. I don't want what broke me to be contagious."

"Hurting and pain isn't like the flu. You don't give it to the people around you. It's like moving furniture. The more people the better. Everyone grabs a corner and gets the job done."

"That's very profound."

"I try."

"Will you come with me to go talk to them?"

"Of course. If you want me there."

"I do. I'm just afraid you'll hear what I have to say and see me differently. I don't want anything to change between us."

"You don't?"

"Do you?"

"We're being honest here?"

"Always."

"I want to be here with you and make sure you're all right. At first I think it was because I cared about what happened to you. Now I think I'm here because being anywhere else doesn't feel as good. If I'm not careful, I'm going to fall in love with you. So if you don't want that, you should say so now."

"And you'll stop?" She smiled at him and watched his eyes twinkle.

"I'll at least try. If that's what you want. I can't promise I'll be successful, but I could try to stop."

"You've never been a quitter, Griff, don't start now."

CHAPTER 19

Gwen

D r. Charmrose was turning out to be pretty cool. She'd opened her office to Gwen's parents and Griff on a Saturday morning. There was no receptionist. No other patients coming or going.

"This is a beautiful office, Dr. Charmrose," Millie complimented as she settled into the loveseat with Noel. Her purse was perched on her lap and her back arrow straight. She was not comfortable here, but she was trying.

"Thank you." Dr. Charmrose pulled up two other chairs for Griff and Gwen, making a U-shape, with her in the middle of them. "I am glad you all decided to come in."

Gwen felt a special connection to Dr. Charmrose now. "Thanks for seeing us on a Saturday. And letting us all come."

"Of course. Can I get anyone anything?" She looked around at each of them and only

Millie spoke up. "It depends why we're here. Maybe tissues?" She let out an uncomfortable laugh.

"I always have plenty of those here. Gwen, why don't you tell us why you asked Griff, and your parents here today."

"Griff is here because he's been involved in this and helping me. I just thought it would be good for him to be here. Plus, he's the one who has been encouraging me to tell my parents what's going on."

Millie looked terrified. Noel looked stoic. Dr. Charmrose looked unflappable.

"What is it you want to share with them?" Again in this visit Dr. Charmrose didn't pick up her pen. She sat back in her chair comfortably and waved as though Gwen had the floor.

"This is hard for me to talk about. And hard for me to ask some of these questions because I'm afraid to hurt you. I love you both so much. I don't want you to think—"

Millie leaned across and grabbed her daughter's hand, sending her purse to the floor. She awkwardly collected it. "We know you love us. And we love you. Nothing you could ever say would change anything. We want to know what's going on so that we can help. Tell us how to help."

"Honesty." Gwen squeezed her mother's hand and looked at her father. "Just be completely honest with me. I have been keeping things from you and I'm here today to tell you everything. Just please if there is anything I ask you, tell me the truth."

Noel nodded. "Of course we will. The Fox family doesn't have secrets."

"But I do. I have kept things from you." Gwen looked down at her shoes as her mother sat back in her chair. She could feel Griff's arm against her on the armrest between them and she took comfort from his touch. "This all started last year."

"When you broke up with Ryan?" Millie asked, with a look of

sudden understanding. "I knew there was more to that story. It was so sudden and you just completely shut down. I've been worried sick but I've been trying to give you space."

Dr. Charmrose cleared her throat. "Gwen, do you want to share with your parents the details of that breakup? Is that relevant in your mind?"

Her chin wrinkled as she held back her emotions. "Yes. That's where so much of this started. I just don't want to make you all sad."

"We're here for you, sweetie," her father said, leaning over and patting her leg. "You can tell us anything."

She wiped her sweaty palms on the thighs of her jeans. "Ryan and I were happy. Things were good. We had a plan. But sometimes things don't go as planned. Remember when I got that sinus infection? The doctor put me on an antibiotic. I didn't realize it could interact with my birth control." She beat back the ache that filled her soul. "I found out a couple weeks later I was pregnant."

Millie gasped and then clapped a hand to her mouth, trying to stay composed. "Pregnant?"

"Yes. It was obviously a shock at first. But Ryan and I had always talked about having kids someday. He was so great with his nieces and nephews. It wasn't how we planned it but we were in grad school, we weren't teenagers. Plenty of people make it work." She was rambling now, meandering through the emotions she felt that day. "Ryan was writing his thesis and working like crazy. Plus, he had his sister's wedding. But two months from then all that would be behind us. So I made the decision to wait to tell him. I even had a little plan in my head for how I'd surprise him with the news."

She was crying now. But she wanted to get it all out. To explain what had changed in her.

Dr. Charmrose handed her a tissue. Then she passed the box

to Millie who of course at the sight of her daughter's tears, started silently weeping herself.

"Do you want to take a break?" Dr. Charmrose asked gently.

"No, it's all right. I want to try to explain so that you can understand how I ended up where I am today. So after I found out, I started taking the prenatal vitamins and I went to see my doctor. She confirmed I was pregnant and she handed me this form. The one I always just write *adopted* on. The family history I can never fill out. I'm on the road to becoming a geneticist and I don't even know what makes up my own genes. Now my child is going to have to deal with a similar void. Never knowing its grandparents' medical history. I left there that day determined to do something to change that. It wouldn't be that hard. I'd buy one of those genealogical DNA kits first. Just to get an idea of my, and in turn, the baby's heritage. Then I had a bigger plan from there. Genetic testing. Research."

Millie sniffled. "I'm so sorry, honey, I never knew it bothered you so much to not know. We should have done more to help you with that."

"It didn't bother me that much. None of this did until I thought about my own child. You and Dad, you were always enough for me. More than enough. I didn't want to go looking at my past because I didn't need to. But the pregnancy, it sparked something in me."

Noel's voice was low and raspy. "What happened? Was it something to do with Ryan?" Whether it was conscious or not, she watched her father's hand curl into an angry fist at the idea that Ryan caused her any pain.

"Three days before I was going to tell Ryan, I had a miscarriage. I'd already bought him a card. And made us reservations at our favorite restaurant. I sat home alone while he was in class, and I lost the baby." She doubled over as she remembered the pain and sadness she felt, curled up on the bathroom floor.

"Oh baby," her mother said, falling to her knees and pulling Gwen in close. "You should have called me. I would have come. I'd have been right there with you."

"I just didn't want anyone to have to hurt about something they didn't even know about. Why should you have to mourn a baby that you didn't know existed?"

"Because it did exist," Millie explained through sobs. "Because you are my baby and I will always be there for you."

Griff put his hand on her back and she could hear him sniffling back his tears. Even her durable father was clearing his throat and wiping his eyes.

Dr. Charmrose gave them all a minute before she began to speak. "I can only imagine the myriad of emotions you are all feeling right now. Miscarriage is an all-too common, but rarely discussed situation that so many people face. It's a loss that requires mourning and grieving. I'm very glad, Gwen, that you've surrounded yourself with people who can not only process the pain with you, but also, when you're ready, cherish the memory of the child you carried. I have resources and support tools for you all if you'd like them."

"Thank you," Millie said, pulling herself back onto the loveseat by her husband. "I'm just so sorry you went through this alone. Did Ryan not take it well? Is that why you broke up?"

"I never told him," Gwen admitted sheepishly. "I just kept shutting him out and shutting down. He tried, but going through that made me realize Ryan and I weren't meant for each other. If our lives were going to have moments of that deep pain, he wasn't the person I wanted next to me for it. He just didn't have enough to weather it. I knew that and I knew I had to move on."

Her father nodded and looked at Millie. They were a couple who could weather anything together and his expression solidified that. "Was the panic attack you had in class not your first one then? It was almost a year later."

"I held on to the DNA test," Gwen explained. "It sat in my apartment for a year. Just like I did. I was sitting around, not doing anything but schoolwork. Waiting for something to happen. Waiting to feel better. On the anniversary of my miscarriage, I mailed the test. I sent it off and then had a breakdown over it."

"Why?" Millie asked, her sweet face stained with tears and worry. "Did you think it would bother us? Because if we ever gave you the impression that we wanted to stop you from finding out more about yourself, I'm very sorry. You didn't seem to want to talk much about any of it growing up and we didn't want to pressure you."

"I was worried that looking into my history would be hurtful to you two. Like I was being ungrateful for all you did for me. I'm very grateful."

Noel's voice boomed. "We know you are. But you don't have to be grateful to us. All we did was love you. Just like any parent loves their child."

Gwen nodded. "I know. But at the time I was feeling very confused and hurt. And I worried what might happen if in this big database I was matched with someone. Someone who didn't want to know me. Or worse someone who never knew I existed and then had to deal with the consequences of finding out."

"You can be matched with people?" Millie said, sitting back in her chair and looking at Noel. "Like matched with people you are related to?"

"Yes." Gwen folded her hands neatly in her lap and drew in a deep breath. "But even before that Griff and I did some of our own research. That road trip, we went to Rhode Island to talk to a nurse who used to work at the clinic where I was left."

"You what?" Millie clutched Noel's arm as though they were just about to go over the crest of a roller coaster drop.

"This is where I'm asking you both to be honest with me. Even if it's hard. She told me that the nurse you guys knew wasn't someone you went to school with. Ivy was much older than both of you. And she alluded to the fact that it might not have been legal, the way the adoption went. I know you've always told me you got a call in the middle of the night and just knew it was meant to be. I'm ready to hear if that's not the case."

Millie pursed her lips so tightly that they nearly disappeared. She hummed and fidgeted in a way that immediately gave Gwen her answer.

"I can live with the truth. Really, it won't change how I think of you. I just need to know the whole story." She fixed her eyes on her father and let her expression plead with him.

He looked to Dr. Charmrose. "I don't know if we should be talking about this in here. There may be some things you hear and don't agree with."

Dr. Charmrose crossed her legs and leaned in. "I am only obligated and compelled to share information I hear in this room if someone's life is in danger, or they cause an imminent threat to people around them. You should feel comfortable to speak freely."

"It was meant to be, Gwen," Noel began, his voice rattling some. "Maybe it's not exactly the story we told you, but I know in my heart you are the child we were meant to have."

"Oh, Noel," Millie lamented. "I just don't know."

"She wants the truth. She told us something that was not so easy to hear, and we owe her the same. I'm just going to come out with it."

"Ok," Gwen nodded. Her stomach rigid as she braced for the cannon ball about to impact her core.

"Your mother almost died giving birth to Nick. That's not an exaggeration, we almost lost her. I was sitting there realizing I was going to have two kids and no wife. Luckily she pulled through. But after a few months of recovery the doctor told us she wouldn't be able to have any more children. At first we thought we'd be all right with that. We were just so happy she and Nick both survived. But eventually, sometime around Nick's first birthday, we started talking about having more children. Your mother always wanted a daughter."

Millie grabbed a few more tissues and wiped at her red-rimmed eyes. She opened her mouth to speak but no words came out, so Noel continued for them both. "We tried beating the odds and seeing if we could get pregnant. Then some science, but it didn't work either. Then one day I ran into Ivy Chantal. She was the school nurse when I was a kid. She and my mother were friendly so we stood in the grocery store having a long conversation and catching up. Eventually she mentioned she was a labor-and-delivery nurse. I must have made a face or something because she knew right away something was wrong."

"So when you said you knew Ivy from school," Griff asked, "that part was true." He looked to Gwen as though, if she were keeping score in some way, she could mark down a point for her parents and their half-truth.

"Yes. Technically. She asked if Millie and I planned to have more kids and I broke down right in the produce aisle. I hadn't let any of my emotions out about the topic of more kids and then, boom, I'm telling a practical stranger in the grocery store how badly we want a little girl."

"You cried?" Millie asked, twisting her face up as she eyed her husband closely. "You never told me that."

"I didn't want you to think I was upset with you. I knew you were trying so hard to make things happen. The last thing I wanted to do was put more pressure on you. Ivy, she saw how badly I was hurting and she talked to me about how many babies she'd delivered that needed good homes. I told her we'd started to look at adoption but honestly, we were overwhelmed by the process. There was so much paperwork. Lawyers. Classes to take. Fostering children with the hopes of maybe adopting but never knowing if you'd get the chance. We thought that process, the starting and stopping might be harder on the boys. We had them to think about too."

Gwen held up her hands to stop him. "You wanted more children? You always told me that you felt your life was complete after the boys. That I was some kind of serendipitous miracle that fell in your lap when you weren't expecting it. Why? Why tell me all that instead of the truth?" She fixed her eyes on Millie. That was who she wanted this particular answer from.

Millie rubbed her hands together nervously. "It wasn't as if we sat down one day and decided to come up with some lie. As you kids got older, we realized how sensitive Nick was. I knew if he thought giving birth to him hurt me in any way, he'd carry that with him. Then we watched you. We saw how you noticed things about you that were different. Other kids would say your skin was too tan for our family. Or that your hair was different than the rest of ours. We knew we wanted to be open with you about being adopted. But we also knew we wanted you to understand that the way you came to our family was special."

"But it wasn't? I wasn't just some exceptional surprise the stork dropped off on your doorstep. The icing on the cake. I was someone else's baby first. And Ivy, she was not some nice nurse who was trying to find me a home with her good friends who she knew would be perfect for me. She was a stranger to you."

Noel raised his hands in protest. "She knew me as a child and still kept in touch with my mother. Yes, we exaggerated the relationship between us and Ivy. But she was a kind woman who loved children and wanted them to have the best opportunities possible."

Griff looked to Gwen and then spoke up. "Was she associated with Mission Crest Adoption Agency?"

Relief flooded Gwen's body as her parents looked at each other curiously. Not seeming as though they'd ever heard the name before. She leaned back in her chair and looked at both of them with a gentle expression. "Did you pay for me? Was it an adoption-for-profit situation?"

Noel cut back quickly. "Heaven's no. Ivy told us if the right situation arose, she'd call us. If we were willing to act fast we could have a child placed with us right away. What we did wrong in this situation was skirt the rules and allow Ivy to help us bypass the normal steps. She had connections and we took advantage of that. She made up some paperwork that showed we'd fostered children before, even though technically we hadn't yet."

Millie blurted out her point. "I was never comfortable with that. That's something she told us after we already had you. I had to swallow the fact that she'd forged documents to show we'd been cleared to foster kids in the past. In my heart I knew we were loving parents with a safe home, so if that's all the paper was saying, I found a way to live with that."

"Did you pay her anything?" Gwen asked her stomach tied in a thousand tiny knots.

"We didn't buy you." Millie whispered as she clutched Noel's arm again.

"But then how did you get me?" Gwen thought of how many times she'd taken comfort in the story they'd told her about her origins. How special she felt every time she imagined her parents getting a call and deciding on the spot they wanted her. Now that was gone. It was replaced by the idea that they'd ached for any baby. Cried over the fact that they couldn't have more of their own. There had always been something consoling to her that her parents could have had a house full of their own children if they wanted to, but instead welcomed her.

"The call did come late at night. Ivy said there was a baby who'd been left at the hospital and needed to be nursed and cared for. We raced down to get you, and when we got there she told us the mother had abandoned you and therefore there would not be all the hoops to jump through. Anything that wasn't done there that night, she had people who could hurry it up and make it all come together quickly. We should have known that she was bending the rules for us. Nothing is ever that simple but we were just so in love with you already."

Gwen held a hand over her heart to protect it. "Did you ever think that maybe you should slow things down and make sure it was all being done the right way?"

Noel dropped his head in shame. "You were in my arms. Holding my finger with your tiny hand. Cooing and I swear you even flashed a smile. I was willing to ignore anything as long as I was walking out of there with you."

"But—" Gwen choked on her own tears. "You didn't know what happened to my birth mother. You didn't know if they took me from her. It all could have been lies. You were trusting Ivy fully."

"We were selfish," Millie answered quietly. "But Ivy was a remarkable woman. She stayed invested in your life for the first couple of years until she got sick. She checked in on you. Brought you little gifts. Called often. I think she wanted to make sure she'd made the right choice too by picking us. If she was duping us, she'd have wanted something from us. She never asked for anything. Maybe we should have told you, or done more. As you got older and you started saying you didn't want to talk about being adopted anymore, we took it as a sign. We tried to put it all behind us."

Noel sat up a little straighter, wincing at a pain in his back. "Your mother wanted to do more. To say more to you about how quick it had all been and how we were hurting so badly before you came along. But I cautioned her against it. This is my fault."

"Why?" Gwen had never seen her father cry very hard, and his damp eyes were blinking quick to try to avoid it now.

"Because at some point, very early on, you were just my baby girl. I would have fought a hundred men for you. Climbed the highest mountain. You had me wrapped around your little finger. Anything that might have taken you away from me, even just the truth, was my enemy."

"But I am legally adopted, right?"

"Of course," Millie said, leaning in closer. "We did everything right, just not in the right order. Maybe not on the right timeline."

Dr. Charmrose had been sitting quietly; leaning back and trying to look like a piece of furniture rather than someone who should partake in the conversation. But all at once she leaned in and spoke. "There is so much to unpack here. I applaud all of you for your candor and responses to each other. Gwen, I think it's important you share all the information you have with them. It doesn't mean you've fully processed what they've told you today, but at least you'll all have the same information as you try to get through this together."

Gwen looked to Griff for encouragement. They were all halfway across the bridge now. Either she had to run back to where she started or cross it the rest of the way. "I had a match on my DNA. I got a message from my birth mother."

Millie looked as though she'd been struck with a club in the chest. Her fingers needled around over her heart and Noel put an arm around her. "Your mom?" she whispered.

"My biological mother. You are my only mom."

"But you heard from her? What did she say?"

Gwen had memorized the email from Leslie. "She didn't go into much detail but she said she was happy she'd heard from me. That she had hoped I had a good life. Most importantly, she said when I'm ready to meet, she'll be there." Gwen kept her cheeks from rising into a smile. She was happy she'd received that email from Leslie, but she didn't want to seem too eager to her parents. They were doing the best they could to keep their footing in this earthquake. She didn't want to be the reason they finally fell over.

Millie forced a smile with all the willpower that was only reserved for very strong mothers. "You want to meet her? If it's what you want, you know we'll support it."

"I do have a lot of questions for her." Gwen attempted to make it all sound very clinical. A business meeting to swap pertinent information. "And she sounds willing to answer them. She has other children. That's the hard part for me to understand. Two are older than me. One is younger."

Millie looked to Noel and crunched up her forehead. "We didn't know that. We were never told she already had children."

"She kept three of them," Gwen reported sadly. "I'm the only one she didn't want."

Griff's hand was still on her back and the pressure was just enough to let her know she wasn't alone. He had her. As he spoke, it was a low whisper by her ear. "She didn't keep you, I'm sure, because she couldn't, not because she didn't want to."

"You don't know that," Gwen said with a sniffle, taking another tissue from the box. "You don't know why she gave me up."

"You're right," he brushed her hair behind her ear. "But I know if she knew you longer, she'd know giving you up was the biggest loss of her life."

Noel reached across and touched her leg again. "And the biggest reward in our lives."

Dr. Charmrose checked her watch. "I find that there's no good way to stop a dialog like this. Everyone has more to say. Needs more time to process. I wish you all could stay here all day and just talk but it doesn't work that way. I don't want you to think just because you walk out this door that there isn't room for these tough talks. You seem like a wonderful family. I encourage you to keep this dialog going and make further appointments as needed."

"Wonderful," Millie said with a long sigh. "I promise we're actually very ordinary people."

Dr. Charmrose stood and when Millie did as well she placed a firm hand on her shoulder. "At the center of ordinary lives, sometimes, we find extraordinary pain. It has to be faced, but it doesn't have to define any of you."

CHAPTER 20

Leslie

Paul had been gone for three weeks. Twenty-one days exactly. He'd done so much traveling over the years sometimes as Leslie sat home alone reading a book she forgot he'd left her. Was he just visiting clients in Orlando? Pitching to an investor in Europe? She'd look at his empty nightstand and remember it was more than that. Their marriage was all but over.

Some of his clothes still hung in his closet. But only the stuff he never wore anymore. His bathroom vanity still had a half-empty bottle of shaving cream and that cologne she bought him years ago and he never seemed to use. Remnants of him Leslie wasn't ready to put away. Not because she wanted him to come back but because there were too many moving parts in the machine that was her emotions at the moment. Engaging in anything else, even just removing Paul's things, could cog the wheel and send her to a screeching halt.

The best news was that Kerry had come back. She'd spent

only four nights at Claudette's house. Four excruciatingly long nights. But Claudette had been generous with her text updates and funny pictures of Kerry smiling and laughing to try to calm Leslie's nerves. There wasn't one particular thing that brought Kerry back. She blamed it on needing some school notes. But ended up staying home instead of returning to Claudette's.

Leslie moved around her daughter gingerly. She fought her urge to push the conversation or reach for a hug. It would have to be on Kerry's time. When she was ready. If she was ever ready.

"You messaged her?" Kerry asked over a plate of pancakes one Saturday morning. Leslie might not be actively trying to pressure Kerry to talk to her, but she knew her daughter. The smell of buttermilk pancakes and the sound of sizzling bacon always brought her down to the kitchen. Kerry punctuated her question by stuffing her mouth full and acted as though she wasn't all that interested in the answer.

"I did. I messaged her through the genealogy site." Leslie poured them both some more coffee. Kerry had apparently begun drinking it last week. More cream than coffee and too many scoops of sugar. But Leslie was picking her battles at the moment. Soon her daughter would be off in the world and a cup of weak coffee would be the least of her worries.

"Did she respond?" Kerry mixed her sugar in and clanked her spoon against her mug. One of those very adult things Leslie hadn't gotten used to seeing her daughter do yet.

"She did respond. We've been chatting a bit. Maybe making plans to meet each other. I know this is a lot for you. For all of us. I'm so sorry to have put our family through this. I won't do anything before you are ready. What you want and are comfortable with comes first to me. It's my priority."

"The boys took it pretty bad," Kerry reported sadly. "Have either of them called you back yet?"

"Not yet." Leslie kept her voice singsong and happy as though the cold shoulder from her sons wasn't eating her alive.

Kerry was trying to soften the pain and Leslie was grateful for that. Her daughter's empathy never ran dry. "It's a little dramatic if you ask me. They're being stupid not talking to you at all. Plus, I think Dad's been in their ears. They go from trying to get as far away from him as possible to now commiserating with him about you. That's shitty."

The Laudon's didn't curse much. She was sure her children did with their friends but as a rule they all tried to be civil around each other and hold a high standard of the language they used. But that had always been Paul's rule. She wasn't that passionate about it.

"Everything is shitty right now," she agreed, letting Kerry see the rules were relaxing now that they were on their own here.

Kerry smirked a bit as she poured more syrup on her bacon. "Dad hates this fake syrup stuff."

"He does. But I know you like it."

"I love it." She drenched her pancakes. "Silver lining."

"To my marriage imploding? Is the syrup that good?"

"I actually don't think you can call it syrup. It's a syrup-like substance. With Dad gone we should go on a full processed food diet. That cheese you squirt out of a can. That pasta you microwave. All the stuff he used to make such a big deal out of us getting every once in a while. I mean, damn, can a kid get a happy meal every now and then?"

"He was a stickler for that stuff. But it was because—" She stopped herself. She wouldn't make excuses for him anymore. "Because he liked to control things. And hated for us to look less than the other snooty people in his life."

"Exactly."

"But I do feel terrible for the secrets I kept from all of you. It was wrong. I should have told him. If he didn't come back to me after that then maybe that's how it was meant to be."

"Whoa, let's not go that far. I kind of like existing. And I never hated those Caribbean vacations we went on." Kerry pointed a fork full of pancakes at her mother. "I get why you did it. At first I thought you did the easiest thing for yourself. Then I realized there was no easy option for you. Either way you gave something up. It was just what you were giving it up for."

"I hope you never have these kinds of regrets in your life. I know you won't. You're a very smart girl. Principled."

"So were you, Mom. What's done is done. We can't change it. We might as well try to make the most of it." She ran her finger around the top of her coffee mug.

"It means a lot to me to hear you say all that. I can understand why your father and your brothers are so upset. I don't want to minimize what they're going through. But part of me is very ready for this next part. The part where I get to see her. To hear about her life. It's something I have spent many days wondering about. Worrying over. I know they don't understand it."

"That's because it could never happen to them," Kerry shot back angrily. "They're never going to understand what kind of choice you felt like you had to make. I was sitting at Claudette's house thinking of what it would be like to carry a child in my body and then have to say goodbye. They'll never understand that."

"I suppose they couldn't. Not the same way you and I would." Leslie was grateful to be standing on even the smallest amount of common ground with Kerry. It was razor thin but somehow holding them both.

Kerry looked sheepish suddenly. "Claudette is worried about you. She said you haven't been returning her calls lately. I haven't said anything to her. I kept telling her it was between you and Dad and I was staying out of it. You know she's going to burst in here eventually all crazy like she does. Some grand gesture of her friendship. You should check in with her."

Leslie laughed. Something she hadn't done in weeks. The image of her friend storming the gates of her house and doing an over-the-top welfare check filled her mind. "I will call her. As a matter of fact, I think I'm going to ask her to come with me to meet Gwen. Whenever that happens. If it happens. I don't think I can do it alone."

"I'd go." Kerry eyed her mother closely, looking for a reaction, moving her next bite of pancakes around mindlessly in her plate.

"That's an awful lot to ask of you," Leslie replied gently. "Every time I think about meeting her I cry. Fear. Shame. Nerves. It's a lot. I don't know how well I'm going to hold up. Or how any of it will turn out. It may not be like the stories they feature on those feel-good news segments. I don't think you want a front row seat to that. I can't make any promises at all."

"You could promise to not keep anymore secrets," Kerry suggested, looking emboldened by the sudden thought. "That's all I really want. I don't mind if what we have is messy. I just want to have the real thing. Nothing superficial. No good dishes or fancy stuff."

Leslie rose with an impulsive idea. "None of that." She moved to the cabinet in the corner of the dining room and grabbed a stack of dishes. "I have a feeling Grandma Laudon won't be coming by for Easter any time soon."

"I doubt it," Kerry said, watching her mother closely. "But what are you doing with those?"

"Trashing them." She pulled the trashcan out from under the sink and dumped the dishes from her arms with a crashing noise that made Kerry cover her ears.

"Mom!"

"Kerry, we don't need those. We don't need half the things in this house. We only need each other. Family. Love. That's all that matters now. I can finally see it. And you had a lot to do with that."

"Well you could still donate the dishes," Kerry protested. "But I guess that would be a lot less fun."

Leslie lifted a dish out of the trash and smashed it down on the others so it broke. "So much less fun. Want to do the teacups next? No one drinks fancy tea here anymore."

Kerry nodded excitedly as she moved to the china cabinet. "I like you when you're a little crazy, Mom."

"I don't know how crazy I'm going to get so hopefully you keep feeling that way. I think this might get worse before it gets better. We're going to have some tough moments. I just hope you're all right through all of it."

"Things don't have to be perfect but there can't be secrets. Plus, I want to meet her. She's my sister."

That was hard to hear. It was true. But it reminded Leslie how she'd kept them apart all these years.

"How are you dealing with this so well?" She was filled with humble wonderment at the sight of her daughter. Leslie knew she'd made loads of mistakes in her life but Kerry was proof she had done something very well. "I would have completely understood if you needed more time, if you stayed upset forever."

"I thought about it. I figured if we didn't talk until I left for school it would be easier to just go and we'd just stay like that forever. Not talking or anything. But I knew I couldn't. That would mean you were alone. You've been alone with this for long enough. No one should have to deal with this by themselves."

"But it's so much change for you. Dad moving out is not something I had planned for. I know we were struggling but I didn't expect us to end up like this."

"Dad's going to have to come to terms with his own choices.

I'm not going to cut him out, but I'm certainly not going to pander to him either. If he's mad at me for sticking by you then it's just one more thing about him I'll never understand."

"Whatever happens, Kerry, I want you to know that I love you and I'm so glad you are my daughter."

"So are we going to go meet her?" Kerry tossed a couple of teacups down into the trash can and reveled in the smashing sound. "Maybe she would like to demolish some of our other family heirlooms."

"She says she's ready for it. We've been talking about meeting at a café in Boston since it's about halfway for both of us. I just wasn't ready to do anything until I talked with you."

"Now you have, so let's do this. What's it going to be like for you to see her?"

"Hard." Leslie said the word before she gave it much thought. "But life's hard. The good stuff usually is. That's what I've been missing. I've been trying to keep things easy. Not letting anything messy happen. It's going to get messy, but I think it's going to be worth it."

"You should invite Claudette too. At least you'd have someone to get a glass of wine with after if you need it. I'm guessing you and I are not going to be drinking buddies just yet."

"Not yet. But I look forward to the time you and I can pop the cork on a nice bottle. It'll be that time before you know it. You were a little toddler with braids about two blinks ago."

"Call Claudette. Message Gwen. Let's do this."

"It's strange to think about telling Claudette. She knew me after all this had happened. When I'd settled things and looked like I had my life together. You were a toddler and I felt like things finally made sense again. This will be a shock for her."

"You know Claudette. She'll take it all in, have some huge outrageous reaction and then fuel the car up for the trip to Boston.

She'll want what you want. Because those are the people we should have in our lives. The ones who rally and show up. Anyone else is just weighing us down."

CHAPTER 21

Gwen

What does one wear to a visit with their mother for the first time? It was a dilemma Gwen was both pleased and annoyed to be faced with. A dress felt overly formal, like she was trying too hard. Jeans were the opposite, as if she didn't care enough. When she'd pulled everything she owned out of her closet, including two bridesmaids dresses she nearly tried on, Millie stepped in. She helped Gwen settle on a pair of khaki slacks and a decent-looking light blue blouse. Some simple jewelry and pale lip-gloss. Which is what Gwen would have worn on most days anyway.

"It's best to be yourself when you're meeting someone new," Millie reminded her. "If they stick around they won't be surprised. Be yourself because I love that girl. She's my favorite."

Griff had been right. Forgiving her parents wasn't nearly the insurmountable task she'd worried it might be. Dr. Charmrose had guided them through a few more tough conversations. Some heated words exchanged. Some painful layers pulled back. Eventually, Gwen was able to see her parents as people, not just infallible fixtures in her life. She drew some previously overlooked parallels. Millie and Noel weren't much older than her when they started their family. Also, like her, they'd experienced a type of loss that changed them on a fundamental level. The loss of her mother's fertility. The loss of hope to have more children. Gone. And left behind was the pain and uncertainty of the future.

They hadn't sought out MCA or gotten mixed up with anything quite that sinister. Could they have done it all differently? Told her and her brothers from the beginning about Millie's infertility and their longing for another child. Their broken hearts. Their pushing of the ethical boundaries. Yes. There was room for more honesty.

But through all of it, she could see what her parents were trying to do. How they were attempting to protect their children from pain. Just like she'd tried to protect her parents by not telling them about her miscarriage. In the end they all carried a burden that could have been shared and made lighter.

Today they were all ready to share the load. The car was full up with nervous energy. Noel fidgeted with his seat belt every few minutes. Griff, who was driving, changed the radio station again and again, switching between country music and oldies. Millie adjusted the temperature so often Gwen had to keep putting on and taking off her sweater. They all looked as comfortable as a flock of seagulls in the desert. But they were trying and Gwen was warmed by the effort.

"Thank you all again for coming with me. I think I'd have backed out a hundred times if we weren't all doing this together." Gwen felt the wings of the butterflies in her stomach beating against her insides.

Millie touched Gwen's leg to calm her. "You can still back out if you need more time. Tell Griff to turn around. You don't have

to do anything you aren't ready for. I'm sure she'll understand."
Millie hadn't yet figured out what to call Leslie. She seemed to
dance around it like a fly, nervous to land on the sandwich right in
front of it. She opted for *she* or *her*.

"With you all here, I'm ready for anything." Gwen covered
her mother's hand with her own. She couldn't imagine what it
was like for her mother. The fear, even if it was irrational, that
your child might abandon you for their flesh and blood. That there
might be some biological bond that would push her out of Gwen's
inner circle. There was no chance of that happening, but it was so
obviously gnawing at the edges of her mother's mind. If Gwen
decided to turn around now, there would be relief for her mother.

Noel cleared his throat and then grunted from an ache in his
back. "We're not turning around for anything. My girl's got it. Is
there anything in particular you want to ask her? I know you've
been emailing back and forth. Has she said much?"

She shrugged. "I've made it a point to be kind of light and
breezy through email. I think the bigger questions are better
answered in person." Gwen knew that wasn't just driven out of
logic, but fear. She'd typed dozens of important questions but
they'd been swallowed up by her fingers on the backspace key.

Griff looked at her in the rearview mirror, his beautiful eyes lit
with optimism. "Do you know if she's coming alone?"

"At first she thought she might but now she's bringing a squad
too. Her youngest daughter Kerry and Leslie's best friend
Claudette. I guess we all need some backup for something like
this."

"Not her husband?" Millie asked, frowning with her eyes.
Quietly fretting over all the unknowns.

Gwen shrugged and pulled her sweater on again for the
hundredth time. "I guess he's not coming today. She did say he
travels for work so maybe he isn't in town right now. I hope
finding out about me didn't cause them too much trouble. I'd hate

to know they were fighting over it. I've been running through so many scenarios of how I fit into their lives and I keep coming up with a lot of square pegs and round holes." Gwen brought her thumbnail up to her mouth and nibbled frantically on it. She'd considered a manicure before this trip but thought better of it once she realized how low she'd bitten all her nails down in the last couple of weeks.

"We can't control what happens with them." Noel reassured her. "Everyone makes their own choices in life. What I want you to remember is whatever happens you've got us and home and everything that's always been there for you. If this adds to your life, great. But you won't have less than you started with."

"Would you forgive Mom if this had happened to us?" Gwen leaned forward practically resting her chin on her father's shoulder in the front seat. "That's the part I can't seem to get my mind around. Can a marriage, even the best kind, deal with this kind of secret?"

"I think I would forgive her," he admitted, a big smile breaking up his wrinkled face. "I've never been able to stay mad at your mother for very long. Every time we did argue over the years, I'd find myself feeling pretty empty without her. Food didn't taste as good. The sky wasn't as blue. You ever feel that way, Griff?" He shot a sideways glance at Griff and then waited for an answer. There had been a bunch of these goading questions over the last couple of days. All tricky ways to try to insert the old *what are your intentions with my daughter* question in.

"No sir. No forgiveness from me. I'm the worst. When I get in a fight I think food tastes better, the birds chirp louder and the sky is a more vibrant blue. I hold a grudge. There's a kid in my neighborhood who scratched my car with his bike. I still have his front wheel in my garage. Every time he walks by I take the thing out and show it to him."

Gwen was grateful for Griff's humor. It had carried them all through the tough moments. Even Noel had to chuckle. The more ways he found to ask, the more humorous and over-the-top Griff's deflections became.

Millie tried to catch Griff's eye in the rearview mirror. "Will you two just admit you're dating already? Your father has a lot of good dad-jokes lined up."

"Sorry to disappoint," Griff sighed. "I haven't won her over yet."

He had completely won her over.

If the situation was different. The timing was better. She knew she'd be in his arms already. But she wanted to run to him for the right reasons. Not for comfort. Not to mend her broken heart. A relationship should be based on so much more than just need.

When the café was in sight Gwen felt a wave of terror over-take her. The kind of fear that made her entire body tingle. There was a collective silence that filled the car.

"What if she doesn't show up?" Gwen hadn't meant to ask the question out loud. It bubbled up from her chest and spilled out of her mouth before she could stop it. Before she could sound unafraid and grown up.

There was a realization that no matter the outcome everything was going to change. Leaning against the car window, Gwen tipped her head up toward the sky and watched the rims of the clouds morph, blooming like over-yeasted bread.

"She'll be there," Millie promised, the way a mother assures her child the first day of school will be perfect. That an abun-dance of friends will be made and fun will be had. A promise to calm the heart but not rooted in any kind of premonition. Just a strong hope, as if her motherly love could will it into reality.

"Thanks, Mom."

Noel, always a little less optimistic grunted. "And if she isn't then we'll have a nice coffee and a muffin while we talk garbage about her."

Her feet felt like cement blocks as Gwen shuffled slowly toward the door of the coffee shop. A small parade of her people who cared about her were marching behind. Pulling the door open, the aroma of strong coffee and sweet pastries filled her nose as she reached back and grabbed her mother's hand. Not since the last time she had to cross a street as a child had she gripped her mother this way. Millie squeezed back. What they were crossing into felt far more precarious than oncoming traffic.

"You'll be all right," Millie whispered.

"I know."

Three women sat in the corner of the coffee shop with looks of excited trepidation. Tables had clearly been pulled together to make room for the crowd. It was probably odd that they'd each brought an entourage to their first meeting, but as far as Gwen could tell there were no real rules for such things.

"Gwen?" Leslie asked, cupping her hands to her mouth the second the word had come out. As if she'd shouted a curse word or screeched at the top of her lungs. Really it had been just above a whisper.

Gwen had wanted to take it all in. Analyze what features she shared with her mother. What mannerism they mirrored. But she was instantly swallowed up by a hug. Tight and unfamiliar. Intimate in a way Gwen wasn't ready for. She had expected they'd fit together perfectly but that wasn't the case.

She could feel Leslie's sobs wetting her shoulder as she pulled away. Gwen didn't cry. There was plenty of emotion to bowl her over, but the tears didn't come. Just her breath catching in her throat and a tremble that kept running up her spine.

Millie was better at the hug than Gwen had been. The two women squeezed each other tightly and stayed close, like yarn that had been skillfully knit together. Words Gwen couldn't make out but clearly things they'd always wanted to say if given the chance.

"Sit," Leslie said, gesturing proudly at the tables they'd pulled together. "We have room for everyone. This is my daughter Kerry and my best friend Claudette."

Here Gwen saw the similarities. Kerry was younger than Gwen but they shared the same large round eyes with long lashes. A point to their chin. Even though her hair was blonde it was the same thickness and even the sweep of their bangs was the same.

Gwen stuck her hand out and Kerry nervously giggled as she shook it, half standing and then settling back into her seat.

Gwen failed miserably at trying to come up with an icebreaker after the introductions. A long stretch of silence overtook them all as they shimmied their seats in closer to the tables. It was Noel who chuckled out some words.

"Looks like we have a set of pretty twins here." He gestured to Kerry and Gwen and they both blushed and smiled.

Claudette adjusted her shiny gold bracelets as she brushed her hair off her shoulder. "Two gorgeous girls."

Millie's back was rigid as she drank down half her glass of water in one sip. The emotion of the initial meeting had worn off and now there was just a sharp unease on her face.

Leslie looked equally uncomfortable but the people by her side seemed to have a calmer energy.

"I just don't know what to say," Leslie admitted. Her eyes were fixed solely on Gwen's features. Her lashes were still wet with tears but she'd mostly composed herself. "I want to thank you both for taking Gwen and giving her such an amazing life and family when I couldn't."

"We were blessed to have her," Millie said, wrapping an arm around Gwen. There was possessiveness to her grip. "She was a joy of a child and makes us proud every day. She's getting a Master of Science in genetic counseling. She has a big career ahead of her."

Griff sat quietly at the end of the table, sizing everything up.

Watching closely like someone sizing up a wave at the beach, deciding if it was worth surfing it to shore. Gwen locked eyes with him briefly and he smiled. It infused her with another ounce of courage.

"Wow, Gwen, that's incredible. Kerry is planning to be a doctor. She's off to college this fall. I'm not sure I'm ready." Leslie pulled her daughter in close to her, mirroring Millie's grip. It wasn't likely intentional, but both seemed to want to lay claim to their maternal love.

Claudette leaned back in her chair and clamped her hands together. She was a beautiful woman. Bright and shiny like her chunky gold necklace. "How do you even do this?"

Everyone turned toward Claudette and eyed her. Even Leslie had a look of concern.

"I just mean, what do you do here? Do you show baby pictures? Spill all the juicy details of how this all went down? How does this work?"

Noel laughed. "I like this one." He pointed at Claudette and his eyes sparkled. "She's right. What exactly do you all think we should do here?"

Leslie gulped. "I don't know. I'll answer any questions you have. And I'd love to hear more about Gwen growing up. What she was like."

Millie beamed at the opportunity. "Gwen was a joy. The perfect baby. My boys were colicky but she never missed a night of sleep. Napped like a champ."

Leslie nudged Kerry. "Well that doesn't run in the family. Kerry and my boys didn't sleep through the night until they were ten. Colic. Ear infections. Then bad dreams. Colds. I swear if it wasn't one of them it was the other. I thought I'd never get a good night's sleep." Leslie looked thrilled at the opportunity to recount her years as a mother to young children.

Noel cleared his throat. "And now your last one is going off to school. Don't think you'll sleep any better in a quiet house. I think it's worse actually."

"That's what I'm afraid of." Leslie covered her face and wiped another tear away. Meeting one daughter and getting ready to say goodbye to another.

Millie kept her voice cool and unbothered but Gwen knew the expression well. It was what came before a pointed question. "How's your husband taking all this? The empty nest and meeting Gwen?"

It was easy to see the question struck the other half of the table like machine gun fire. Claudette hummed out a noise and gave a look as though, that was a long story.

Leslie righted herself and didn't flinch as she explained. "Paul and I are separated right now. I don't want you for a second to think it has to do with you, Gwen. It doesn't. We had a lot to work out before this and unfortunately we weren't able to."

"Seriously," Kerry said, trying to reassure her. "Really it wasn't you."

"I'm sorry to hear that," Millie said gently. "I'm glad you have support here. I kept trying to imagine what this day would be like for you."

"I've been wondering the same with you," Leslie admitted. "I never wanted to barge in on your lives. Or disrupt anything."

Gwen felt a spark of recognition. "I never wanted to disrupt your life either. I thought me showing up out of the blue would put you on the spot or ruin your life."

Leslie smiled gently. "You couldn't ruin anything. It was a very complicated time in my life back then. I was overwhelmed. The only solution I could think of was adoption."

"It worked out amazing for me," Gwen glowed as she looked at her parents. "I couldn't have ended up with better people. My life has been very blessed."

"I'm so glad about that." Leslie forced a smile. "Ivy assured me they were wonderful people. That they would be perfect and loving. I'm so happy it turned out to be true."

Griff leaned in closer and cleared his throat. "There were whispers of Mission Crest Agency being somehow involved. But Ivy, she wasn't a part of that?" Griff had promised Gwen he'd bring this up. He'd wait for the right opportunity and make sure someone answered the question.

For the first time Leslie looked genuinely thrown. Her eyes narrowed and her posture changed suddenly. "Whispers? From who?"

Gwen licked her dry lips. "Before I had the DNA results I talked to a nurse at the clinic where I was born. She thought that maybe Ivy was working with MCA."

"She wasn't," Leslie cut back quickly, shifting in her seat. "I originally reached out to MCA before I realized they were not reputable. No one knew at that point how bad their practices were. The moment I caught wind of that I backed out. Or I tried to. They had some very strong tactics to try to convince, no, downright pressure women to sign their contracts and do things their way. I fled to the clinic and counted my blessings that I found Ivy. She was an angel. My angel and your angel."

"Is that why you abandoned me?" Gwen asked, holding her breath. "Why you didn't give your name or anything? I always wondered why you just left."

Leslie had to roll her eyes up toward the ceiling to catch the impending tears. "That was the only way. Because I'd gotten involved with MCA I couldn't chance them knowing I'd given birth. I couldn't chance them coming for you." There was earnestness in her expression. A flash of the fear she must have felt back then.

"I understand." Gwen said the words before she really felt them. She couldn't understand what it must have been like. She'd fallen in love with her own baby at the first sign of two lines on the pregnancy test. Gwen had formed dreams around the potential. Let her mind wander to names she'd always loved. Imagined what it would be like to mother. To love that intensely. She felt all those things, and never held her child. Leslie had to make a choice to leave the clinic that night with empty arms. So no, she couldn't understand how it felt, but could see how it could happen. How it could be the only way.

"You don't have to be kind about all this." Leslie dipped her head, seeming weighed down by shame. "It's all right to feel angry. To feel anything you want. There is no right or wrong way to do this. No playbook."

"I don't feel angry," Gwen admitted, sounding surprised. "I have so many questions. I don't want to bombard you with them and honestly I don't know where to start. I don't want to just start blurting things out."

Kerry laughed. "That's how we always talk. It's fine."

Claudette's singsong voice cut in. "Let's order some drinks and then you pepper this lady with questions. Honestly, we're all dying to hear some of the answers." She tapped her long finger-nails expectantly on the table.

Gwen gave Leslie a look, questioning if she was up for it and was happy when she nodded back her approval. "It's been hard for me to realize you have older boys and a younger daughter. I didn't expect that. I didn't understand how that happened."

It wasn't really a question. It didn't get to the heart of anything, but somehow Leslie understood. "My husband Paul and I were married and had my two older boys."

"They're sort of being dicks about this right now," Kerry cut in. "But they will come around."

Gwen liked Kerry. She was forward and open. Her sister. Something she'd never had before. "It's all right. I'm sure it's a lot to take in."

Leslie nodded, patting Kerry's hand. "I think this is the

hardest part for them to understand too. You would think as a mother of two already I could figure out how to make it work. But Paul was gone and I didn't expect he'd be coming back."

Claudette leaned in and smiled proudly. "So she had a torrid affair with a handsome coworker."

They all snickered as Leslie scolded Claudette like a bad puppy. "It was not exactly like that at all. Torrid is a poor representation."

"Does my father know about me?" Gwen asked, the word *father* causing her stomach to flip with nerves. She wanted to know more but somehow felt as though it would wound her dad to see the look of desperation in her eyes.

"He didn't know I was pregnant." Leslie lowered her voice as the waitress delivered a tray full of drinks and a couple of snacks they'd ordered. Gwen couldn't think of eating and her coffee was only so she had something to hold. Something to keep her hands from jittering. "Mark had done so much for me. Helped in many ways. He lived on the other side of the country and I wasn't sure how him knowing would help the situation."

"Did you keep in touch?"

"No." Leslie pursed her lips. "Soon after Paul and I were talking again. Trying to make things work. I knew I had to close that door tightly in order to move forward. Mark and I weren't looking to keep in touch. It was only meant to last a few weeks while we worked on a project."

Claudette hooted. "And look how great that project turned out." She gestured at Gwen. "I'd say you did a lovely job. All of you. All of you had something to do with this beautiful girl."

Kerry poured a ton of sugar into her coffee and Gwen couldn't help but smile. She remembered how desperately she'd wanted to drink coffee only to find out it tasted gross. She remembered being seventeen.

"You have two brothers too, right? Older?" Kerry's eyes were bright and inquisitive.

"Yes. Dave and Nick."

"We both have two older brothers. Which means I'm sure you always wanted a sister as much as I did."

Gwen beamed. "I always wanted a sister."

The conversation moved from cordial to overly personal and then back again. No one knowing exactly where the lines were. What to say, or what to leave out.

Two hours flew by, feeling much more like two minutes.

When they were all standing on the sidewalk, bundled in their coats, Gwen felt her heart thudding. The goodbyes passed between everyone. Only one left. Leslie and Gwen hadn't mustered up the courage yet.

"We'll do this again?" Leslie asked, touching Gwen's hair gently. "I hope we do."

"Maybe dinner next time?"

"Maybe just the two of us?" Leslie shrugged, looking so unsure of herself. "I know you probably had a lot more you wanted to know."

"I'd really like to find my biological father," Gwen whispered. She didn't know why she didn't want her dad to hear.

"I don't know much, but I'll message you any information I have. I think he might still be in California." Leslie pulled Gwen in for a hug and this time it felt much more comfortable.

"I'm sorry about Paul." Gwen refused to believe she wasn't the cause of their break-up.

"I'm sorry for Paul," Leslie replied flatly. "He has no idea what kind of joy he's going to miss out on. My boys, your brothers, they'll come around. Kerry will make sure of that."

"When they're ready."

Leslie looked at Millie and Noel who were wholly entertained by a story Claudette was telling. "You are a very lucky girl. I couldn't have dreamed up a better family to adopt you. I'm only sorry I couldn't be that for you."

"Don't be sorry for what you did." Gwen spoke into her mother's shoulder. "Just be glad for what we might be able to have now."

They parted ways and drove back home. At first Gwen thought she wanted to be dropped off at her apartment on the way. But last minute, she told Griff she would rather go back to Redwood Road with her parents. Maybe they could talk more about her taking over the house for them. She thought of the redwoods. The way her father had relayed the story. Gwen wanted that type of stability back in her life.

Noel held his excitement at bay. "It's a strong house. It needs an even stronger owner. You'd be perfect."

When they arrived back home her parents went inside and Gwen stood on the front steps with Griff. A sense of, *now what*, overtook her. Griff had been everything she needed to get to this place. But what would they be now? He'd likely be leaving for a job soon. Old Wesley wasn't where he wanted to settle.

"You're kind of my hero in all this," she said coyly, raising on her tiptoes to kiss his cheek. He looped his arm around her and pulled her close, brushing his lips to hers, just for a second.

"You're the hero. I'm the guy who drove you around." They stayed like that, their bodies pressed together. "So now what?"

She laughed at how he'd read her mind. "I'm going to find my father next. Leslie thinks he's in California. Do your driving services go that far?"

"I'd drive you to the moon." He let her go and reluctantly took a step back. "And leave you there."

"I wouldn't ask you to do that. You need to get back to your life. I know some of those interviews have turned into job offers. Just like I said they would."

"There's a surf shop in California that's considering launching a franchise. I might look into that while we're there."

"You want to run a surf shop?"

"No. But I want to go to California with you. A thinly veiled excuse will have to do."

"It might not turn out great," she reminded him. "We got pretty lucky this time. My father might be harder to find. And he didn't know I existed. It could be bad."

"It could be a disaster," he agreed. "But being with you never is."

The End
Continue with Book 2: The Pier at Jasmine Lake

ALSO BY DANIELLE STEWART

Missing Pieces Series:

Book 1: The Bend in Redwood Road

Book 2: The Pier at Jasmine Lake

Book 3: The Bridge in Sunset Park

Book 4: The Stairs to Chapel Creek

Book 5: The Cabin on Autumn Peak

Broken Mirror Series:

Book 1: The Way Down

Book 2: The Way Home

Book 3: The Way Back

Piper Anderson Series:

Book 1: Chasing Justice

Book 2: Cutting Ties

Book 3: Changing Fate

Book 4: Finding Freedom

Book 5: Settling Scores

Book 6: Battling Destiny

Book 7: Unearthing Truth

Book 8: Defending Innocence

Book 9: Saving Love(includes excerpts from Betty's Journal)

Edenville Series – A Piper Anderson Spin Off:

Book 1: Flowers in the Snow

Book 2: Kiss in the Wind

Book 3: Stars in a Bottle

Book 4: Fire in the Heart

Piper Anderson Legacy Mystery Series:

Book 1: Three Seconds To Rush

Book 2: Just for a Heartbeat

Book 3: Not Just an Echo

The Clover Series:

Hearts of Clover - Novella & Book 2: (Half My Heart & Change My Heart)

Book 3: All My Heart

Over the Edge Series:

Book 1: Facing Home

Book 2: Crashing Down

Midnight Magic Series:

Amelia

Rough Waters Series:

Book 1: The Goodbye Storm

Book 2: The Runaway Storm

Book 3: The Rising Storm

Stand Alones:

Yours for the Taking

Love in a Paper Garden

Multi-Author Series including books by Danielle Stewart

All are stand alone reads and can be enjoyed in any order.

Indigo Bay Series:

A multi-author sweet romance series

Sweet Dreams - Stacy Claflin

Sweet Matchmaker - Jean Oram

Sweet Sunrise - Kay Correll

Sweet Illusions - Jeanette Lewis

Sweet Regrets - Jennifer Peel

Sweet Rendezvous - Danielle Stewart

Short Holiday Stories in Indigo Bay:

A multi-author sweet romance series

Sweet Holiday Wishes - Melissa McClone

Sweet Holiday Surprise - Jean Oram

Sweet Holiday Memories - Kay Correll

Sweet Holiday Traditions - Danielle Stewart

BOOKS IN THE BARRINGTON BILLIONAIRE SYNCHRONIZED WORLD

By Danielle Stewart:

Fierce Love

Wild Eyes

Crazy Nights

Loyal Hearts

Untamed Devotion

Stormy Attraction

Foolish Temptations

Surprising Destiny

Lovely Dreams

Perfect Homecoming

You can now download all the Barrington Billionaire books by Danielle Stewart in a "Sweet" version. Enjoy the clean and wholesome version, same story without the spice. If you prefer the hotter version be sure to download the original.

The Sweet version still contains adult situations and relationships.

Fierce Love - Sweet Version

Wild Eyes - Sweet Version

Crazy Nights - Sweet Version

Loyal Hearts - Sweet Version

Untamed Devotion - Sweet Version

Stormy Attraction - Sweet Version

Foolish Temptations - Sweet Version - Coming Soon

FOREIGN EDITIONS

The following books are currently available in foreign translations

German Translation:

Fierce Love

Ungezügelte Leidenschaft

Wild Eyes

Glühend heiße Blicke

Crazy Nights

Nächte, wild und unvergessen

Loyal Hearts

Herzen, treu und ehrlich: Die Welt der Barrington-Milliardäre

***

French Translation:

Flowers in the Snow

Fleurs Des Neiges

NEWSLETTER SIGN-UP

If you'd like to stay up to date on the latest Danielle Stewart news visit www.authordaniellestewart.com and sign up for my newsletter.

AUTHOR CONTACT INFORMATION

Website: AuthorDanielleStewart.com
Email: AuthorDanielleStewart@Gmail.com
Facebook: facebook.com/AuthorDanielleStewart
Twitter: @DStewartAuthor
Bookbub: https://www.bookbub.com/authors/danielle-stewart
Amazon: https://www.amazon.com/Danielle-Stewart/e/B00CCOYB3O